TWO
FEET
IN

a novel

SCARLETT ADAIRE

TWO FEET IN
Copyright © 2022 by Scarlett Adaire
Published by

 red bird books

ePUB 978-1-7372015-1-9

www.scarlettadaire.com

Author Photo by Kelli Boyd
Interior Format

For Diana, Korie, and Kristen

Here's to The Power of Love…

"Oh, you can't make yourself stop dreaming
Who you're dreaming of
If it's who you love
Then it's who you love"

-John Mayer and Katy Perry

CHAPTER ONE

Charlie

IN HER NEARLY two decades of dating, Charlotte Compton had perfected the hypnotic skills of Cleopatra, able to seductively convince any and every man she desired to bow down at her feet. The problem was finding the one *she wanted* to keep for good. That was until Gabe Adams. For the life of her, she couldn't figure him out. Charlie had been trying to weave Gabe into her web for months now, but to no avail. Something, whether it be stubbornness, competitiveness, or just plain stupidity, kept her trying despite the lack of success. He was different, that's for sure. Charlie had every reason to believe that Gabe wasn't *The One*. He wasn't even her type, whatever that was these days. He was older, shorter, and quirkier than any man she had ever been attracted to. But Charlie was currently batting zero on the ultimate commitment, so flexing on the must-haves-list of marital partner traits seemed to be the smartest thing to do. Afterall, she had nothing to lose in her efforts, except for time. No boundaries. No limits. No walls. Leave no stone unturned. And maybe, just maybe, her Mr. Right would appear.

Charlie watched her coworker, project partner, and intended target of nearly half a year make his way to the front of the conference room to the sleek black podium. The quiet, sterile room was filled with a dozen

men and women in over-priced suits that surrounded a
just as pricey mahogany conference table clad with brass
detailing. Their piercing focus was on the large screen
projecting the presentation at hand: Charlie and Gabe's
research for the nation's largest spa and wellness company,
the Sabo Group. The unlikely pair had been assigned to
the prominent client by their company's board of direc-
tors. Gabe and Charlie couldn't be more different. He
was rigid, calculated, disciplined. She was bold, spontaneous, and loved to color outside the lines. But Charlie
figured it was their dichotomous differences that had
gotten them selected as partners for the task in the first
place. Everyone knows contrary forces make for a great
well-rounded result. Charlie held her breath as she eyed
the first slide of the PowerPoint that beamed on the
screen. She prayed their opposite forces had done the job.

In typical Charlotte Compton form, she was soon distracted by something much more enticing. Her focus
wavered from the screen, shifting to Gabe's hand as it
grabbed the thin silver pencil microphone, his voice
turning into a low hum of white noise in her ears. Her
mind flashed back to last week when he'd merely grazed
her with a simple touch to her back. Whether it had been
intended as an act of affection or not, Charlie was fixated
on reading into any possible smoke signal she could deci-
pher. Despite Gabe's strict self-proclaimed co-worker
dating rules, they had developed a great friendship. He
needed her validation, and she needed his discipline to
keep her spinning creative mind on track. It was a muddled, symbiotic, almost co-dependent relationship—one
that was way past platonic and skirting the lines of an old
married couple. Gabe had always been known around
the office as nice, but aloof. He was the guy that was
hell-bent on keeping his personal life separate from his
workplace. Some had even wondered if he had a personal
life at all. He practically lived at work. But Charlie had

come to know a different side of Gabe. Maybe that was because her relentless extroversion pulled it out of him, kicking and screaming. They had confided in each other about nearly everything—*so she thought*.

Charlie's mind drifted further away as the lights of the conference room dimmed and Gabe continued to rattle off the familiar presentation that he had recited to her more instances than she could count. She had heard his voice so many times over the phone, in meetings, in conference calls, and sitting right next to her. She had often wondered what it would sound like with his lips touching her ear. Charlie's mind reeled, imagining her hands moving slowly over the navy-blue collar of his suit coat. As her fingers crept under the edges, grasping them with intent, her fantasy shifted to his lip—that bottom lip that was so perfectly framed with the sexiest gray stubble. Mentally tracing it with her thumb, she couldn't help but crave to give it a tender kiss.

The lights abruptly flipped back on way sooner than she would have liked, stealing her away from her mental excursion.

"Charlie, do you agree? Any thoughts?" Gabe asked, innocently unaware of the intimate moment he had just been the star of in Charlie's dream world.

Panicking, she realized she had heard none of his presentation.

"Um, yes. Brilliant. Bullseye." Charlie awkwardly scrambled to reply with a little too much zest. His eyes narrowed at her, indicating he was pissed, and she was busted. Charlie smiled nervously back at him, hoping her cuteness would ignite forgiveness. In her defense, she didn't really need to listen. Their thoughts were always in sync. Well, almost always. Except for that one pesky incongruity that entailed them dating each other.

The room buzzed with satisfied whispers and nods. Despite her lack of attention, it appeared to Charlie that their hard work had paid off. The Sabo Group looked pleased. Hopefully that would be enough to distract Gabe and stifle his annoyance with her.

"You didn't hear a word I said, did you?" Gabe asked with agitation in his voice as the two of them stepped out of the conference room together after a plentitude of diplomatic smiles and commending handshakes. As fast as her gait normally was, Gabe's pace was double time as he hastily headed for the elevator back to their office floor. Charlie's long legs raced to keep up with him.

"What? Of course, I did. I told you it was brilliant," Charlie defended, blushing with guilt, knowing where her mind had drifted off to in truth.

"Charlie, I know you like the back of my hand. Where was that little mind of yours? In Anthropologie's shoe section?"

"Ha-ha, very funny. Something like that." Charlie laughed sarcastically as the pair stepped through the elevator doors simultaneously. Now shoulder to shoulder, Charlie realized this battle wouldn't be won easily. "Gabe, how many times have you gone over the Sabo development strategy with me? At least a hundred. Hell, I could have given the presentation verbatim, I've heard it recited so much," she contended with an added eyeroll as they both stared firmly ahead at the stainless-steel elevator doors in front of them.

"I know you could have. But whether you realize it or not, I need you. I need you to be ready to defend our ideas and have my back. What if someone had thrown out a curve ball question? You are my right-hand woman. I need you in the room with me mentally, not trying on red velvet stilettos," Gabe said sternly, his face finally turning to her. She watched his austere expression soften as their eyes met. He couldn't stay mad at her for too long, and she knew just how to speed up the forgiveness process.

"Oh, I most certainly know you *need* me," she responded in a sexy tone, nibbling on her lower lip, crossing her arms, and kicking her curvaceous hip out to the side. Her long, tone legs jutted out of a red pencil skirt and were finished off with the sleekest, sexiest black patent heels. She wasn't the slightest bit shy in making passes at him. Charlie figured he had to cave at some point; they all did.

Gabe's gaze darted immediately back to the closed elevator doors that would soon be opening now that they had reached the floor to their offices. His hands fidgeted around in the usual nervous shuffle that always appeared when her forward gestures were putting too much pressure against his emotional boundaries. He shoved them safely into his pockets, attempting to wrangle them down inconspicuously with little to no success.

Clearing his throat from an obvious nervous tickle, he replied, "You know what I meant. And while I am most certainly flattered that a woman like you would ever think twice of being with a guy like me, you know my rules. I can't date people I work with. Never have, never will."

"Correction: you *can*. You just *won't*. There's no rule stating coworkers can't date," Charlie retorted more than confidently as the two stepped off the elevator and headed past the maze of cubicles toward their private offices.

"I know, but I don't think the higher ups in this company would look too fondly at a man who can't separate work from play for a promotion to an executive position. It's not a risk I'm willing to take right now."

"Well, your loss," Charlie muttered as she reached to open her office door. "Oh, and by the way, I wasn't in the Anthropologie shoe section." She gave him a sexy smile. "I was in the lingerie section at Nordstrom." Charlie threw out a wink as the cherry on top of the visual painting she had just created in his mind, leaving him to shake his head in self-defeat.

As she cockily marched to her desk, feeling overly confident that she had just successfully burned yet another hole of doubt into Gabe's flimsy, self-righteous wall, she felt her phone vibrating in the purse that still hung across her shoulder. Fumbling to find it, she answered just in time.

"What's up, B?" Charlie chirped to her just-as-sassy and borderline-bitchy friend, Bianca. Charlie had always chalked Bianca's quick tongue and blunt nature up to her friend's deep Italian roots. But while Bianca's fierce words were sometimes hard to swallow, her amazing authentic chicken parmesan and Italian cream cake were not. And, more importantly, Bianca was an unwavering, loyal friend—once you got on her good side. And that task wasn't for the faint of heart.

"Hey, chick. I wanted to call and remind you about our girls' gazebo night tomorrow. I would've shot you a text, but I'm driving. I'm surprised you answered. You're not working right now?"

"Yep, I'm still at work. Gabe and I just finished up a meeting," Charlie mumbled with a bored tone.

"Sounds super exciting. Hey, have you convinced him to get in your panties yet? I've never known a man to be able to withstand the sexual aura of Charlotte Compton for as long as he has. You sure he's not gay?" Bianca snickered through the phone.

Shaking her head at Bianca's per usual crude question—and even more so at the frustrating thought of how much time and energy she had wasted on trying to conquer Gabe's heart, or mind, or penis, for that matter—she responded, "No action yet. And no, he's not gay. He's just ridiculously stubborn. Should I bring anything tomorrow besides the usual?"

"No. Just you and your famous batch of French martinis. Sadie's handling the cheese and grapes, and I'm bringing chocolate-covered strawberries from Lulu's Bakery. I figured we needed a special treat after what the three of us have been through the past few months."

Charlie concurred with her friend's statement, feeling a twinge of pain as she hung up the phone. Chocolate-covered strawberries from the beloved Lulu's Bakery were a delicacy that could fix almost any ailment, from hormonal mood swings to bad days at work. But even the most coveted dessert would be hard-pressed to mend the most recent wounds of the three neighbors-turned-friends. The past few months—or rather, the past year—had been difficult for the trio. Charlie's mind slipped back to how easy life used to be when she'd first moved into their quaint little cul-de-sac just a couple of years ago.

Sadie and Levi had lived in their home for almost a decade. Bianca had moved into the house across the street with her husband, Tom, about five years after them. Charlie was the newest addition, only having lived in the "sac," as they called it, for a little over two years. She had decided to stop waiting to check off all the boxes, like marriage and kids, before buying her dream home. After all, she was successful in her own right and could easily afford the country club address. Charlie knew she stuck out like a sore thumb amongst the picture-perfect families, but she was never one to fit into molds anyway. She believed her presence to be a valuable contribution to diversity amidst cookie-cutter suburbia; but others thought differently. She didn't quite receive the warm welcome she had hoped for. Charlie had made every effort to befriend the two women across the street, despite their initial resistance. Charlie knew being a third wheel was never a pleasant assignment, but that hadn't stopped her from inching her way into the already-established duo. Bianca and Sadie had become fast friends immediately upon Bianca's move to the sac, despite the fact that they were polar opposites. Sadie was a stay-at-home mom with two boys and a typical white-picket-fence life. She was petite and soft spoken. Bianca was everything opposite. She was a boisterous, workaholic oral surgeon, running a business and trying to conquer the world all in one day. The two women had learned to appreciate their opposing energies, becoming each other's proverbial yin and yang. And when the mysterious single gal moved into their territory, Charlie was fully aware that the established pair was suspicious of her intentions. After all, having a single, attractive female on the block meant only one thing: keep your husbands close and your enemies closer.

Bianca's fiery tongue had been no match for Charlie's quick wit as the suspicious surgeon rattled off questions about Charlie's motive for moving into a family-oriented suburban neighborhood as a single female. Charlie slapped back with an answer even the sassy Italian couldn't help but wave the white flag of defeat to: "Bianca, I don't know you well. But I can see what your questions are trying to uncover. If you're wondering if I'm husband trolling, the answer is *no*. Sweetheart, I don't want your husband. Hell, I'm sure *you* don't even want your husband most days." And with that fencing finale, the two bowed to each other in mutual respect, knowing they had found a soulmate friend for life—one that could strike a sword equally as precise as the other. Sadie was a guaranteed package deal once Bianca was on board. And so, the unlikely trio of friendship, with divergent backgrounds and interests, was founded. Bianca had solidified their friendship by presenting Charlie with a housewarming gift, calling a truce: a wine glass that read *Bitchy Besties*. And the rest was history. The three friends still laugh at how Bianca's plan at unveiling "the snake in the grass," had completely backfired, and ultimately, "the snake" wound up expanding their duo into a triple threat armed with wine and the finest charcuterie board in the low country.

But only a year later, their friendship would be faced with most vicious test of all: Sadie's husband Levi was diagnosed with terminal bone cancer. Their Thursday gazebo nights had morphed into a therapeutic necessity rather than an update on Charlie's spicy dating life. Evan, Levi's brother, had been kind enough to come sit with his dying brother and his two nephews while the three ladies uncovered pain and fear that no human should have to endure.

As Charlie packed up her things and headed down the hallway toward the elevator to leave, she wondered how Sadie was holding up. She hadn't talked to her in a few days with this Sabo project closing in. She was sending her friend a quick text letting her know she was looking forward to hanging out tomorrow, when she heard Gabe's voice bellowing from his office.

"You headed out?"

"Yeah, you about to wrap it up?" Charlie yelled back, raising her head from her phone to see him making his way to his office doorway.

"No, not yet. You know me. Got a million things to finish." He smiled before beating her to her usual response. "I know, workaholic."

"Geez, Gabe. The only person that works this late is Batman. Why don't you at least do some work in the comfort of your own home? You keep bragging about this amazing balcony that you have. Why not put that view to good use? Seems like a perfect office backdrop to me."

"You know I get too distracted at home. Too many projects calling my name. And then there's my wine collection." He snickered.

Charlie shook her head in annoyance. "Once again,

your self-inflicted rules. Not mine. I'm ready to kick off these high heels and slip into something a little less… restrictive." She smiled coyly at him before stepping onto the elevator. "See ya tomorrow, Batman," she chirped, adjusting her form-fitted jacket making sure it hung perfectly to accentuate every curve. Their eyes stayed locked in a tight stare until the elevator doors severed the connection, only allowing the sound of his voice to sneak its way in through the crack.

"Sleep tight, Robin."

CHAPTER TWO

Sadie

*T*HUMP, THUMP, THUMP.
The heavy pounding in Sadie's chest beat in perfect rhythm to the pace of her feet on the asphalt. As she
rounded the corner of her street to the cul-de-sac, she
caught a glimpse of the dim light of her bedside lamp
beaming through her bedroom window. Her aching
heart sank deep into the pit of her stomach as she tried
her hardest to suck in the heavy, humid Savannah air.
Her escape from reality was over and the unbearable pain
would soon return. No amount of endorphins could
overcome the massive weight of her broken heart.

As her tennis shoes crossed onto the familiar brick pavers of her driveway, she collapsed onto her knees, not
from the exhaustion of the run, but from the unbearable
trek she had been on the past year of her life. Rolling
onto her back, Sadie splayed her limbs out like a snow
angel, gazing helplessly up at the clear night sky. The
ground felt strong underneath her body, connecting her
to the earth. She swore she could feel it spinning on its
axis. Stars lit up the sky like fireflies that seemed close
enough to catch. She hoped Levi was looking down at
the same ones tonight from Heaven. This was when she
felt closest to him. This was where she hoped he could
see her, here, on these pavers, staring up at the night sky.
Warm tears pressed out of the corners of her eyes as

she closed them and pictured his face. She smiled at the image, despite her pain.

Footsteps quietly shuffled behind her head. She didn't need to open her eyes to see who was there. It was Bianca. Over the past few months, everyone in the sac had come to know her sacred nightly routine. The guest quietly lay down beside Sadie on the ground, and she felt the comforting grasp of Bianca's hand squeezing hers.

"How is he tonight?" her sincere voice asked.

"He's beautiful," Sadie whispered. She knew Bianca believed her. That's what friends do. They believe in whatever helps your heart heal, even if the stretch in reality is far.

"That's good, sweetie. Tell him hi for me, and we miss him," Bianca squeaked out, obviously unsuccessful at fighting back a tearful break in her voice. Sadie knew Bianca's heart ached for her, that she wanted so badly to change the story for her, to delete the most recent chapter of her book—but that wasn't possible, even in fairytale land.

"How long will this pain last, B? I mean, I know it will be here forever in some fashion, but surely it will ease up some, right? It has to," Sadie pleaded, turning to look at Bianca for reassurance. Despite Bianca's best poker face, Sadie could see the uncertainty and pity in her eyes.

"Sweetie, I don't have all the answers. My only assumption is that the pain will morph into a new form that becomes more livable, and that somehow, time will heal the wound. But probably still leaving a scar."

"You know, I would rather feel this pain constantly than to ever forget one thing about him. Even the annoying stuff like his terrible grilling skills or his relentless snoring." Sadie chuckled affectionately. "I think I'm most afraid of forgetting."

"Oh, you don't have to worry about that. You have two amazing boys that look just like him and have his horri-

ble sense of humor." Sadie laughed at Bianca's accurate
description, thinking of all of Levi's bad jokes. "I'm sure
he'll live on through them. How are the boys, by the
way? Are they handling all of this okay?"

"As best as one could expect. Evan has been so good
to spend time with them. Of course, their uncle isn't a
replacement for their father, but they need a male figure in their lives. I'm clueless on everything they love,
like sports and the outdoors." Sadie's heart broke, thinking of all the moments Levi would miss—soccer games,
teaching the boys to shave, fishing and hunting expedi-
tions. These were all things Levi had dreamed of for years
when he and Sadie were planning their family. He had
been so excited to have two boys, just like him and Evan.
His big brother was everything, and he couldn't wait for
his sons to have that same bond.

"They are so lucky to have Evan. I can only imagine his pain too. Watching Levi suffer had to be hard to
watch as a protective big brother that had always helped
him fight his battles." Bianca sighed.

Maybe Bianca was right. Maybe the pain would just
always be like this, but they would eventually all become
numb, making life tolerable. Whatever the answer was,
there was currently no good conclusion. Sadie watched
as Bianca stood from the pavers, reaching her arm out to
help her up. With a tight grip on her hand—and more
importantly, her soul—Sadie caved to Bianca's pull as
she rose to her feet from the safe ground. Hugging her
tightly, Sadie felt Bianca's lips kiss her sweaty cheek.

"You're going to be okay. I promise," Bianca stated
matter-of-factly, grasping Sadie's shoulders tightly. Bianca
sounded convincing, and deep down, Sadie wanted to
believe her words. She genuinely believed that God's
plan was better than any she could have designed. But
in this moment, it was hard to see the path for the smog.

Nodding, Sadie turned to the baby-blue front door

of her home. The boys were inside doing last-minute schoolwork and prepping for bedtime. She needed to pull herself together for them, like she had so many times over the past year. She hoped the pain in her eyes was masked by the sweat and fatigue of her jog.

"Don't forget, tomorrow night is gazebo night. Get your run in early," Bianca yelled as Sadie strolled to her front porch.

"I know. Charlie already texted me about it a little earlier," Sadie replied, turning to give a thumbs up to Bianca's final shout. She was looking forward to the weekly girls' gazebo night this time. She needed a big cocktail and good company. Giving a rare genuine smile to her friend, she blew a kiss at Bianca as she closed the door for the night.

Sadie could hear the shower running in the boys' bathroom. They had both done way better with their dad's death than she had ever imagined they would—or better yet, way better than she had. They seemed to have matured a decade in the past year, having watched their once super-human father wither away before their eyes. Sadie's heart ached at the thought of them having to grow up too soon. The boys had always been under Levi's wings though, so they had been groomed from an early age to be tough, honorable, and reliable. Levi had wanted nothing more than to raise his sons to be even better than he was, which seemed like an insurmountable task to Sadie, who honestly believed her husband had been pure perfection.

"Boys!" Sadie yelled over the shower's echo. "Time to wrap it up. You both have twenty minutes of reading to do before bed tonight."

"I'm already reading, Mom," Tad yelled back proudly from his bedroom. That left Max to be the one showering, by default. Tad was eleven going on forty. As the first born, he took his duties and responsibilities as the new man of the household very seriously. Sadie had reminded him on multiple occasions that while she appreciated his help, he was still a kid. She and Levi had pondered for hours after he was born on what to name him. Nothing had seemed to fit. Levi had spent the entire pregnancy referring to their unborn child as "the tadpole," and she wasn't sure if it was delirium setting in from the delivery, but she sarcastically suggested Tad, short for Tadpole. She would never forget Levi sitting on the edge of her hospital bed, the proud new father holding their son wrapped up in a blue blanket, both them crying with laughter at the idea. "I actually like it." Levi smirked. "Well, Tad— not the full name Tadpole." And the rest was history.

"Okay, baby. I'll tuck you in as soon as Max is out of the shower," she confirmed. As she headed toward the kitchen to pack lunches and load the dishwasher, she heard a ping on her phone.

Tell the boys GN for me. I'll be there to pick them up for baseball practice around 3:30 tomorrow.

It was Evan. Her heart sank at the sight of his text, despite how grateful she was for him. She hated that Levi wasn't there to take the boys to practice. Having Evan around was a double-edged sword. Evan was just a four-year-older version of her late husband, with a few more inches in height and a handful more gray hairs, so the sight of him was comforting yet eerie. His voice was an exact replica of Levi's. She could close her eyes and be fooled that somehow her husband was standing there talking to her.

Will do. Thanks, E. Give the girls kisses from me.

Sadie loved her nieces, Ava and Lainey. They had given her the opportunity for tea parties and dress-up dolls that her sons had not. She had been so preoccupied lately, though, that the scale had been tipped unevenly. Evan had been way more present for Max and Tad than she had for his girls recently. Sadie hoped they understood the reasoning and that this season would pass. Maybe a good spa day with them would help make up for lost time. They were both in junior high now, so anything pampering related would surely be a hit.

She made a mental note to text Kate, her sister-in-law, about it later. Sadie was certain she would be up for that escapade. Kate was much more self-indulgent than she was. Kate loved all things fancy and elite. Sadie wasn't sure exactly what had drawn Evan to his wife. They were so different. He was so humble and grounded, and she seemed so flighty and vainglorious at times. Levi had always struggled with his brother's choice in a spouse. He claimed to get an unsettling vibe from her, like she wasn't reliable. Sadie had always taken up for Kate. After all, she hadn't done a single thing that would imply any foul play or lack of commitment. Just because she liked expensive things and seemed to feed on drama didn't mean she had any less love for her family. Maybe it meant she was bored or had too much time on her hands—or too much money, with her uber-successful husband's bank account at her fingertips. Maybe she had her priorities a little out of line with all the years she spent at supper club parties and country club socials. However, secretly, Sadie had the same deep-rooted suspicions as her husband. But keeping the seas calm was way more important to her than rocking the boat with unsupported accusations.

Sadie heard the water stop and made her way to the boys' bedrooms to tuck them in. The two ultra-masculine kids were all things boy, but never had they turned their nose up at nighttime snuggles with their mom. Sadie hoped this wouldn't end any time soon. She was so grateful for a husband that had never been afraid to show his love with touch or words. The boys had seen what a good marriage should look like. Levi had never been too busy for a hug or a long kiss. And it was never the wrong time or place. He'd loved limitlessly and she was so thankful her kids had seen that in the flesh.

"Night, Mom," Max boasted as he smacked Sadie's cheek firmly with a kiss.

"Love you, my baby. Uncle Evan is taking you and Tad to baseball tomorrow. Make sure to have your things ready to go by three-thirty after school, okay?"

"Sure thing, Mom," Max confirmed, reaching for the book on his nightstand.

Sadie made her way into Tad's room. It was quiet. He had fallen asleep with his glasses on, and his book tucked under his chin. She chuckled at the sight that lent proof to his old soul. How many times had she seen his father in that same position? She took off his glasses and laid his book down on the bedside table, then placed a kiss on his lips.

"Night, my sweet Tadpole," she whispered, fighting back tears. He didn't move an inch as she turned off his lights and headed to her room.

As she slipped in between the sheets to her own nesting place, Sadie's hand slid across to the empty side of the bed. Touching Levi's pillow, she sighed. "Night, baby. I love you," she whispered while her pillowcase slowly became damp from tears. She couldn't remember the last time she had fallen asleep with a dry pillow. Life had been so simple and good before Levi's cancer diagnosis. She longed to relive just one night from before that time. But that would never happen.

CHAPTER THREE

Bianca

THE BRIGHT SUN was beaming straight through the car window onto Bianca's skin. She could feel the temperature rising inside her body and wasn't sure if it was the direct ray of light or her anxiety building that caused a bead of sweat to run down her back. Casting a quick glance over to her husband, she could sense from Tom's stern expression that he, too, must have been fighting a case of the jitters. Grabbing his free hand, her sweaty palm squeezed his, lending a comforting touch to her partner of seven years. Tom was a quiet man, the polar opposite of "larger than life Bianca," but they complemented each other well. Tom appeared content to let Bianca take the lead in most aspects of their union. He had gracefully volunteered to move to Savannah after their engagement, allowing their long-distance relationship to take the next official step toward marriage. After all, his engineering consulting firm could be run from anywhere. Bianca, having a well-established oral surgery practice, couldn't as easily pick up and move without having to start again from scratch. Logistically and theoretically, it had made sense for him to move to her.

Over the years, their careers had grown, but the one thing that hadn't was their family. They had been trying for what felt like forever to get pregnant with no such luck. In all transparency, Bianca had never really wanted children before Tom came along. She had always been satisfied with her career being her "baby." But Tom, and her uber-traditional Italian Catholic father, had taunted her into seeking motherhood. And like the competitive, goal-driven surgeon that she was, once she had set her sights on something, there was no stopping her at attaining the prize. But there had been conditions set. Tom had agreed that Bianca's work schedule would be priority and that the bulk of the childcare would fall on his watch. Bianca, not being the most maternal despite being the oldest female in her large Catholic family of five, had long professed her dislike of small children. But she had made an exception for her husband. That was a sacrifice of marriage, right? And boy had she sacrificed, so she thought. Between fertility trackers and ovulation kits, Bianca was ready for a bullseye. And today was the big day. Bianca's heart pounded. Tom placed the car in park and shut off the engine in front of the large white stucco building of the South Georgia Fertility Center.

"This is it. Are you ready?" Bianca asked her husband sheepishly.

"As ready as I can be," Tom muttered through a deep nervous breath. Bianca cupped Tom's cheek with her hand, leaning in to give a reassuring kiss. As they walked hand in hand into the sterile doctor's office, Bianca smiled up at her tall, shaggy-haired husband. Apparently sensing that she needed affirmation, he gave her a quick wink back.

Paper after paper was placed in front of them to sign as they sat wide-eyed at the consultation table across from the medical team that currently had the fate of their family in their hands. Most of the forms centered around the financials of the medications and egg retrieval procedure. Bianca initialed away what seemed to be her life. Tom sat beside her in silence. Her fearless personality was much more equipped than Tom's to handle the curveballs that life whirled. The worry and fear expressed in Tom's furrowed brow told the story of what was going on inside that mathematical and calculating mind of his. As the doctor ran through a list of all the risks and possible side effects of the medications and procedures, Bianca could see him wiggling around in his seat uncomfortably.

The doctor must have noticed too. "Tom, do you have some concerns? Something I can help you with? I know this is a lot of information, but it's crucial that I give you all the possible outcomes, no matter the minimal risk," the doctor stated, looking sternly over the top of his wire framed square readers.

"Um, no. I guess I'm okay," Tom answered hesitantly. "Well, actually, I do have one. Did you say that death was a possibility during the egg retrieval surgery?" he squeaked out with broken syllables.

"Every surgical procedure in medicine has that possibility, whether from infection, post-op complications, or anesthesia-related issues," the doctor confirmed. "It's a legal obligation for us to state that. I promise that your wife will be well taken care of and the risks for complications are low."

Bianca's heart broke. She knew the root of her husband's fears was coming from Levi's recent death. While the two hadn't been the best of friends, he had still watched the horrific story unfold from across the sac. Everyone in their neighborhood circle had been affected in some way. They had all pitched in to cook meals, help with Sadie's boys, and mow their lawn when Levi got too weak to do it himself. Bianca knew that despite Tom's typically stoic, almost numb demeanor, Levi's death was still a tender wound.

"Babe," Bianca whispered, squeezing his thigh in reassurance, "I'm going to be fine. Couples do IVF all the time."

Tom nodded, acknowledging the sincerity of her words. "Yeah. You're right, B."

But Tom's disposition seemed anything but convinced as their appointment wrapped up, and they headed home with a cooler full of expensive medications in the front passenger floorboard. Bianca's intuition was telling her something was off. He wasn't committed to the idea, which baffled her since he was the one that had wanted children in the first place. Maybe it was stress or fear of the unknown. Surely every couple in their situation went through the same rollercoaster of emotions...so she hoped.

———————

The car ride home felt longer than the usual fifteen-minute drive from the hospital to their house. The silence in the car added what seemed like hours onto the trip. Bianca realized that this entire process was stressful, but they were finally getting somewhere. She couldn't help but be a little disappointed in Tom's lackluster demeanor.

"Tom, are you sure you want to do this? It's going to change our lifestyle completely. We've been together for seven years without having to so much as think about whether we come or go. This baby, or babies, will change everything."

Tom's hands tightly gripped the steering wheel. "Sure, babe. I know. I just wish we could do it on our own, without help from a doctor. But you obviously think this is the right direction to go in." He smiled at Bianca, his wavy blond hair shining even brighter than usual with the sunlight streaming through the sunroof.

"This is a marriage, Tom. It's not *my* decision. It's *our* decision. I realize this isn't what we had planned, but nothing in my life has ever come easy. I've had to take twenty extra steps to get to where most people get with one. I guess having a baby is no different, par for the course," Bianca said snidely as they pulled into the garage of their two-story stucco home.

Bianca's heart sank, thinking of the congruent story lines of her life. Being the oldest child of a fiercely driven physician father, she had spent her life trying to keep up with his expectations for her. There were rules. So. Many. Rules. Then there was her tiny, spicy grandmother, constantly pecking on her shoulder, reminding her of what a good Italian woman should portray: homemade pastas strung over kitchen chairs to dry, Sunday Catholic Mass appearances with Holy Days of Obligation to boot, and providing enough sex for your husband to keep the goomahs away. And while she had successfully met all expectations, they had by no means been attained on the first go-round. She had made her high school basketball team on the second try her sophomore year, gotten into her father's college alma mater off the wait-list, and matched with her oral surgery residency only after having to retake the endodontic portion of her dental exam boards as a formality, even though she would never have to do another root canal in her life. Bianca was wildly successful, but not without some trips and bruises along the way. Having a baby was yet another hurdle she would have to jump. She just wondered if Tom had the stamina for the race.

Tom cut off the engine, then turned to her, grabbing her hand. "Bianca, don't worry about me. I've been off the mark lately mentally. Not quite certain what's going on. It's stress, I'm sure. It's nothing you've done. I'm sorry, babe." He smiled reassuringly. "Now don't you have a gazebo night to get to?"

"Yes. Crap! I totally lost track of time." Bianca quickly looked down at the clock on her phone to see if she had any missed messages from Sadie or Charlie. Her screen read five twenty-five and thankfully no missed messages.

"I'm good. We don't meet up until six thirty. What do you say we give the old school-natural-way one more try?" Bianca winked as she stepped out of the car, motioning him inside the house with as sexy a stroll as she could muster with the cooler of fertility medications tucked under her arm. Bianca watched as he shrugged his shoulders in defeat. The look on his face was heartbreaking. She had to fix this.

Despite Tom's body language of rejection, Bianca didn't give up. Grabbing his hand, she pulled him out of the car, through the back door and into their bedroom, but not before quickly unloading the medicine into the freezer, which did seem to derail her sexy efforts a tiny bit. But that didn't stop her. Tom had never been one to be forward in the bedroom anyway. Bianca had always taken that role upon herself, much like every other situation in her life. But something was different this time. His confidence was gone. His desire was absent. And his soul was guarded.

As Bianca seemingly forced her husband through the motions, she was making love to a stranger. He sank farther away the closer she got. She wanted to talk more. But she knew better than to press him. The day had been heavy, and any extra weight might make him break. She opted to leave him alone to process. Besides, she needed to get cleaned up and down to the gazebo. Sadie wasn't remotely forgiving of a tardy appearance. She kissed Tom softly on the lips, and his closed eyelids didn't flinch. She took that as his request to be alone. If there was one thing she knew about her husband, he was king of internalizing. And there was no way to pry out his thoughts until he was ready. And now obviously wasn't the time. She just hoped he figured it all out soon…

CHAPTER FOUR

Bianca

THE GRAVEL PATH to the gazebo had been tram-
pled down more times than any of the three women
could collectively count. The large, white, wooden venue
had been a staple for date nights, birthday parties, picnics,
and more. When the tide was high, the Moon River covered the marshland separating the gazebo from the iconic
low country landmark. For the most part, the breeze off
the water kept the sand gnats away, but just in case, the
builders had brilliantly placed two large ceiling fans to
ward off any unwelcome tiny distractors, while the light
blue ceiling played a supporting role in the backdrop—
that, of course, had been chosen to deter evil spirits, as
low country folklore had so believed for generations. On
summer evenings, when sunset was delayed far into the
day, you could catch glimpses of dolphins jumping and
hunting for their evening meal. Boats were aplenty, mostly
fishing, but sometimes the occasional shrimp boat or sail-
boat could be seen off in the distance of the intercoastal
waterway. All in all, it was the perfect little niche for anyone from families and couples to friends and strangers to
enjoy one of the earth's most picturesque scenes.

Bianca could hear the gravel rustling behind her at a
steady pace as she made her way down the palmetto and
pine-lined trail. She had left her house early, hoping for a
little time alone to clear her mind of the heaviness of the

day. Something wasn't settling right with her about Tom's reaction at the doctor's appointment earlier. She couldn't quite put her finger on it, but she knew there was more to his apprehension than simply worrying about her wellbeing. But as she turned to see who was trailing her, she spotted Sadie, with her shoulder-strap cooler in tow, smiling and waving. Sadie Carson was always early. For everything. Her calendars were perfectly organized, and her grocery lists immaculately crafted. She was every Southern man's dream—a true, loving housewife with a genuine smile and an open kitchen, welcoming guests for coffee or wine anytime—depending on the time of day, of course. Only, sadly, now she was alone, which seemed like such a waste of her talents.

"Slow down, geez," Sadie barked breathlessly as Bianca watched her trying to catch up. The heavy humidity made even the most physically fit gasp for air in the moisture-dense climate. "I barely finished my run earlier in this God-awful heat," Sadie professed with small droplets of sweat starting to trickle down her temples.

"Which is exactly why I don't run, sister." Bianca snickered.

"Trust me, once you have kids, staying fit and trim isn't as easy as cutting calories for a few days. The pounds stick and stay. Plus, it clears my swirling mind. Speaking of, how did your appointment go today with the fertility doctor?" Sadie pried innocently.

"Fine," Bianca answered half-heartedly as she stepped into the shaded destination. She wasn't ready yet to discuss all the details. She needed a good cocktail before letting her two friends dissect and analyze her suspicion that something was wrong with Tom.

"Fine?" Sadie questioned as she sat the cooler onto the wooden bench and unpacked the perfectly organized containers full of fruit and fancy cheeses.

"Yeah, a lot of information to take in at once. For both of us," Bianca mildly clarified.

Just as Bianca was about to attempt to change the subject, a loud whistle bellowed out from the trail behind them. "Wow. She's actually here on time. I can't believe it. She's never able to pry herself away from work—or that *man*, for that matter." Bianca snickered, knowing that Charlie was bound and determined to conquer Gabe's heart. She had never been rejected by a man in her entire life that they knew of. Since Charlie had marked her target, it was apparent she had taken every single minute possible to drag out their time together at the office, whether it be critical to the project at hand or not.

"Can you believe it? I'm on time. Don't ever bust my balls about being late ever again," Charlie stated proudly, placing the large martini-filled thermos in the center of them as if it were the Olympic torch.

"First of all, you have no balls to bust. Secondly, once on time does not make you a punctual person, my dear. But the rarity will be noted, for sure." Sadie patted Charlie's cheek with maternal approval, giving her a snarky smile.

"Geez. There's no winning with you two." Charlie huffed with the skill of a teenager, pouring a magenta concoction into a plastic martini glass.

"So why *are* you on time? Was there a fire alarm forcing you out of your office or something?" Bianca chuckled, stealing the just-filled martini glass from Charlie's grip.

"Um, you're welcome," Charlie stated with fake agitation, grabbing two more plastic inverted cones on stems. "No. No fire alarms. I was ready to see you two. And… Gabe left early, so I had no reason to linger." She chuckled as she handed Sadie an overly filled glass.

"Any progress on the Gabe front?" Sadie quizzed, taking a sip.

"Ugh, no. That guy's asshole is drawn tight as a drum. I

swear I've used every man-hypnotizing tactic that I have single-handedly perfected over the years, and none seem to be working," Charlie frustratingly admitted.

"Maybe he isn't into you. Maybe you aren't his type," Sadie stated nonchalantly.

"What? I'm everyone's type." Charlie huffed again, flipping her long straight brunette hair back over her shoulder in true diva style, giving her best Cher imper-sonation. "Besides, I see the way he looks at me. I catch him staring out of the corner of my eye. And he gets all sorts of nervous and starts to fidget when I flirt with him. I know he wants me. I think I intimidate him. Not too many chicks are as forward as I am."

Bianca watched as Sadie smiled endearingly at her friend. "True statement. I only wish I had your self-con-fidence, Charlie. He'll come around. Give him time. Just promise me you'll keep your options open to seeing other people. I hate to see you put all your eggs in one basket," Sadie pleaded.

Bianca could guess what Sadie was thinking: *if only my life was as simple as yours.* Bianca was proud of her heavy-hearted friend for always taking the high road and not comparing Charlie's bachelorette struggles to her own widow trials and tribulations.

"Enough about me. B, what happened today at your appointment? How did it go?" Charlie pressed.

"She says it was *fine.*" Sadie sarcastically beat Bianca to the punch.

"Well, it *was* fine," Bianca responded protectively. "It seemed like we were signing our lives away with all the paperwork and documentation. And…" She trailed off, taking a long sip of the raspberry concoction.

"And?" Charlie pried. "No one likes a cliffhanger."

"And Tom choked. Even the doctor asked him if he was okay. I think the list of possible complications sent him into a tizzy," Bianca continued after gulping down her hefty swig.

"Is it really that risky?" Charlie asked innocently.

"Not any riskier than any other outpatient-type surgery. They list the worst that can happen. It's a formality. Not to bring up Levi, Sadie, but I think Tom is still scarred over his death like the rest of us. All medical lingo sounds worse after you've watched one of your friends die." Bianca made eye contact with Sadie, giving her a comforting smile, knowing that the worst pain still resided in Sadie's broken heart.

"So, are you still going through with it?" Charlie pushed the conversation past death, and for that, Bianca was thankful.

"I guess. I asked Tom on the way home if he was sure he wanted to do this. I have the medications and am set to start them on Monday. The last thing I want to do is load myself up with hormones and then have him balk. Or worse, get pregnant and then have him decide it's not what he wants. We've been together just the two of us for so long, it'll be a big adjustment having a baby."

"Would you be okay if he backed out and changed his mind?" Charlie pried.

"You know I never really considered having kids before Tom. My career was plenty for me to manage. But he's always wanted them so much. To me, just the two of us is plenty. So, I'm fine either way. I just need him to be fully committed to the idea because after Monday, there's no going back."

"Having kids is a big adjustment for sure. Especially when you jump through the hoops you two have. I'm sure he'll be fine," Sadie replied in a comforting tone.

"I sure hope so. We're about to see what he's made of." Bianca chuckled. "Or more importantly, what he can tolerate. I hear these medications bring the beast out of your soul. If he's scared now, wait until he sees me all hyped up on hormones." Laughter echoed through the gazebo. Bianca took pride in her extra-large personality, and it was comical thinking of what it could look like getting any more exuberant.

"If he kicks you out, you can stay with me, B. You don't scare me." Charlie fist bumped her friend. "Although Sadie would make a much better roommate. She's a way better cook."

"Yeah. I love you, Charlie, but I would absolutely pick Sadie's house over yours. Speaking of your house, is Evan there with the boys?" Bianca was happy to divert the subject away from her and Tom.

"Yes. Max and Tad were looking forward to it. I know they miss their dad terribly. And it doesn't take much to feel Levi's presence when Evan's around. They look, act, and sound so much alike its spooky." Bianca watched as Sadie's eyes drifted down to her empty martini glass. Bianca quickly reached to refill it. After all, Sadie needed to drown her sorrows more than anyone. Bianca's heart sank a little deeper with guilt knowing she was going home later, a little tipsy, to snuggle in bed with her husband, and Sadie would never again have that luxury.

"What's Kate been up to lately? It's odd that she never comes over and brings the girls to hang out while Evan's there," Charlie inquired as Bianca topped off her drink and handed out the coveted chocolate covered Lulu's strawberries.

"Now that you mention it, I haven't seen her since the funeral. I was thinking yesterday about how I need to set up a girl's outing with Lainey and Ava. I feel like I've totally dropped the ball on aunt duties the past year. Kate stays so busy with all her country club social activities and running the girls to after-school activities that she probably hasn't had time to stop by. Plus, she and I don't have that much in common. We get along and are cordial, but she isn't someone I find overly comforting. So, I'm not super heartbroken that she doesn't come by to visit."

"True. She's probably one of the shallowest women I know," Bianca stated matter-of-factly before shoving an entire strawberry into her mouth.

"B! That's not nice," Charlie barked with a sarcastic smile, following suit taking her own dive into chocolate strawberry heaven. "Yummy! These never disappoint."

Bianca shook her head at Charlie's lash, who was obviously playing up the opportunity to be the honorable of the three women, when she herself was typically just as quick to cast condemnatory remarks about Kate. "Give me a break, Charlie," Bianca retorted, rolling her eyes. "We all know Kate would rather be prancing around the Savannah Golf Club in pearls and a Lilly Pulitzer sundress, Bellini in hand, than spending time comforting her recently widowed sister-in-law."

"Guys, its fine. Honestly, I would rather it just be Evan anyway. It's easier to swallow the pain of not having Levi around when there isn't another married couple staring me in the face, reminding me of my loneliness. And go easy on Kate. Deep down, I think she means well."

Bianca watched as Sadie turned to gaze over the water. The tide was rolling back out, revealing sandy mud covered with tiny little air bubbles and fiddler crabs scattering the surface. The sun had finally taken its place below the horizon, and a crescent moon was beginning to appear. Bianca knew what Sadie was craving. It had become as predictable as the streetlights clicking on at dark.

"Speaking of Evan. I need to get back to the boys. I'm sure Evan's ready to be home after a long day at work. I don't want to keep him," Sadie explained, packing up her cooler.

But Bianca knew better. Evan was in no rush to get home to a presumably empty house. Truth was, it was Sadie's favorite time of day. Bianca figured she couldn't wait to get home and lie in her driveway, stare at the heavens, and find some sense of peace with the possibility that she might feel Levi's presence. To Bianca it looked crazy, but who was she to judge? After all, life was crazy. And sometimes you did what it took to survive in this crazy world. Even if it meant selling your soul to the *Looney Tunes* gods.

CHAPTER FIVE

Charlie

GABE WAS IN full-blown *Rain Man* mode. Long pieces of white butcher paper hung on any free wall space available in his immaculately organized office. They looked so out of place with their haphazard placement and irregularly torn edges. As he zipped around like a squirrel with ADHD, scribbling ideas onto the blank canvases, Charlie sat coolly in his chair, stiletto-adorned feet propped comfortably on his pristine desk watching the show. Gabe was a minimalist. And his completely bare desktop was only the beginning. No pictures, no memorabilia, not even a name plate was allowed to invade his workspace. Each day, there were three Post-It notes placed perfectly on the upper right corner, each stating one task to accomplish by the end of the day. Then, the next day, those three were removed, and three new ones placed. This extreme display of systematic behavior drove Charlie insane. She did anything she could to disturb Gabe's perfect order. Whether it be papers, a coffee mug, or currently, her high heel shoes, she loved disrupting the clean slate. She made it her duty to be the antithesis of his compulsive ways.

"Charlie, can you please take your overpriced shoes off my desk? You know how I despise that. I'm trying to concentrate here, and you're being no help," Gabe stated with agitation.

"Well, it looks like I'm going to be here awhile, so I would prefer to be comfortable. But yes, I will remove the shoes if you insist," she rebutted, keeping her feet on the sleek black desktop while popping off the expensive cheetah print beauties and dropping them onto the floor, exposing her perfectly manicured toes. She gave them a relaxing wiggle as they stretched out over the surface. Charlie knew Gabe meant both the heels and her feet, but she couldn't resist the urge to play dumb and take his direction literally to push his buttons more. After all, he looked so cute when he was frazzled with his pursed lips and wrinkled forehead.

Gabe huffed and rolled his eyes. "You're unbelievable, Charlotte Compton." Turning back to the white sheet plastered with his chicken scratch, he continued, "What do you think about a holiday promo?"

"Holidays? Seriously, Gabe? I'm currently dreaming of floating in a swimming pool with a delicious umbrellaed-bevy in hand. Newsflash, it's April. Plus, holidays are so overdone." Charlie tipped her sunglasses down from their positioning as her headband and onto her nose as she leaned back into his chair in full-blown sun-goddess mode.

"Let me help your imagination slip to the winter holidays, bathing beauty," Gabe snickered, moving quickly over to the thermostat, turning the air conditioning to a frigid cool.

As much as she pushed his buttons and tested his theories, she knew he loved her complete opposite perspectives. Otherwise, why would he keep asking for her opinion? He could just as well confide in another coworker. Something about their chemistry apparently made him come back to her, even if she was a huge pain in his ass.

"Yikes, that's cold! Okay, point taken. Now can you please turn that off?" Charlie begged, defeated in her attempt to procrastinate. "Listen, I know you're hell-bent on winning their trust, but Gabe, you need to slow down. You're going to go into cardiac arrest if you don't stop worrying about Sabo's approval. You've been at it non-stop. Did you even go home over the weekend?" Charlie quizzed, eyeing Gabe's wrinkled shirt.

"Yes, I went home. And yes, I did come in and work this weekend," Gabe defended, tucking in the shirt that had come untucked as he maneuvered from one edge of his office to the other. "Charlie, now isn't the time for you to lecture me on how you think I should operate. If you're going to do that then you can leave," he barked, eyeing her over the top of his dark-framed glasses.

She knew it was no use. She might as well dig in and help him. Otherwise, he would be here all night. "Okay. Want my opinion?"

Gabe nodded, egging her to go on.

"What am I going to get in return?" She jokingly winked and blew him a sexy kiss.

"Come on, Charlie. I don't have time for this," he retorted.

"You're no fun. Fine. You're totally missing a huge opportunity. The holidays are hectic, yes indeed. However, Sabo is a company that caters to stressed-out, spread-thin moms. Do you want to know the most stressful time of year, second only to the holidays for parents? Back-to-school time."

Gabe's eyebrows lifted and she knew he was intrigued by her concept.

"There's nothing that moms dream of more than dropping their kids off at school on the first day and heading home to crash on the couch until two thirty-five when it's time to go get the hoodlums from carpool. Want to give the Sabo board something fresh? Give them a back-to-school 'Mom's Turn' promo." And with that, Charlie stood up, straightened her form-fitting black slacks, slipped back into her heels, and tossed her red blazer over her shoulder with flare, poised for any designer catwalk. As she strutted out of Gabe's office, she heard him chuckle at her blatant display of arrogance.

"Must be nice to be so smart," Gabe yelled from behind her.

"I'm not all that smart. I'm just bold," she corrected him, turning to face him, her eyes sending a laser beam to his. "You prefer an office with minimal clutter. Well, I prefer a brain with minimal clutter. You're so distracted and fixated by the stacks and stacks of rules and guidelines that reside in your head that you can't see the valuable gems that lie underneath. My mind is wide open. No restrictions, no guidelines for as far as the eye can see. That makes it easy to see the valuable stuff." Charlie smiled and batted her lashes, spreading her arms wide, insinuating the valuable stuff was indeed her. She hoped someday he would opt to make his mind as clutter-free as he had made his tangible world. And maybe, just maybe, he would see what a sparkly gem she was.

"Thanks, Robin," Gabe called out as Charlie made her way back to her office.

"Yep. Anytime, Batman." Charlie could hear her desk phone ringing as she approached the door. When she was close enough to see the name on the caller ID, her stomach dropped for a second. *Moretti Oral Surgery. Why would Bianca be calling my work number? I didn't even know she had it.* But as Charlie jumped to answer the ring from across her desk, she was too late. She picked up her cell phone that had been charging next to her laptop and was greeted with five missed calls and three texts. All from Bianca.

"Does anyone answer their phone these days, damnit?" Bianca yelled into Charlie's ear rather than the standard *hello* that graced most conversation introductions.

"Geez, B. What's wrong?" Charlie asked, slightly

annoyed that no one was dying or injured, which would have resulted in Bianca sounding more frantic than angry. "I am at work, you know."

"Ugh. I know. Sorry. It's just that I have been trying to get ahold of Tom all day long. He won't answer and I need him to move my IVF medications from the freezer to the refrigerator. I totally forgot to do it this morning before work. I'm supposed to start them tonight when I get home." Bianca's voice sounded equal parts annoyed, worried, and nervous.

"Ask Sadie to go move them for you. I'm sure she's home," Charlie suggested.

"Nope. Of course, the one time I need her to be at home, she's with Tad on a school field trip somewhere in the middle of Claxton at some damn free-range chicken farm. I was hoping you were headed home for lunch and could run by and check things out. I'm really worried about Tom more than anything. I have a sinking feeling something is wrong. I have back-to-back sedation surgeries all day and I really can't leave," Bianca explained.

"B, I wish I could. I'm up to my ears in this Sabo pitch. I'm sure Tom will call you back in a little bit. He's probably just outside in the yard or something," Charlie reassured her high-strung friend.

"Yeah. I hope so. I guess I'll run home for a quick minute if I don't hear from him soon. The patients will just have to wait. Thanks anyway, Charlie."

Charlie ended the call, and her gut sank. She couldn't put her finger on it, but she too felt like something was off with Tom. But now wasn't the time for her to dwell on drama at the sac. She had an epic back-to-school promotion to curate.

CHAPTER SIX

Bianca

BIANCA'S HEART POUNDED. Thankfully, from the outside, her gray stucco home looked normal. Tom typically parked in the garage, so she wasn't expecting to see any signs of him as she drove up, unless he happened to be fiddling in the yard, which he wasn't. The door to the garage rose in what seemed like slow motion, like a stage curtain waiting to reveal an epic scene. And epic it was. No car. No sign of Tom. The large two-car space was empty. Really empty. As she scanned the shelves lining the walls, they were nearly bare. Confused, and slightly disturbed, Bianca's feet felt like concrete blocks as she pulled in and headed to the door leading to their home.

Peeping into the kitchen, her familiar domain, all seemed untouched. "Well, that looks normal," she muttered to herself, relieved to find that the inside seemed okay.

"Tom? Babe? Are you okay?" Nothing but silence responded back to her. "Thomas!" Bianca tried once more, feeling a knot forming in her stomach. Her mind started to race with the worst possible scenarios. *Oh my God! Have we been robbed? Is Thomas tied up dead?!*

As she raced to his office, fully expecting to find him mutilated, the hallway echoed more than usual. She rounded the corner to his workspace. Something was wrong. Very wrong. The room was empty. Not even a picture was left hanging on the walls. And not one sign of Tom. Bianca's hands started to tremble. *What the fuck was going on?*

"Bianca?" a voice echoed softly from behind her.

Startled, she turned to see Mrs. Gibson standing in the doorway. "Oh, hi, Mrs. Gibson," Bianca gasped, relieved to see the sweet elderly neighbor that had obviously let herself in through the open garage entrance.

"Is everything okay here? I got your voicemails to see if I would come check on Tom. I was at the gardener's club monthly luncheon today, so I wasn't able to call you back, but when I left this morning, there was a huge moving truck in your driveway. It seemed a little odd, but I just assumed you were maybe moving things to storage or getting new furniture…" Mrs. Gibson trailed off nervously as she scanned the half-empty room.

"A moving truck?" Bianca gasped, her mind swirling with what was becoming apparent. Bianca bumped past Mrs. Gibson, bolting from room to room. Bianca was slapped with the reality of what had happened: Thomas was gone. Out. And with him, his things. Bianca's chest tightened, making it hard for her to breathe.

She collapsed onto the living room floor, her body tingling with weakness. Stars raced in front of her pupils. And just before she started to see black, she caught a glimpse of a familiar face.

"Shit. Shit. Shit!" Charlie yelled. "Bianca, just breathe. You're going to be okay. Mrs. Gibson," Charlie continued with a forced calm in her voice, "I'll handle this. Thank you so much." Bianca was thankful, even in her distracted condition that Charlie had the courtesy to ask the elderly neighbor to excuse herself so that she didn't see her mental breakdown. It wasn't every day that a stonewalled Italian surgeon lost her composure—but it also wasn't every day that her husband apparently moved out on her without so much as a goodbye or fuck you. Bianca continued to struggle to breathe, but as the seconds passed, she began to regain her clarity and vision, which wasn't a sight she even wanted to see as she scanned the room.

Charlie's phone rang, and before the tone had a chance to complete one full alert, Bianca heard Charlie's frantic voice bark to the person on the other end. "Hell no, it's not okay. Where are you? When can you be here?" Bianca watched as Charlie's eyes darted to hers. She didn't have to ask who it was. It was Sadie. "Tom moved out. All his shit is gone. Well, half of *their* shit is gone, which I guess means he took it upon himself to take half of what he thought was his," Charlie answered bitterly, followed by nodding as Sadie's voice became audible from the cell phone. "Yes. Gone. What a cowardly bastard. You've gotta get here quick. Okay. Bye," Charlie replied, squeezing Bianca's hand tightly.

"What are you doing here? I thought you were in the middle of that big Sabo project?" Bianca asked.

"After you called, I had a sinking feeling I needed to come home and check on things. I'm glad I did. Work can wait." Charlie smiled tenderly at her.

"I'm glad you did too," Bianca replied. "I've never had a panic attack before. I've seen plenty of patients have them. Now I know what they mean when they say they feel like they're dying." Bianca's heart sank as she panned the room, taking in the view of what was left of her home. She *wanted* to die. It was such massive destruction that if she didn't know better, she would have called it a robbery. And in some ways, it was. It was as if someone had plucked deliberate pieces out of a completed jigsaw puzzle, leaving only a portion of the now-unidentifiable image.

"Are you okay?" Charlie asked cautiously.

"Unbelievable. Un-*fucking*-believable," Bianca whispered as she rose to her feet, finally feeling stable, and started to assess the damage room by room, completely ignoring Charlie's question.

"I'm not trying to be insensitive, B. You've got to believe me. But you seriously had no clue he was this unhappy?" Charlie pried further. Bianca felt like a zombie as she forced herself through the painful journey of her abandoned home.

"If you're asking if I knew my husband was miserable enough to pack up his things and secretly desert me while I was at work, then no. I had no clue." Bianca turned to Charlie, tears welling up in her eyes. Bianca could only remember crying once in front of Charlie—at Levi's funeral. And even then, she had managed to harness her typically stoic surgeon demeanor, keeping a loose grasp on her true emotions. But currently, she was about to lose it, and she was nervous to see what that might entail.

Bianca heard the door to the garage slam and footsteps quickly coming toward the master bedroom where the two friends had paused their tour through the echoing house.

"I got here as fast as I could. What in the world?" Sadie said breathlessly, obviously trying to assess the fallout as she scanned the room.

But as Bianca started to speak, she felt her phone vibrating in her pocket. Staring at the screen, she pulled together her best tough-girl persona. Even as badly as Bianca was hurting, there was no way she would give Tom the satisfaction of hearing her fall apart. She hit the ignore button, sending him straight to voicemail.

"I'm not ready yet. I need a minute to figure out what to say to him," Bianca said as she started to pace the room. Both friends sat quietly on the bed, apparently waiting for her next move. Surprisingly there was the ping of a voicemail.

"Oh, this should be good," Bianca muttered as she turned on speaker mode and hit the play button.

"B, it's me. Um, I was hoping to catch you before you got home, but I guess you're still in surgery. Um, I need to tell you something..." His voice trailed off. "When you get home, I won't be there. It's nothing you've done, nor is there anything you can do to fix the situation. I hate to do you like this. I'm sorry, B."

"What the actual fuck? A voicemail? To end a marriage? This isn't junior high! This is a lifelong commitment here. A sacrament!" Charlie screamed at the phone.

"Are you really surprised? He's obviously a coward if he packed up and moved out while she was at work. I don't think a voicemail divorce plea is much of a stretch. What a fucking bastard." Sadie stood up, moving to wrap her arms around Bianca. Numb, she just stood there, letting Sadie's embrace support her.

"I guess we can leave those medications in the freezer. Looks like I won't be needing them," Bianca sarcastically announced, shaking her head in disbelief. Picking up a photograph from her wedding day sitting on her dresser, tears started to stream down her face. As the drops flowed heavier, Bianca threw the picture frame hard at the wall, causing it to shatter and fall to the floor in a dozen pieces. The photo laid on the ground, covered in shrapnel. Bianca collapsed to the ground, her body heaving for air as she buried her head in her hands. Her mind raced with questions and guilt that only a person with a true Catholic upbringing could conjure up. For the life of her, she couldn't imagine what grave sin she had committed to deserve this penance.

CHAPTER SEVEN

Sadie

SADIE SCRAPED THE last bit of eggs onto Evan's plate as he sat, fork in hand, at one of four barstools in her kitchen, ready to devour her famous breakfast. While he was there to get the boys for school, he was also reaping the rewards of her amazing cooking talents.

"Yum. Thanks, Sadie," Evan mumbled, with his mouth full of the cheesy concoction she was known for.

"You're welcome." She chuckled, seeing his face contort to move the steaming eggs from one scorched place in his mouth to the next. "Like your little brother. Impatient." Sadie's heart broke remembering how much Levi loved her cooking. He, too, had been guilty of eating food straight from the burner. "He must have learned that from you. It's not going to run from your plate, you know," she reassured him, placing a large glass of cold milk next to him, well-versed in the cure for singed gums.

"So how is Bianca holding up? Has she heard any more from Tom?" Evan pried after taking a large gulp of milk.

"She's not good. She's basically been in bed all week. She canceled all her surgeries and closed all the blinds in her house. She told Charlie and me to only check on her once a day to make sure she hasn't died from a broken heart. Otherwise, she wants to process this alone," Sadie stated coldly, mimicking Bianca's tone.

"I take it that you won't need me to come hang out

tomorrow for your usual girl's gazebo night?" Evan quizzed.

"No, I guess not." Sadie laughed at how ridiculous Evan looked, all dressed up for work with his glasses slid halfway down his nose, completely fogged up courtesy of the steaming eggs on his fork. "But you're more than welcome to come hang out here anyway. Why don't you bring Kate and the girls? I haven't seen them since the funeral. It would be nice to have some time to visit."

"Kate's taking them to a cotillion prep class at the golf club. She's on her own agenda lately. But I'll ask her." Evan shrugged.

"Lainey and Ava are old enough to be prepping for cotillion? Man, time sure does fly." Sadie shook her head, thinking of the pigtailed little girls that used to love hanging out with Aunt Sadie. Time had moved in fast-forward without her while Levi had been sick. Sadie cringed at all she had missed. "What do you mean, 'Kate's been on her own agenda'?" Sadie pried, wondering what her superficial, self-indulgent sister-in-law had been up to recently.

"She signed up for acting classes downtown with some of her girlfriends. I think they're prepping for *Real Housewives of the Lowcountry*, or something ridiculous like that." Evan snickered, shaking his head. "Anyway, she's been either with her new acting buddies, or in front of a mirror in her dressing room reciting lines. It annoys the shit out of me, so I've been avoiding the whole situation. I'm hoping this too shall pass as another one of Kate's fanatical hobbies."

"Acting? Well, that's interesting." Sadie tried to sound supportive. She had never been one to gossip or feed into drama, but she couldn't help but think to herself how perfectly fitting the concept was. After all, Kate was used to acting. And she was good at it. How many times had Sadie seen her sister-in-law flash a bright, welcom-

ing, convincing smile to an acquaintance, only to turn
away with the vilest eyeroll and muttered comment of
how annoying so-and-so was? Acting was fake. And the
word *fake* had Kate Carson's picture beside it in the *Web-
ster's Dictionary*. Sadie had been eerily impressed over the
years at how counterfeit her sister-in-law could be, and
how quickly her persona could change depending on
her momentary agenda.

"Interesting is one way to put it. I hope she doesn't sink
a ton of money into this endeavor. I have funded many
"Ventures de Kate," as I like to call them." Evan stood
and moved toward the sink to rinse his plate. "Boys!" he
yelled over the running water. "Time to go. We don't
want to be late."

Sadie heard the pitter-pattering of tennis shoes down
the stairs as her perfectly groomed sons made their
way to the front door, grabbing their book bags. "Give
Momma kisses," she ordered, smiling at their gelled hair
and preppy, button-down shirts. "Did you brush your
teeth after breakfast?"

"Yes, ma'am," both Tad and Max said in unison, each
giving Sadie a quick peck on her cheek. "Bye, Mom,"
they chimed in perfect timing.

"Thanks, Sadie, for breakfast. I'll let you know about
tomorrow night. Maybe I can convince Kate to come
hang out, or at least let the girls skip their class for once."
Evan extended his arm toward her for a quick hug. A
twinge of pity filled Sadie's heart for Evan. For the first
time, she saw a bit of sadness in his demeanor. Sure, he
missed Levi terribly, but this was different. It occurred to
her that maybe his loneliness stretched past that, though,
and into his marriage. Sadie was determined to get more
information about Kate's new hobby. For over a year, she
had been so focused on Levi that she hadn't paid much
attention to anything else. It was time she got back into
the family loop. After all, Evan had done so much for

her, Tad, and Max, that the least she could do was get a pulse on how he was doing in his own life. As Evan pulled out of the driveway, she grabbed her phone and shot a quick text to see if by chance she could catch Kate early enough in the day to maybe sneak in a lunch date, though she knew it was a long shot.

S: Kate, long time no see, sister. Wanna grab lunch today?
K: Yes! Noon, okay? Gryphon Tea Room?
S: Perfect. Can't wait.

While she was shocked that Kate had responded so quickly and had no prior engagements scheduled, her more overriding emotion was anxiety. Sadie hadn't been out of the house socially but for a handful of times since Levi's funeral. What if she ran into someone who asked how she was doing, or something triggered her emotions over Levi's death? Would she break down? Would she be able to muster up a fake smile and move on? *Well, I have to do this at some point. Might as well be today.*

Another speed bump would be her attire. Kate would be dressed to the nines as she always was. Thankfully, Sadie had plenty of maxi dresses that billowed out enough to hide her nearly emaciated frame. She hadn't had much of an appetite since Levi's diagnosis, so finding clothes in her closet that didn't make her look like *she* was the cancer victim was a feat in itself.

As she placed her phone down on the counter, she caught a glimpse of Bianca's house across the sac. The curtains were still all drawn tight and three packages sat on her front step, further acknowledging the fact that she hadn't left the house in days. It was time to make Bianca talk. If she was going to force herself back into society today, then by God, she wasn't going to do it alone.

Sadie marched across the pavement and bypassed the front door, grabbing the extra key from the fake rock under the azaleas to let herself in. She knew Bianca wouldn't answer, so she would use forceful action straight out of the gate.

"Knock, knock. Any one home? B, I'm coming in!" Sadie shouted as cheerfully as she could, but not wanting to sound too chipper as to seem insensitive. After a moment or two of silence, she shut the door behind her and made her way to Bianca's bedroom. The room was pitch black.

"Go away. I told you I didn't want to see anyone," Bianca muttered from under a heavy stack of blankets and comforters that were pulled over her head so far that all Sadie could see from the minimal light shining in from the hallway was a messy brunette crown of hair.

"You aren't the boss of me, missy. I can break into my best friend's house if I please." Sadie snickered, making her way onto Bianca's bed.

"Ugh. You and Charlie are so annoying. She's texted me nonstop. I'm going to run out of storage on my phone from her relentless messages," Bianca barked as she pulled the covers down, revealing puffy eyes and a red nose raw from tissue wipes.

"I don't recall being this nasty to you when the tables were turned, and you were stalking *me* after Levi's death. Would you rather us not give a shit and let you wilt away in this bed, growing bed sores?" Sadie patted Bianca on the leg, signaling tenderness despite her pseudo harsh words.

"That's because you're a nicer person than me," Bianca huffed, pushing herself up to a seated position and leaning back onto the tufted gray linen headboard.

"True, but you're tougher than me, so you don't have a legitimate reason to still be hiding. It's time. Let's talk." Sadie clapped her hands together, signaling Bianca to begin speaking pronto.

"Okay. What do you want to know?"

"First off, did you ever speak to him?"

"Yes." Bianca's short answer dug under Sadie's skin. "He says he's been evaluating everything in his life since Levi's death, and that includes our marriage. Of course, he claims that it isn't anything I've done, blah blah blah, but that he didn't want to lead me on any further, much less bring a child into a marriage that wasn't sound." Bianca's voice cracked as she pushed out the last few words of the sentence.

"I guess I'm in shock. I know that I've been distracted over the last year, but he never seemed unhappy or undevoted to your marriage," Sadie replied in disbelief. "Did he mention maybe doing counseling or trying to take some time apart, or is he gone for good?"

Bianca shook her head in despair. "I honestly have no clue what happened. I asked if it was someone else, or if he was hiding anything, and he said no. I asked if there was any way he would come back home and let us talk this through. I told him if the fertility treatments were scaring him then we could look at other avenues like adoption or surrogates or just stop trying to have children completely, but that my marriage to him was most important. He didn't seem at all interested in those ideas. I don't know, Sadie. I'm as shocked and confused as you are. This is all so unfair. I devoted my life to that man. I am a fucking good wife!" Bianca screamed pounding her fist into the bed firmly. "I provide for us—and a huge salary at that. I cook for us—and not just anything. It's all homemade from scratch, just like my grandma told me a good Italian wife should do. I wash his clothes and leave him love notes in his car. Hell, I even make a point to give him at least two blow jobs a week, plus guaranteed Sunday afternoon sex. I followed all the rules. What more could I have done, for Christ's sake?" Bianca's voice raised as tears began to fall. "When I left for work that morning, everything was the same as it always was. He kissed me. Told me I looked beautiful and wished me a great day at work. And then this…" Bianca trailed off, spreading her arms sarcastically.

"I know, B. You're right. You're an amazing wife. You don't deserve this." Sadie moved to her friend, pulling her close in a tight embrace. She stroked her hair and rocked Bianca just like she had done so many times to comfort her own tearful boys, then kissed the top of Bianca's head. Sadie was determined to solve the mystery. "There's more to this story. I don't know what it is, but sooner or later, it'll all come out in the wash. Trust me."

CHAPTER EIGHT

Sadie

SADIE EASILY SPOTTED Kate as she nervously scanned the restaurant for any other possible familiar faces that may be lurking around the room. She had given herself a long pep talk on the drive there. *Take deep breaths, smile, and say thank you if anyone offers condolences for Levi's death. Nothing more, nothing less. Don't break down. You can do this.* She coached herself silently, dreading the thought of running into any of her and Levi's friends or acquaintances.

Luckily, she didn't recognize anyone else in the packed, cozy venue. The Gryphon Tea Room was one of Savannah's most enchanting restaurants. Once an apothecary and pharmacy, the owners had kept the antique medicine jars and glass-paned cabinets along with the original wooden bar that once served ice cream. The adjacent walls were lined with bookshelves that housed old books and trinkets. One could sit for hours and let their eyes wander around the room, in awe of the history. Kate had taken a table in the far back corner. Sadie spotted her bright pink blouse and platinum blonde hair before Kate raised her head up from her phone, probably texting a fellow Stepford wife about plans for the evening. As Sadie made her way to the table, she was thankful she had decided on the strapless maxi dress. The summer weather had already reared its ugly head despite only being the end of April.

"Hey, Kate," Sadie said endearingly to her sister-in-law. While they were as opposite as day and night, she still felt connected to Kate somehow. Maybe it was the love they had for Levi and Evan, who were, for the most part, clones of each other. It was surprising that two women so different could fall in love with the same type of man.

"Sadie, you look great. How are you holding up? I don't think I have seen you since, umm..." Kate trailed off and Sadie's heart dropped at the thought of where Kate's sentence had been headed. Luckily, no tears flowed and no gasps for air were required as the subject of the funeral was skirted.

"Thank you. I still have some weight to put back on, but I think I came to the right place to start." Sadie smiled as she sat down, grabbing the menu from the table.

"Fill me in on Bianca. Evan told me Tom moved out unexpectedly. Is she okay? Did she say why?" Kate dug. Despite her sincere tone, Sadie could see right through to her true intentions. While Kate effectively channeled her well-versed acting skills, Sadie knew that she really wanted the inside scoop to share at the ladies' tennis courts. Nothing would be juicier than finding out why Dr. Moretti's husband abandoned her while she was at work doing surgeries.

"Bianca's doing as well as could be expected. She's kept private about it, so I can't comment too much on what happened and why." Sadie had never been one for gossip, especially when it pertained to her friends, and even more so when she knew who the beneficiaries of the information would be.

"Oh, come on, Sadie. You're her best friend. She didn't say anything as to why?" Kate coaxed.

"Honestly, she was so blindsided, I don't even think she understands why he left. He only mentioned that Levi's death made him reevaluate life." Sadie shrugged as she took a large sip of water.

"I can't say I haven't done the same thing…" Kate trailed off, alluding to a secret.

Sadie peered at her sister-in-law over the top of her glass, catching a look of hesitation. "I'm sure we all have. Death has a way of making us self-examine, and rightfully so," Sadie concurred, trying to make eye contact with Kate, but the bright blue eyes of the platinum blonde were still fixated on her hands that happened to be grasped tightly together with fingers intertwined. Over perfectly arranged salads, the two women continued to catch up on life. But Sadie sensed over the entire conversation that there was something more that Kate wanted to disclose. As the check was paid and Sadie stood to leave, she was startled by Kate's sudden jolt, grabbing her by the arm and pulling her back down onto the green velvet seat.

"Sadie, I need to tell you something," Kate whispered. The mere abruptness of her grasp was disturbing enough to send Sadie's stomach sinking into her feet, much less the eeriness of her tone.

"Okay," Sadie muttered slowly in a concerned and suspicious tone.

"Please. I know you and Evan are close, and he needs to hear this from me. But I want you to know my side before he blurts out his rendition to you." Kate looked firmly at Sadie, as if seeking her approval to proceed with the understood agreement of secrecy.

Sadie nodded, agreeing to the silent contract.

"I know Evan mentioned to you that I've been taking acting classes over the past few months. Well, truth be told, I've been taking them secretly for quite some time now. I knew he would think it was silly, so I didn't tell him." Kate's eyes drifted down shamefully. "I guess there are worse things I could have kept from my husband, right?"

Sadie nodded, thankful that this conversation didn't seem to be going in *that* direction.

"I didn't tell him about the lessons until I started realizing how much I loved them, and how good I actually am at it. I know this is going to sound crazy, but I want to pursue a career in acting."

Sadie quickly mustered up an excited expression to paint on her face as Kate's eyes darted to her, seeking her reaction. "That sounds great! I don't understand why you think Evan wouldn't support that. I am sure there are plenty of local venues that host plays and other outlets. Have you tried auditioning at any of those places?" Sadie asked.

"See, that's the thing. I like doing…more along the lines of commercials and television, you know, reality TV-type things. And those don't exist here in Savannah." Kate swallowed hard, her neck tensing firmly as the muscles fired in sync beneath overly tanned skin, before setting her next sentence free. Sadie's stomach tensed as to what was about to be unleashed. "So, I signed up for a summer acting session…in California. And I signed the girls up too. I think it would be great for them to see the other side of the country, and to learn a new skill." Kate paused.

A mix of emotions flooded Sadie's mind. Quickly, she crafted some sort of response, trying not to appear too baffled. "That sounds like fun, but Evan doesn't know that you and the girls are going away for over two months?" Sadie's tone turned worrisome. "I can't imagine him not supporting you in your dreams, but he'd be alone all summer." Sadie's heart sank at Evan being abandoned. He was already missing his brother. Now, to have his immediate family desert him, seemed a little insensitive on Kate's behalf. Sadie tried hard to stifle the agitation that was rising within her.

"He won't be alone. He has you, Tad, and Max," Kate reassured Sadie in an upbeat tone. "And his golf and boating buddies. I bet he'll love getting to have the entire summer to play without having to answer to me."

"You know him better than me," Sadie admitted, trying to calm herself down and bring her loyalty back to neutral. "I know the boys will love having him around even more. I'll make sure he's fed and behaving." Sadie chuckled as she realized she sounded like a babysitter reassuring parents as they left for dinner for the evening. "When do you plan on telling him? Just so I can be prepared."

"Tonight. That's why I was so thankful when you texted this morning about lunch. I was going to see if you wanted to grab a coffee this afternoon, but you beat me to the punch. Please act clueless when he tells you. And if you can find it in your heart to maybe say a few supportive things about the trip to Evan, I would forever be grateful. That is, of course, only if you want to." Kate's face turned into that of a begging puppy and Sadie decided that despite Kate's selfish decision to leave Evan while he was still mourning his brother, everyone had the right to follow their dreams. Sadie smiled tenderly, agreeing to keep the secret and lend a few supportive words if the conversation called for it.

But on her ride home, Sadie's heart ached thinking about Evan. She knew how lonely her house had been since Levi's death. She couldn't imagine how deafening the silence would be if Tad and Max were gone too. The good news was that she and Evan had each other, and for that, she was thankful.

CHAPTER NINE

Charlie

THE BOARDROOM BUZZED with firm hand-shakes and congratulatory praise. Charlie beamed proudly as Gabe accepted the signed contract from the Sabo CEO. He had done it. Well, *they* had done it. The two of them had worked up an entire campaign centered around back-to-school moms. The plan was brilliant. He had taken her crumb of an idea and expanded it into a four-week overhaul of promotions, advertisements, and social media buzz. It was sure to send sales soaring. Charlie's eyes met Gabe's, and he winked, acknowledging her help. Sure, he had given her credit in the presentation, but that simple, endearing, fleeting body movement meant more to her than any words ever could. She felt her face flush with heat like a teenage girl. Thankfully, his gaze was pulled away by another member of the Sabo team before he noticed her vibrant shade of red.

As the room began to finally empty, she made her way over to the star of the show. "Congratulations. You knocked it out of the park." Charlie smiled, locking arms with him.

"It was all because of you. What would I ever do without you, Charlotte Compton?" Gabe said, shaking his head in awe.

"I often wonder the same thing," Charlie replied flirtatiously. "I was wondering when you were going to realize that you are *way* better with me by your side." She returned the wink as he tucked his chin bashfully.

"I think this calls for a celebration. Wanna go grab a drink? I owe you one or two," Gabe asked. Charlie watched proudly as he snatched up his briefcase with much more tenacity than he had sat it down with prior to the presentation. She loved seeing him ooze with confidence.

"Sure. I usually have my Thursday gazebo night with Bianca and Sadie, but for obvious reasons, it's canceled this week. Jaded Bianca and alcohol are never a good idea. I can only imagine the drunk texts and calls she would send Tom."

"Well then, let's go." Gabe practically trotted to the door, holding it for Charlie's exit as she shuffled past his baited gesture.

The Grove Lounge was a hip little restaurant conveniently located right across the street from their downtown office, making it an easy walk for after-work drinks. Surprisingly, no one else had mentioned wanting to go for a cocktail, but then again, neither Gabe nor Charlie invited anyone else. Charlie secretly hoped that was intentional on Gabe's part. The fact that he'd made one-on-one time for her after hours gave her the ammunition and the opportunity she needed to convince him to bend his rules.

"Let me guess, you want a New Zealand sauvignon blanc," Gabe stated as he pulled out the barstool for her.

"You know me well. My turn. Let me guess, you want an Oregon Pinot Noir," Charlie said confidently.

"And you know me well." The two happily snagged the filled wine glasses from the bartender, clinking them in unison, cheering their day's success. "To the smartest, sassiest, most creative woman I know, who also never fails to push me to my limits. And for that, I am grateful. Here's to my partner in crime. I am constantly in awe of

you, Charlotte Compton." Gabe finished his toast and
Charlie smiled, locking eyes with him. He had never spoken to her like that. Of course, he had complimented her
and shown respect to her as a coworker, but these words
were deeper, more precise. She knew they weren't off
the cuff. Gabe didn't work that way. He was calculated.
He had carefully selected the verbiage. After all, he could
have as easily simply said *thank you.*

"Wow. I'm flattered. Those words mean a lot coming
from someone that I admire." Charlie smiled, bashfully
letting her eyes fall to her glass.

"Well, they're sincere. I know you think I'm stubborn
and close minded…" Gabe trailed off, giving Charlie
time to chime in.

"Yep. Sure do," she chirped as she looked to him in
total confirmation.

"But I have boundaries for a reason," he finished.

"We all have boundaries, Gabe. We humans form them
to protect ourselves from hurt, pain, failure, or whatever
may disrupt our normal lives. I have them, too, believe it
or not," Charlie snickered, aware that for most of her life,
she had been pegged as the renegade. "But they're flexible…fluid, per se. And most importantly, within those
boundaries, I have zero limits." Charlie raised one of her
long, thin arms high into the air. "Your boundaries and
limits are in a tight, rigid box, Gabe. How will you ever
live your full potential with such strict restraints?"

"Who knows? I guess I'll die in my tight, rigid box,"
Gabe said sarcastically.

Charlie knew she'd struck a chord. Maybe she should
have been a little nicer after his sweet toast to her. She
decided to lighten the conversation and switch to sports,
which they both loved. Her gaze shifted to the big screen
that floated behind the bar.

"Hard to believe it's time for the NFL draft already.
Seems like just yesterday was Superbowl Sunday," Charlie

said, hoping to not be too obvious in her tactic. But her heart skipped a beat as a face that she knew all too well appeared on the screen. A smile plastered across her face, just as it always did anytime he crossed her mind: Dominic Houston.

"Time flies. I remember when that guy right there was just a rookie. Hard to believe he's retired," Gabe said as he pointed to the television, oblivious as to Charlie's long-standing connection to the famous NFL quarterback.

"Yeah. He's a good one," Charlie replied, unsuccessfully trying to stifle the sentiment she had in her heart for him.

"You say that like you know him." Gabe chuckled as Charlie's mind raced. She hated that she always fought this battle in her mind before letting the cat out of the bag. But she was exhausted by it—the fame, the questions, the star power that always surrounded her relationship with him. She had chosen years ago to keep what little piece of him she had, to herself. She liked it that way. But when the time was appropriate, she sometimes revealed her biggest treasure.

"Because I do," Charlie replied confidently as she lifted her wine glass to her red tinted lips.

"Bullshit. You're telling me you know Dominic Houston, one of the most famous football players in history, and you haven't talked about him once since I've known you? Prove it." Gabe's demeanor was a mixture of disbelief and resentment to her secret.

Charlie smiled snarkily, reaching for her phone. As her fingers moved to her Favorites photo album, rows and rows of images of her and the massive, handsome, brown-skinned man flooded the screen for as far back as high school and as recent as last season. She could feel Gabe leaning over her shoulder to see the proof.

"Let me see those," he barked, snatching her phone out

of her hands. "Unreal. Why didn't you tell me?" Gabe said in a tone that alluded to betrayal.

"Maybe I thought you would just befriend me for an autograph," Charlie said timidly.

"No way. I would ask for way more than that. Can I meet him?" Gabe replied through a chuckle.

Charlie rolled her eyes, snatching the phone back. "Case in point," she replied matter-of-factly.

"How do you know him? Looks like you went to high school together or something from those pictures."

"Yes. Lexington Catholic. He was the star quarterback. I was the cheerleader. We were unconventional best friends. I like to call us soulmates," Charlie said, trying to stifle an endearing smile.

"Ohhhh. So you dated," Gabe prodded.

"No way! Never. Why does everyone always think that? It's so annoying. See why I keep him a secret?" Charlie barked. The conversation always proceeded like this.

Gabe appeared to sense her frustration. "Simmer down, Robin. Geez," Gabe huffed. "It's pretty cool that he's *your friend*. And I guess I can understand why you kept it from me. Is there anything else I should know about you, Charlotte Compton? Are you an heiress to a throne or Picasso's granddaughter or anything?" Gabe chuckled.

Charlie shook her head at him, annoyed, but also sympathetic to his doubts.

"Well then, let's go home. We still have work to do tomorrow. And now that the contract's been signed by the Sabo Group, it's off to the races on executing the campaign."

"Thanks again for the drinks. This was fun." Charlie smiled, reaching for her bag. "Damnit! I must have left my bag in my office. I've got to run back up and get it. It has my keys in it."

"I don't want you going back into the building by yourself. It's late. I'll walk you up," Gabe insisted.

"Oh, Gabe, don't be silly. I'll be fine. You go ahead and go home. I know you're exhausted."

"Not a chance," Gabe argued as he grabbed her by the arm.

The two slightly tipsy friends made it up the elevator to their floor. It was apparent that everyone was gone. Even James, the custodian, had called it a night. The after-hours emergency lights were on, casting enough light to illuminate the hallway to Charlie's office. As she reached down beside her desk to grab the leather handle, she could feel Gabe close behind her. Closer than he had even been at The Grove when he'd peered over her shoulder at pictures of Dominic.

She turned to find him within inches of her face. Numb, she wasn't quite sure how to react. This was so out-of-the-blue. All the while she had spent chasing him, she hadn't quite pictured what she would do if he actually caved. Her heart raced as she looked into his eyes that had softened with desire. Stroking her face gently with the back of his fingers, they brushed past her cheek and landed, tangling in her long, dark hair. As his palm grasped her scalp, pulling her in close to him, she felt his lips on hers. They were just how she had imagined they would be—soft, warm, and delicious. Pushing herself back onto the top of her desk, she felt him slide her red skirt up around the tops of her thighs, his hands firmly gripping her skin. Grabbing his belt buckle, she pulled him in close between her legs, feeling him hard against her. As he kissed the nape of her neck, his heavy breathing echoed in her ear. She moaned as his hand landed between her thighs and moved under her black lace panties. His touch ignited a wave of pleasure that she had only dreamed of. As she pressed herself even closer to his touch, she thought her heart might pound out of her chest.

"Gabe," she whispered, stopping suddenly, grabbing his

face to meet her stare. As much as she wanted him, she didn't want any regrets tomorrow. Especially for him. She knew her desires, but just as well she knew where his two feet had always stood until that moment. And that was in the hard *no* camp. "Are you sure?"

He looked sincerely into her eyes. She could almost see the battle occurring in his brain. Charlie watched his gaze fall from her face. His hand stopped its exploring and he kissed her gently and softly on the lips. "You're right. This may not be the best idea."

Charlie's heart sank. She had thrown salt into her own game. Why couldn't she have kept her big mouth shut? She literally hated herself in that moment. Standing up from her desk, she pulled her skirt back into its proper position.

Gabe wiped his face and straightened his tie. "Come on. Let's go. I think we've had enough excitement for one day," he said, grabbing Charlie endearingly by the waist. The silent walk to the garage was more awkward than any bad date conclusion Charlie had ever experienced in her decades of pursuing the opposite sex.

"See ya tomorrow, Batman. Thanks again. I really am proud of you." Charlie forced a smile, pushing past the uncomfortable goodbye as she got into her car. He nodded softly and gave a quick wave as she watched him follow suit.

Charlie sat in her running car, her mind swirling. *What the fuck just happened?* She needed to talk this out. She prayed Sadie's lights would still be on when she got home.

As she rounded the corner to the sac, she was relieved to see the faint glow of Sadie's bedside lamp through her blinds. Turning off her headlights, she pulled onto the brick pavers of Sadie's drive. Grabbing her phone, she held her breath as she texted her friend.

C: Hey. You up?

Thankfully, three dots appeared.

S: Yep. You ok?
C: Can I come in? I need to talk.
S: Sure. Not sleepy anyway.
Charlie heard the click of the deadbolt as she approached the front door. Sadie stood behind it in her long gray robe, her hair in a messy bun, still damp at her temples from her standard nightly run.

"What's going on? Where have you been?" Sadie asked.

"Sadie, you won't believe this. I'm not sure I do."

"You need a drink? Sounds like I do." Sadie turned, waving Charlie into the kitchen.

Taking a seat on the leather barstool, Charlie's head collapsed into her hands. "Remember I told you that Gabe and I had this huge pitch today for the Sabo Group?"

Sadie nodded, pouring them both a glass of wine.

"Well, it went amazing. Like, better than amazing."

"Good. So, what's the hang up?" Sadie quizzed as she took a seat on the countertop, facing Charlie.

"Afterward, Gabe and I went to The Grove for a celebratory drink. No big deal, the usual us, bickering and poking fun at each other in our typical flirtatious way. When we went to leave, I realized I had forgotten my bag in my office. Of course, Gabe insisted that he walk me back up to the office rather than me being in the building all by myself." Charlie took a huge gulp of the wine sitting in front of her, then a deep breath. "The next thing I know, I have my skirt up around my waist, my bare ass on my desk, Gabe between my legs, and his hand in my cookie."

Sadie nearly spit out her wine. "What?! Well, that's out of the blue. Isn't that what you wanted? Did you have sex?"

"Yes, it's what I wanted, and no, we didn't have sex. Something stopped me. Maybe it was my guilty conscience knowing how adamant he's been about us not dating. But now what? I have to go into the office tomorrow and work right beside him. Do I act normal, like nothing happened? Do I try to talk to him about it? Ugh. This is so weird. Why couldn't he have simply asked me on a date? Then I would've been prepared. I would've known from the get-go what his intentions were."

"Sounds like to me he has feelings for you that he's in denial about. I obviously haven't been in the dating game for years, but I would try to play it cool and see how he acts. It'll come up at some point, and you two can address it then. You're both adults. You'll figure it out." Sadie shook her head in disbelief. "Wonder what made him suddenly change his mind? It's so odd. So impulsive."

"Who knows. He's usually super predictable. Maybe I don't know him as well as I think I do." Charlie shrugged. "Maybe I finally broke down those boundaries of his with my relentless pressure. And for what, to deliver immediate rejection?" Charlie slapped her forehead with the palm of her hand.

"How the hell do you get yourself into these situations? Never ever a dull moment with you, Charlotte Compton."

"Sometimes, dull sounds amazing."

———◆———

The office was lit up by bright speckles of sunlight creeping in through the windows. Charlie's stomach turned as she rounded the corner. She could see Gabe sitting at his desk through the glass partition. She scurried quickly to her desk, trying to get there before he had a chance to see her. Heart pounding, she made it safely into her office unnoticed, closing the door silently behind her.

What the hell is wrong with you? Why are you so nervous? He's the one that initiated the make-out session, not you. Chill the fuck out, Charlie. Her pep talk ended just in time. She heard a light tap on her door and could see Gabe peeping in through the glass. She waved him in, gathering herself as best she could.

"Morning," Gabe chirped in what seemed like a forced tone, making his way to the seat in front of her desk. "So, I wanted to come on out about last night."

Charlie's heart pumped as her mind raced. She wanted to tell him that it was okay, and that while she didn't want to do anything that made him uncomfortable, she had feelings for him and that she knew he did for her too, and that somehow, they would work through it all and figure it out as they went along.

"I'm really sorry about last night. I'm not quite sure what happened," he said nervously.

"Oh, it's okay. We had a little too much to drink and were maybe a little too excited over the Sabo contract," Charlie said, trying to downplay the elephant in the room.

"No, it's not. I need to tell you something. I've been dating someone for a few months…" Gabe trailed off.

Charlie's stomach sank. Part of her wanted to know more, and part wished he would stop right there. "Oh, well, congratulations, I guess. Who is this lucky lady?" Charlie somehow mustered up the tiniest inflection of excitement in her voice, despite the rage that was festering below the surface.

"You don't know her," Gabe stated sheepishly.

"Well, that's obvious." Charlie couldn't help but sound snide, thinking of all the opportunities he'd had in the past few months to disclose this bit of information to her.

"Um, well, yes," Gabe stuttered. Charlie's face must have said one thousand words because Gabe turned a shade of bright red.

"So let me get this straight. You've been seeing someone for months, and despite the fact that we talk every single day, you've failed to mention anything about her to me even once. I'm confused." Charlie couldn't help but laugh at the absurdity as she leaned back in her office chair, arms crossed, waiting for Gabe's answer.

"I didn't say I was getting *married* anytime soon. And besides, it's nothing. But what happened last night wouldn't be fair to her, and I wanted to come clean."

"Sounds like you don't need to come clean to me. You should probably come clean to *her*. I'm sure she thinks she's more than 'nothing.'" Charlie shook her head in disgust. For the first time, she was completely disgusted with him. She knew he was a private person, but they confided in each other. He hadn't lied to her per se, but he had definitely been untruthful by omission. She needed some air. "I'm gonna grab a coffee downstairs. If you'll excuse me," Charlie stated as she pushed past Gabe.

"Charlie," Gabe barked as he grabbed her arm, turning her around to face him. She could see the desperation in his eyes. "You're not so innocent either, you know. You didn't tell me about being friends with Dominic Houston."

"Are you being serious? That's apples and oranges, Gabe. You led me on, knowing how I felt about you. You could have come clean and confessed, and I would have bowed out gracefully. I'm not a man-thief." Charlie was growing angrier with each passing second. She couldn't believe his audacity to compare her friendship with Dominic to his flimsy dating status.

"Charlie, I know that. But why me? Why do you have to want *me*? I just didn't know how to handle all of this…" Gabe trailed off, waving his hands back and forth between the two of them.

"Trust me. I'd rather not. Honestly, you're a huge pain in my ass." Jerking her purse over her arm, she headed to the doorway of her office. Turning back, she added, "I can't compete with what's innate within you, nor can I relate to all of your excessive self-inflicted rules and lim itations." And with that, she turned her back to him—and to the idea of ever being *with* him—as she felt something new and unfamiliar: walls stacking up around her heart.

CHAPTER TEN

Bianca

BIANCA SQUINTED FROM the bright sunlight. She hadn't been outside the house in what felt like decades. As she stood on her front porch, wrapped in the same robe she'd been wearing for several days now, the world was different, scarier. She decided to head to the safest place she knew: Sadie's kitchen. It was ten in the morning, so that meant school had started, and work hours had begun. No boys and no Evan would be present to see the state of distress she was in. Maybe, if she was lucky, Sadie would make her some food. After all, pizza delivery, cereal, and popcorn had been her only nutrition recently. As she knocked on the door, she saw Sadie standing in the kitchen, her eyes popping wide as if she had seen a ghost as she caught a glimpse of Bianca at her doorstep. In practically a sprint, Sadie rushed to let her in.

"Oh my goodness! You're alive!" Sadie wailed, wrapping her arms tightly around her friend. Bianca stayed silent, melting into Sadie's arms. "Come on. Let's get you some coffee. You hungry?" Sadie asked.

Bianca nodded and headed to the brown leather barstools.

"You look better."

Bianca flashed a sarcastic smirk. "I really didn't have anywhere to go but up. I saw my reflection in your glass door. If you think this is better, then I must've looked like a gremlin when you saw me last." Bianca watched Sadie for what felt like an eternity as she displayed her near professional barista skills at the prized espresso machine. The loud sound of steam indicated the end of the process was near. Sadie handed the cup to her gently, careful not to spill any of the precious liquid. Taking the coffee cup in both hands, Bianca took a deep inhale through her nose, absorbing all the comforts that come with the warmth and aroma of Sadie's coffee. She wasn't quite sure how she did it, but Sadie made everything better than anyone else. Of course, her super-duper expensive espresso machine that Levi had gotten her three years ago for Mother's Day did help elevate her skills. But still, any big-named coffee shop had nothing on Sadie Carson.

"How do you want your eggs? Scrambled? Cheese?" Sadie quizzed, taking ingredients from the refrigerator.

"Yes and yes." Bianca nodded, feeling her stomach start to growl at the thought of some actual nutrition. "I may need some veggies thrown in there, too, if you have any. I haven't had the best diet the last few days."

"No problemo, kid."

Bianca suddenly started to feel a little more human. It was obvious Sadie was avoiding the hard conversation, so she decided to make the move to the inevitable topic.

"I have a meeting today with our banker. We're separating our accounts," Bianca stated matter-of-factly in her professional oral surgeon tone.

"Really? Will Tom be there?"

"No. He's too chicken-shit for that. He's attending via phone. I'm sure the last thing he wants to do is face me. And honestly, I look so bad right now, it may be for the best. But part of me wants him to see me this broken so he knows what he's done to me. I've always been the stoic one. The alpha female. The thick-skinned Italian. I never imagined I'd fall so low. But then again, I never imagined my husband would leave me without warning while I was at work." Bianca shrugged as she began to devour the food Sadie placed in front of her. "Yum. This is great, Sadie. Thank you."

Sadie nodded. "Have you two talked anymore? Does he want to reconcile?"

"No and no. And I won't beg anymore. I do still have a smidge of pride left."

"I never expected this out of him. It's unbelievable that someone you think you know so well could have such a Dr. Jekyll and Mr. Hyde personality switch like that," Sadie huffed in shock.

"Yeah, you're telling me. So, enough about me. How's Charlie? I texted her back last night and she hasn't responded yet. With the way she was blowing up my phone this week, I figured she would be Johnny-on-the-spot with responding." Bianca chuckled, ready to switch the subject of conversation to anything but her and Tom.

"She was a little, um, pre-occupied last night, I guess you could say," Sadie snickered.

"What's that mean? Do tell."

"I probably should let her have the pleasure of telling you."

"You can't do that to me. I can't handle any more so-called surprises in my life right now," Bianca pleaded.

"Okay, so last night, she and Gabe went for drinks after work. I guess they nailed the big project they've been working on together and decided to go to The Grove to celebrate. And... they ended up making out in her office."

"No shit?! I thought he was totally adamant about not mixing work with pleasure," Bianca squeaked, eyes wide open. "Did they fuck?"

"No, as a matter of fact, Charlie got a little spooked for some reason and it ended prematurely, if you know what I mean. But she did wind up half naked sitting on her desk, so there was certainly some action. I will give her

the pleasure of filling you in on all the intimate details.
She showed up here last night all busted up and freaking
out, not knowing how to act toward him today at work.
I told her to play it cool and just try to be normal. I'm
fairly certain that won't happen, though. I'm sure there'll
be some sort of Charlotte Compton drama that unfolds."

Bianca joined Sadie in laughter. It felt good to use those
muscles again. Unfortunately, the sensation was cut short
by a slam coming from the front door. Bianca turned to
see Charlie stomping in with her brunette hair flying, red
lips pressed together tightly.

"Speak of the devil," Bianca muttered as she turned to
see Sadie just as baffled at the grand entrance.

"Charlie, it's ten in the morning on a Friday. Aren't you
supposed to be at work?" Sadie quizzed in a somewhat
worried tone.

"I know what fucking time it is," Charlie barked.
Bianca watched, confused still, as Charlie made her way
to the fridge, pulling out orange juice and champagne.
Bianca locked eyes with Sadie. *This must not be good.*

Pouring way too much champagne and only a drip of
orange juice into a cup, Charlie plopped down at the bar
next to Bianca, huffed, then turned to her, giving her a
peck on the cheek. "Good to see you're alive," Charlie
whispered, only changing her tone for that one sentence.

Bianca smiled, fully aware that when her friend was hot,
calming herself down for a simple moment of affection
wasn't typical or easy for the spicy Charlotte Compton,
which made her effort even more endearing.

"Do you want to tell us what's going on, or should I
guess?" Sadie asked bravely. "And she knows about last
night. I filled her in." Sadie tipped her head to Bianca,
who still sat quietly in her state of shell shock.

"Well, that didn't take long. News travels fast around
here." Charlie rolled her eyes but continued her ram-
page. "Un-fucking-believable. That man has been seeing

someone for *months* and hasn't even *hinted* at having a girlfriend. I've talked to him, texted him, and sat beside him for nearly a *year* now, and he has never *once* mentioned even so much as going on a *date*. And he's known the *whole* time how I felt about him, and he dragged me along. I feel so stupid. I'm pissed as hell," Charlie grumbled.

"A girlfriend? He never mentioned anything at all? That's so bizarre," Sadie said, puzzled as she leaned onto her countertop.

"Right? And here's the worst part: he totally fessed up, but then followed up with 'it's nothing though.' That's terrible to say." Charlie took a huge gulp of her mimosa.

"Sounds deceitful to me. But it also sounds like you dodged a bullet, Charlie. The last thing you want is a man that's good at conveniently deleting parts of his life from you. Take it from me," Bianca said while she sarcastically patted Charlie on the back. "Otherwise, you end up deserted, lying in your bed for days in the dark, and eating three-day-old pizza, wondering what Mack truck ran you over. Trust me. Better to find out now."

"I know, B. You're right. I feel so bamboozled. My intuition's usually better than this."

"Excuse me? You don't have the best record with relationships, dear. I wouldn't say you have good intuition with men. Friends, yes. The opposite sex, no," Bianca firmly corrected.

"I can't disagree with you there, but I really thought Gabe was different. I wasn't attracted to him at all when we first met. I liked him as a friend first, so when I developed an attraction to him, I figured I was safe for once, because I'd used my friend intuition rather than my boyfriend intuition," Charlie explained in frustration, dropping her head into her hands in despair. Bianca listened, selfishly thankful the drama wasn't hers this time. "I stormed out of my office. I told him I was going for coffee, but instead, I came here. We have a huge day planned at work. How am I supposed to go back there and be productive when I really just want to spit in his face?"

"I'm not trying to rub salt into your wound, but maybe this proves Gabe's exact point of why it wouldn't be good for you guys to date and work together. Can you imagine mixing regular lovers' quarrels with daily tasks? He kind of has a point." Sadie shrugged her shoulders as she stole Charlie's mimosa. "How about I finish this, and you head back to the office with your head held high? You don't have anything to be ashamed of. I promise you will laugh about this in a few months."

"Ugh. You're right. Gotta put my big girl panties on. I've never let a man get the best of me yet, and I don't plan on allowing it this late in the game," Charlie concurred. "What's on the agenda for you two today?"

"I'm having a movie night with my boys tonight, so chores here until then. Bianca is taking it one step at a time." Sadie winked at her, obviously protecting her from any further discussion about Tom. Now wasn't the time to get Charlie even more fired up at the male population by bringing up her banking separation with Tom. Bianca could just hear Charlie now—*Don't let him have a fucking penny. He doesn't deserve a red cent.* She didn't disagree with her friend, but she also needed to save her own energy for the real battle this afternoon.

"Okay, girls. I'm headed back to Awkwardville. I guess this will have to count as our gazebo night for this week." Charlie gathered her things, popped a piece of gum in an apparent effort to hide her champagne breath, and kissed both Sadie and Bianca on the cheek.

For a moment, Bianca felt like her old, feisty self again, determined to give her friend one last jab at the situation. "I hear your bare ass was plastered all over your desk. You may want to grab some sanitizing wipes, too, if you plan on continuing to do scandalous shit in your office. Don't let Monica Lewinsky's life lessons go in vain!"

Charlie quickly flipped her the bird and slammed the door, leaving Bianca and Sadie to snicker at the complete absurdity of their love lives.

My, how quickly things could change in the blink of an eye.

CHAPTER ELEVEN

Charlie

FIVE O'CLOCK FRIDAY couldn't have come soon enough. Somehow, Charlie had managed to get through the rest of her workday without bitch-slapping Gabe, despite her increasing desire to do so every time she saw his face—which was a lot that day, seeing as though they had tons of planning to do for the back-to-school campaign she was now regretting ever mentioning to him. She was thankful she hadn't finished the stiff mimosa she'd poured at Sadie's house that morning, otherwise, she might have had just enough of a decreased threshold to do it. Despite her quick temper and even quicker tongue, she'd learned through the years that sometimes, silence was the best payback, especially for someone that valued your words. And she knew Gabe valued hers, or at least had appeared to. But who knew? Maybe that wasn't what it seemed either. Charlie wondered if anything he'd said to her had been legit. What other things had he *conveniently* left out in their conversations?

As she flopped down onto her light blue, velvety couch, a large glass of sauvignon blanc in hand, she couldn't help but feel sorry for herself. After hundreds of dates and failed relationships, when would it be her turn? She had gotten really good at finding Mr. Wrong. Luckily, that hadn't sabotaged her determination to find her person.

Her heart had managed to still be nearly unscathed and
open, despite the heartbreaks—until today. For the first
time, she felt a twinge of guardedness. Charlie wasn't
quite sure what had happened differently this time, but
she figured it had something to do with friendship being
involved. She and Gabe had been confidants first before
any sort of attraction. That was a line she had never been
taunted to cross before. She and Dominic had never even
considered a romantic status, and she couldn't recall any
other friends of the opposite sex that she had had any
particular attraction to.

Charlie took a big sip of wine, letting it swirl in her
mouth to drench every single tastebud. *Maybe it's me.
Maybe I'm the problem.* Was she meant to be alone for
forever?

She caught a glimpse of Sadie through her front windows, jogging past her house, and her heart sank. While
it might suck to not find your person, what if you found
him and then lost him? Or worse, what if you thought
you'd found him, then he changed his mind and deserted
you, like Tom did to Bianca? Suddenly, her little pouting
session seemed selfish. The sun was already set, and the
sky was turning a shade of navy blue. The stars would be
out soon, and Sadie's run would be wrapping up. And she
also knew where that would lead her.

Making her way to her kitchen, she grabbed another
wine glass and filled it for her friend. Barefoot and double fisted, Charlie walked to the edge of Sadie's driveway
and dropped down to the ground in a cross-legged position, waiting for Sadie's return. Charlie could see her
way-too-skinny body making its way around the sac one
last time. As Sadie's pace quickened toward the finish line,
Charlie saw a smile flash toward her.

"Hey, hot stuff! Can I buy you a drink?" Charlie called
out, raising the overfilled wine glass to her breathless
friend.

"Charlie, I need water first." Sadie laughed, breezing past and over to the water bottle sitting on the front porch.

"Water. It's so overrated."

"I didn't say I didn't want it; I said water *first*. Now, gimme that wine." Sadie snickered, yanking the wine glass from Charlie's grasp, still trying to catch her breath and beginning to stretch her legs out into wide splits.

"Now I see why you do this every day. I didn't even run, and I feel better watching you stretch." Charlie laughed, then mimicked Sadie's position, spreading her legs into a V shape.

"Don't overexert yourself there, sister." Sadie laughed as Charlie started to grimace at the tug of her muscles fighting the position.

"The last bit of exercise I got was running out of the office as quickly as I could to escape the huge bullet I dodged all day."

"How *was* the rest of the day? Sounds like about as much fun as my lunch date with Kate yesterday," Sadie confessed.

"Kate? Why in the world would you have lunch with her? That's plain torture. If you're *that* desperate for daytime company, I can always meet you for lunch downtown." Charlie wrinkled her nose and furrowed her eyebrows looking as if she'd thought of something foul, creating an expression that made her friend quickly pinch her lips together in an apparent effort to keep from spitting out her wine with laughter.

"You know I've always taken up for her, but after yesterday, I have to agree with you and Bianca. She's something else." Sadie shook her head in disbelief.

"What has the wicked Stepford sister-in-law done this time? To have actually ruffled Sadie Carson's feathers must mean it's something epic. Let me guess…she hired a bodyguard? Or maybe she's flying to the South Pacific to harvest her very own strand of saltwater pearls to adorn her neck at the next golf club event."

"Neither of those would surprise me. But what she confessed sure did," Sadie muttered over the crickets that were starting to sing.

Charlie waved her hands, encouraging Sadie to divulge the big bang.

"You have to swear you won't say anything." Sadie raised a pinky finger up to Charlie asking for a pinky promise. "I'm not even sure Evan knows yet. She was supposed to tell him last night at some point, but since he didn't come over like he usually does on gazebo night I didn't have the chance to find out any details. I offered for him to come hang out anyways and bring Kate, Lainey, and Ava, which is what prodded me to call and ask her to lunch yesterday. I wanted to try and reach out to her, knowing that sometimes people have a hard time in awkward situations. Not everyone knows how to handle a widow. I was hoping that if I took the first step, she might feel more comfortable. Well, I quickly found out that her comfort level with me is obviously not the problem. Little did I know, she was planning on reaching out to *me* for coffee yesterday too."

"I smell a rat. Kate Carson never 'just reaches out for coffee' without an agenda. What did she want? This should be good." Charlie leaned back with her arms crossed, waiting for the narcissistic reasoning.

"Kate has been taking acting lessons for some time now, which Evan is aware of," Sadie clarified. "She wants to pursue it further, so she's enrolled herself *and* the girls in a summer-long-acting class in California."

"So why did she feel the need to confide in you about this? I don't get it." Charlie needed more details.

"See, that's the thing. Kate hadn't told Evan about her plans as-of lunch yesterday. She wanted my promise to support her and help convince Evan that it was a good idea if he balked at it. And she wanted my word that I would look out for him while she was away."

"You mean to tell me she's leaving her husband for two months, taking their children, and probably putting all of this on his dime, without even asking him about it first? This proves my point about that selfish witch. She doesn't deserve Evan. Not for one single minute. So you said you didn't know if she told him yet?" Charlie asked, finishing off the last drop of her wine.

"No. I didn't see him last night. I'm assuming she told him then. I took the boys to school this morning because I had a meeting with the school counselor to check in on how they've been doing in class since Levi's death. So, I didn't see him this morning either. I haven't a clue as to what went down."

"Something tells me you're about to find out..." Charlie muttered as she saw Evan's truck pull into the sac. As he parked it near the curb in his usual parking spot, Charlie heard the engine shut off and his door slam closed. His gait was smooth and confident as he made his way over to them. Charlie eyed his ruggedly handsome face adorned with crow's feet and a tightly trimmed goatee speckled with a few gray whiskers. She was always surprised at how much he looked like Levi. She couldn't imagine how hard it must be for Sadie to see such a clone of her late husband all the time. Maybe it was comforting. She sure hoped so, otherwise it could only be pure torture.

"Did you need us to move?" Sadie laughed as she started to stand up, alluding to the fact that she and Charlie were blocking the entrance to the drive.

"Don't get up on my behalf," Evan urged, motioning for Sadie to stay seated. "I'm stopping by to see how the meeting with the school counselor went this morning."

Charlie's heart dropped at how thoughtful Evan was. Sure, Max and Tad were his nephews, but he'd taken his role as the male figure in their lives to blue-ribbon status since his brother's passing. It was so sweet seeing Evan still watching out for his kid brother, even after he was gone. Who knew? Maybe it was Evan's way of healing. Charlie couldn't imagine his grief, but she also couldn't imagine what the world he had seen in Kate. How thoughtless of her to leave Evan at such a critical time. She stood up, despite Evan's demands for them to remain seated, and grabbed her now empty wine glass. Sadie was still nursing hers. But there was an ample amount of sensitive material for them to discuss, and Charlie selfishly didn't want any part of that heavy conversation.

"Don't run off yet," Sadie begged as Charlie brushed off the backside of her shorts.

"I'm zonked from the hectic work week. More importantly, my wine glass is empty, and I need a refill. You guys have important things to discuss." Charlie fist bumped Evan, high-fived Sadie, and headed back to her house across the sac. As she grabbed a chilled bottle of wine from the fridge and made her way to the screened porch to listen to the crickets, she heard her phone ping in her pocket. A huge smile stretched across her face when she saw the name that appeared: Dominic.

Hi…

It always amazed her how just two little letters from him made her whole world stop spinning. A simple *hi* was all it took to turn the corners of her mouth up in an instant. It didn't matter how much time had passed since their last conversation. Whether a day, a week, or a month, they never missed a beat.

Hi… she wrote back.

In typical Dominic style, his timing couldn't have been more perfect. Whether it was throwing a laser sharp pass to the end zone or sending a late-night text, his game was always on point. After a week like the one she'd had, there was nothing more comforting than hearing from her best guy friend—the one and only Dominic Houston.

You up? Let me guess… two glasses of wine in so far?

Charlie could almost hear him chuckle through his text, knowing he was spot on.

C: One and a half, to be exact. How is my favorite football star?

D: Depends… How is my favorite badass?

C: Wish I could say I was a badass, but after this week, I feel more like a dumbass.

D: Uh oh… Trouble in Charlotte Compton paradise?

C: Nah. Nothing I can't get past with a little wine and a hot bath.

D: Who's at fault? Need me to come straighten them out?

C: No one important. It's Friday. Don't you have some unassuming hot chick piece of trash to entertain tonight? Must be desperate or you wouldn't be texting me.

D: Geez. That's harsh. Don't take your man-hate out on me.

C: Sorry…

D: It's cool. I just missed you. Wanted to check in.

C: Aw. Miss you too, boo.

*D: So, I'm headed to Jacksonville for a little bit of business next week. Hoping I could
see you on my way down from Charlotte.*

C: What? Of course! You need a place to crash?

D: That would be amazing. Monday night, okay?

C: Nothing like the last minute. Guess some things never change about you. Good thing I love you. I'll have dinner and a bed ready for ya.

D: Can't wait…

C: Oh, it's just you, right? No hoes coming with?

D: Hoe free…

C: K. Good.

Charlie smiled. She hadn't seen Dominic in over a year, which was atypical for them to go so long between visits. She gone to his last home game in Charlotte before he retired last season, but they hadn't been able to get their schedules to sync since then. With Levi's sickness and her work schedule, life had been unusually chaotic. She'd gotten to see him a lot more when he was still playing in the NFL than since his retirement. It had been easy for her to hit the Atlanta or Jacksonville games to see him. Sometimes, he'd even surprised her with tickets and airfare to other cities if they had gone too long without a visit. But that usually only happened if he was in between girlfriends. Their friendship wasn't the easiest thing to explain to any of his "ladies of the moment," so she usually only got invites if there wasn't some drooling over-Botoxed and over-plumped gold digger taking up his VIP seats. But Charlie didn't mind waiting her turn. She loved any minute she had with him. He was her favorite man, and she honestly wouldn't have wanted to share his attention with some bimbo anyway. She dreaded the day he might actually decide to keep one for good, but Charlie wasn't going to think about that right now. Instead, she finished the second glass of wine, then went upstairs and snuggled into her sheets, thankful for Mr. Houston.

CHAPTER TWELVE

Sadie

E VAN'S DEMEANOR WAS oozing with dejection. It took all Sadie had not to scoop him up into a big bear hug, but she had promised Kate that she would play dumb when Evan revealed the California trip to her. And if there was one thing Sadie was good at, it was honoring promises.

"What did the guidance counselor say about Max and Tad? Does he think they're coping okay?" Evan's questions were sincere, but he seemed distracted by some hidden agenda. Sadie watched as he paced back and forth in her kitchen, his hands tucked deep in his work slacks. She could only assume that he was buying time to figure out when to disclose Kate's bomb.

"He's shocked at how well they are doing. "Thriving" was his exact word. He said it must be from how stable we've kept their schedules and daily activities. Kids need consistency, and Mr. Jenkins said with the way you and I have committed to keeping their lives as normal as possible, they're better than he would've ever imagined." Sadie smiled a thankful grin to her brother-in-law while she rattled the stainless-steel cocktail shaker filled with the vodka tonic she anticipated Evan needed at the moment.

"*We?* I don't deserve any of the credit if that's what you're insinuating. That's all you. I'm a carpool helper."

"Stop it, Evan. You know that isn't true. I couldn't

have managed a single day without your help. I feel bad that I've taken up all your attention over the past year. I couldn't be more grateful to Kate and the girls for sharing you with me." Sadie deliberately made the transition, hoping to bridge the conversation and nudge Evan to spill the beans.

"Yeah. I guess they have been pretty accommodating. But I'm not sure Kate's missed me being around anyway." Evan shrugged and took a large gulp of the vodka tonic she'd just handed him.

"What in the world do you mean by that?" Sadie played dumb, but she couldn't help but secretly agree with him.

"Kate booked a summer-long-acting class for her and the girls," Evan admitted.

"Oh. That seems fun. I didn't realize Lainey and Ava were into acting," Sadie replied innocently.

"In California…" Evan continued.

"Oh. And leave you here? By yourself?" Sadie couldn't help but tee up the conversation, hoping to hear how Evan really felt about the situation.

"Yes. Honestly, I couldn't care less about Kate being gone for the summer. She and I barely talk anyway, so not much will change in that realm. We just pass each other in the halls of our house with a nod. Our marriage has been dying a slow death for years. But what angers me is that she's dragging Lainey and Ava into her scheme. If I had to guess, this is really all about her. The girls are a decoy to keep me from shooting down the idea. She knows I'd never agree to her going two months in the summer without seeing them. Somehow in her twisted mind, she thinks I won't say no if there is a chance for the girls to experience something new or enlightening. But she's wrong. So very wrong." Evan tipped the highball glass back and took another large swallow.

Sadie knew his every word was spot on, but she had promised Kate she would back her up if Evan balked at the idea. "I think it's a great opportunity. It can't hurt anything, except your wallet, and you'll have the summer all to yourself to fish and golf. It's a win-win."

"Yeah. I guess. I *have* been wanting to take Tad and Max fishing. Levi and I spent every summer on the water together, catching fish and crabs and shrimp. I know he'd want them to have the same memories." Evan's eyes filled a smidge with tears as he quickly changed the subject. "But Lainey and Ava don't belong across the country. They need to be here, with their friends, doing teenage girl things. The last thing I want is for my daughters to wind up like Lindsay Lohan, mixed up in sex and drugs and exposed to adult life way too young," Evan argued, his voice becoming more stern.

"So, what did you say?" Sadie pried.

"I said no. For the first time in our marriage, I told Kate Carson no," Evan said with pride, a victorious smile spreading across his face.

Sadie was stunned. She couldn't coax a single word to exit from her mouth. She was positive her facial expression said it all anyway. Never in a million years had she expected Evan to veto his wife's plan. From expansive trips to elaborate home renovations, Kate Carson had always gotten what Kate Carson wanted.

Sadie didn't press him to change his mind. It was pointless. It was apparent he'd made his decision. And if she knew one thing for sure, once a Carson man put his feet in the concrete, they weren't moving. "You have to do what you think is best for your kids. No one will fault you for that." Sadie couldn't bring herself to argue Kate's side any more than the minimal effort she had already put forth. It was enough to uphold her promise.

"I guess I better head on home. Don't want to keep you up too late. Thanks, Sadie. I can always count on you to talk me off the ledge."

Sadie chuckled as she grabbed Evan's empty glass. "I

don't think anything I said was very profound, but I'm happy to help. Besides, I'm at peace with the ledge. Been hangin' out on it for some time now."

Though she hated to admit, it was nice to have a companion there with her on the brink of plummeting.

CHAPTER THIRTEEN

Bianca

IT WAS FUCKING hot. Way hotter than it should be at the end of April in Savannah. Bianca threw the covers off her sweaty body and cursed the Low Country and its vicious humidity. Her favorite Huey Lewis T-shirt was drenched, and her recently highlighted brunette hair was plastered to her forehead.

"Ugh! What time is it anyway?" Bianca muttered to herself, grabbing her phone. eight fourteen. Way too early to be this scorching in her bedroom. She jumped up and headed to the thermostat in the hallway. Maybe the setting had gotten changed accidentally. She had finally let the housekeeper back in yesterday. After her weeklong sabbatical on lockdown-in-mourning, the house had developed a stench that she could only liken to a boy's dorm room. Maybe the housekeeper had changed the setting and forgotten to move it back. The screen on the hallway thermostat read eighty-five degrees—entirely too high of a temperature for anyone other than her tiny Italian grandmother who had kept her house a degree shy of an inferno.

"What in the hell? Literally—*Hell*…" Bianca tried tapping some buttons, but it was no use. Of course, perfect timing. The AC unit was broken. Tom had always handled these types of things. He was the one with the flexible schedule while working from home. Taking care of maintenance was his job, and Bianca had been happy about that. She preferred blood, guts, and a patient schedule booked tighter than a vise grip. Not this. She grabbed her phone and texted the one person she knew could help her: her office manager, Jane.

Hey. AC is out at home. Who do we use at the office?

Jane was always ready at any moment to come to her doctor's rescue.

J: Lowcountry Air. Ask for Luke.

B:You're a lifesaver. Saturday hours?

J: For the right price, I'm sure.

Bianca didn't care if it cost one million dollars. There was nothing she hated more than being hot. She Googled the number quickly and asked for Luke as Jane had advised.

"Luke's out on a call. Can I take a message?" the female voice with a heavy smoker's rasp replied.

"This is Dr. Moretti. He's the technician that services my office. I have a problem with my AC at my residence. Could you see if he's available to come take a look?"

The raspy voice agreed to take her number and address and see what she could do. But she did reinforce that it was the beginning of summer in Savannah, and she wasn't the only one begging for AC attention. "Tell him I'll make it worth his while." Bianca was ruthless at this point. The awkward silence coming from the phone made her realize that her comment could be taken in multiple ways.

"I will see what I can do," the doubtful voice said.

Bianca ended the call and decided she must escape the heat. Stripping down to nothing, she jumped into a cold shower and marveled at how good it felt. There was no doubt she was going to be spending the day at the neighborhood pool, despite the glares and whispers from the stay-at-home moms that she knew were well aware of Tom's abrupt exodus. There was a nice tiki bar that would help lower her give-a-shit threshold to them and their gossip. And she bet that Sadie and Charlie would be up for a pool day too.

———◆———

There were perks to living in sunny South Georgia. One was the climate. The neighborhood pool was open year-round and heated during the cooler months for the frequent occasion that a random eighty-degree day may appear in the middle of winter. It wasn't abnormal to see kids with their little blue lips swimming on a sunny day in February. By the time spring rolled around, most weekends were guaranteed at least some pool time. Most of the year-round partakers were parents with children, but despite not having kids of their own, Bianca and Charlie had fallen into that parental category by default with Sadie as their friend.

"B, I really hate it that your AC is on the blink, but this last-minute pool day sure is a great by-product," Sadie admitted as she wrangled Max for one more swipe of sunscreen. He grunted and wiggled his way out from her grasp.

"I agree. Especially since we didn't have our gazebo night this week," Charlie chimed in as she spread out three beach towels, claiming their seats under an umbrella.

"Well, it takes care of the problem for today, but if this Luke character doesn't call me back, which one of you is going to let me spend the night at your house? You both know there's no way I can sleep in the heat."

"You're more than welcome to stay with me, B. You know that," Sadie confirmed.

Bianca turned to Charlie, waiting for her obligatory offer as well. When she didn't respond, Bianca saw Sadie raise her eyebrows and stare at Charlie too.

"Wow. Thanks, Charlie. I see where I'm welcome." Bianca snickered and shook her head.

"Listen, we all know that you would never choose to stay with me anyway. Sadie is a better cook, a better hostess, and she has fancier sheets with a higher thread count than mine. So why bother? Besides, I have company coming on Monday night, and I've got to get the guest room ready for him," Charlie admitted.

"*Him?*" Bianca quizzed suspiciously.

"Yes, *him*. Dominic. He's coming through town on his way from Charlotte to Jacksonville. He texted me last night. He's so last minute on everything. Drives me insane. But he hasn't been to my house since I moved here, so I've got to get things in order…" Charlie trailed off, appearing to wait for the firing of questions.

"Oh? Are we finally going to get to meet this mysterious superstar bestie of yours?" Bianca asked with a sarcastic tone. She wasn't much into sports, but everyone knew Dominic Houston. His was a household name.

"Maybe. You know I don't like to share him when I finally get his full time and attention. But maybe I could make an exception for you two, so long as you don't act like drooling superfans," Charlie replied with narrowed eyes.

"You don't have to worry about that with me. You know I don't do sports. That's your thing. I wouldn't know Tom Brady from LeBron James. And I only know those names from hearing Max and Tad talk about them," Sadie confessed while she scanned the pool for the two boys. "But it would be nice to meet this man that you seem to think hung the moon and are adamant on keeping tucked away and protected in that back pocket of yours."

"I don't understand, Charlie. If I had a so-called best friend for two decades that happened to be an NFL quarterback, I would tell everyone that I met about him. 'Hello, my name is Bianca Moretti, Dominic Houston's best friend. Nice to meet you.'" Bianca stuck her hand out to Sadie for a handshake.

"You guys don't get it. Star power isn't everything. It's exhausting. And it always makes you wonder who's genuine and who has an ulterior motive. Dominic's always embraced the stardom. He eats it up. The fans adore him. But not me. I'm happy just sitting on the back bleachers watching everyone swoon over him. I'm excited to have some one-on-one time with him, though. I'm usually fighting off the news reporters and bimbos for his attention." Charlie laughed and smooshed her boobs up high, creating massive cleavage, mimicking the swarming gold diggers.

"Why isn't he flying?" Bianca pressed. "That's a long drive from Charlotte to Jacksonville. I'm sure there's a direct flight. Hell, he probably has enough money to charter a private plane."

"Who knows. I didn't even think to ask that. But I'm sure he has a good reason. Dominic Houston is calculated with every decision he makes, on *and* off the field. And yes, the man has more money than God. After a decade in the NFL, he's set for life."

"He's never married? No kids?" Bianca pried, surprised that some model or actress hadn't lassoed him.

"No and no. Well, no kids that he knows about yet." Charlie laughed, insinuating his player prowess.

"Ugh. Men are gross. Just out there spreading their seed like it's nothing," Bianca huffed.

"It may be gross, but if you saw him, you'd understand why his seed is in such high demand. The man is *gorgeous*. Always has been. Google him," Charlie barked. Sadie obeyed the orders while Bianca leaned in from the other side to see the screen.

"Damn. He's fine," Bianca chirped. "Y'all ever hook up?"

"No way! We're just friends. Besides, you have to

remember I grew up in Kentucky. It wasn't kosher back in the 90s for the white cheerleader-slash-homecoming queen to date the black quarterback. He went to my overpriced private high school on scholarship for his football skills. There were enough whispers and rumors of our scandalous friendship back then that any question of a romance would have sent the entire school reeling. I dated Bradley, the all-star wide receiver. They were always together, and I was their third wheel. That set up made it tolerable for my friends and parents that Dominic and I hung out so much. He rarely dated back then. He was determined to get a football scholarship, which he did, to the University of Louisville. So, to answer your question, no, we never fucked. I admit, though, he *is* hot as hell."

"Sooo you *would* fuck him?" Bianca pried.

"Ugh! Stop it! Can't guys and girls just be friends? I've had to have this conversation with every single man I've ever dated. They've always been so intimidated by him and our friendship. I can promise you that if we were going to go down that road, we'd have already done it years ago. Besides, I'm not his type," Charlie defended.

"But wait. I thought Charlotte Compton is every man's type, right?" Sadie chimed.

"Dominic is the exception...In more ways than one," Charlie clarified.

"I agree with Sadie. What's not to want? Does he not like white chicks?" Bianca added.

"He likes white chicks, but not professional, independent, self-sufficient, and smart

Ones—like me," Charlie answered.

"Maybe he does, but that type never gave him a chance?" Sadie smiled and winked at Bianca, alluding to a secret crush.

"You guys are hopeless. Let's focus on something else. B, check your phone and see if Luke the AC dude has called," Charlie encouraged.

Bianca grabbed her phone, obeying the order. "Ah! Yes! Two p.m. Thank God for Jane. What would I do without her? I've always referred to her as my work wife, but now that Thomas is gone, she's my default husband too. Poor thing, having to help me take care of catastrophes at home."

"I'm sure she's happy to help. For as much of a pain in the ass as you are, you're totally worth it." Charlie chuckled and patted Bianca's cheek.

She responded with an eat-shit smirk and turned to Sadie. "Have you heard from Evan? What's he doing this weekend?" Bianca quizzed.

"Oh yeah, did he say anything about the California trip?" Charlie asked. Bianca saw Sadie shoot Charlie an eye-jab. There must be some secret that Bianca wasn't privy to for Sadie to have reprimanded Charlie like that. "Whoops. Sorry, Sadie," Charlie apologized, covering her mouth with her hand.

"It's fine. Just don't repeat any of this. Promise?" Sadie commanded.

"Promise." Bianca was always good to keep a secret. She might have gotten a bad rap over the years for being a loud and mouthy Italian, but when it came to confidential information, she had been HIPPA trained to the max. She was as sealed as Fort Knox. Secrets weren't hers to tell.

"Kate registered herself and the girls for acting lessons this summer in California," Sadie explained to Bianca. "And did so without any discussion with Evan."

"But conveniently with his wallet, I bet." Bianca huffed and shook her head at the typical display of Kate narcissism.

Sadie confirmed her supposition with a nod.

"Who goes off for two months and leaves their husband after he just lost his brother? As tough as Evan is, I'm sure he's lonely and sad without Levi. To leave him all alone in their big, historic, downtown monster mansion is wrong. She never ceases to amaze me—or rather, disappoint me."

"I agree it's insensitive. But I haven't told you the rest of the story. Believe it or not, Evan vetoed it," Sadie confirmed.

Bianca watched as Charlie's eyes almost burst out of her skull. "No way! He told her no? Man, I'd hate to be living inside those walls. I bet it's as cold as ice." Charlie rubbed her hands together, mimicking cold weather. "Hey, B. Maybe you can stay there with them until your AC gets fixed. Should be good and icy," Charlie said with a snicker.

Bianca shook her head at the outlandish idea. "No thanks. I'd rather die of heat stroke."

"Oh, I'm sure she's pouting. But I'm starting to think that's the norm—him being lonely even when Kate *is* getting her way. I assumed he was spending time with us the past year because Levi was ill and he wanted more time with him, which I'm sure *was* the case, but sometimes he's with us when I think he should be spending time with his wife. I know that he wants to help with Max and Tad, and while I don't want to make any unfair assumptions about their marriage, he alluded to the fact that they have two separate lives. I feel sorry for him," Sadie confirmed as she waved Max and Tad over for another coat of sunscreen.

"One thing's for certain: Kate has no clue what a prize husband she has. I would give anything to have someone like him," Charlie added.

"I agree. A good and faithful husband is hard to come by. Now if you will excuse me, since mine deserted me, I've got to go take care of home maintenance. It's one forty-five. I don't want Lukey waiting on me."

"He has a pet name, and you haven't even met him yet?" Charlie snickered.

"If he fixes my AC, he can have anything he wants," Bianca stated matter-of-factly as she stood to put on her swimsuit cover-up.

"Roarrr! Go get 'em, tiger," Charlie said, motioning a cat scratch.

"I most definitely didn't mean it like that, Charlie," Bianca said snidely, placing her hand on her hip.

"Gotta start somewhere. Might as well have a little fun." Charlie winked.

"You're impossible." Bianca rolled her eyes right before she tipped her sunglasses down onto her nose from the top of her head. "I don't think I'm quite ready for the dating scene just yet. My soon-to-be ex-husband's side of the bed is still warm."

"I said absolutely nothing about dating," Charlie defended with a coy smile.

Bianca pretended to ignore her friend's proposal of a boy toy as she turned to Sadie, who seemed to be silently enjoying the banter. "I'll keep you posted, Sadie, on whether I'll be your house crasher tonight. Hopefully it's an easy fix."

"Whatever you need, B. You know where to find me," Sadie assured her with a smile and a thumbs up.

And with that, Bianca skirted off to meet the hero of the moment.

———◆———

The Lowcountry Air van was blocking the door to her side of the garage. Her agitation for the thoughtlessness of the driver was quickly overridden by the quick sinking realization that now both sides of the two-car garage were hers to park in. Tom wouldn't be needing his bay anymore. She quickly hit the second button on her garage door car settings and took a deep breath as she ripped the bandage off, pulling into his bay for the first time. She quickly dismissed the lack of consideration for parking when she saw the ruggedly handsome savior step out of the van.

Bianca's eyes were glued to the young, handsome, bearded figure that was making his way to the entrance of her garage. She could see his face in her rearview mirror as he swayed in and out of her vision. Stepping out of her car and closing the door softly behind her, she now had a better view of this Luke character. *Why haven't I noticed him before in my office? I'm sure I would remember that face. Geez, I'm such an ass sometimes. I really should make it a point to introduce myself to contractors, especially if they look like this.*

Bianca smiled coyly at him and made her way to shake his hand. She was pleasantly shocked that she even still had the capacity to find attraction in the opposite sex under her current circumstances, even if they were a decade younger than her. In her mind, she should have all but been numbed enough for celibacy.

"Um, ma'am, I don't think you want to shake my dirty hand." Luke smiled, holding his palm up so she could see the dirt caked into the calluses and cracks that even Lever 2000 wouldn't touch.

"Doesn't bother me. I'm an oral surgeon. Now if you were a plumber, I would take your advice." Bianca snickered and high-fived the palm that he still had raised.

The corners of his mouth turn up into a perfect beam at her joke. "I'm Luke. Peggy at the office said you were having some AC trouble." She smiled at his deep southern accent. Even after all her years in the South, she still loved the unique sound of it humming in her ears.

"Yes. I'm Bianca Moretti. You do work at my office."

"I know who you are," Luke mumbled softly, making Bianca's stomach surprisingly fill with butterflies. She stood there for a moment, staring into his green eyes, speechless at his unexpected overt charisma. "Um, can you let me in? I need to see the thermostat," Luke continued.

"Oh, um, yeah. I guess that would be helpful." Bianca laughed nervously as she quickly turned to the door leading into the house. The heat generating from her blushing face was no match for the heatwave that blasted her as she walked into the mudroom. Bianca could barely breathe in the thick air.

"Yep. You definitely have a problem," Luke confirmed as he buzzed by her confidently and headed to the hallway to look at the thermostat. As she stared at him walking ahead of her, she noticed the wallet in his back pocket was causing one side of his blue jeans to hang lower than the other. He had enough ass support, though, that he wasn't showing any boxer or underwear waistbands, or worse... Bianca would have hated for a plumber's crack to ruin a good piece of eye candy. And no chewing tobacco ring imprint on the other pocket either. Good thing. Being an oral surgeon, Bianca had removed her share of tobacco-causing oral cancers from the mouths of men just like him. There wasn't anything more unattractive to her than a tobacco yuck-mouth.

"Do you know where your unit's located?" Luke asked, catching her off-guard as she checked out his backside. She could see him hiding a smile as she shook her head guiltily.

"Let's try the attic first. Where is the access?" Luke asked.

Bianca led him to the stairway and the walk-out attic door.

As he opened it, he turned to Bianca. "You don't have to follow me in here. It's hot. I'll come grab you when I know what's going on. You okay with that?"

"Of course." Bianca nodded in agreement. She couldn't get over how commanding he was towards her. There was something so confident, so alpha manly about his aura that drew her to him. It was completely obvious that she had no experience managing these types of crises, not at work or at home. She was as awkward as a schoolgirl on a first date. She hadn't felt this way in years. And she kind of liked it.

After she made her way downstairs, per Luke's orders, she rummaged through the hall closet and found a large box fan that Tom had thankfully left behind, despite it originally being his from his old bachelor pad. It was dusty and dated, but it worked. She plugged it in and sat it on top of her countertop. Pulling up a barstool, she faced the high setting and like a kid, started talking into the blades, causing a vibrating voice that made her laugh. "I ammmm sooooo hoooottttt. Heeellllppp meeeee."

Luke's chuckle from behind her made her jump. Mortified, she turned to him with a forced smile. Surely catching such a polished oral surgeon in such childlike behavior was the highlight of his day. "By all means, don't let me stop you. This is very entertaining. I bet your patients would love a video of this." He smiled.

"I'm starting to think the heat in here has caused me to become delusional," she defended with a nervous laugh. "What did you find? Can you get me up and running? Otherwise, no telling what other crazy activities I might try next."

"I *did* find the problem, but it's not good news. You need an entirely new unit. Yours is completely shot," Luke said with regret.

"I'm assuming that means a lot of money and more time in the heat," Bianca stated, burying her face in her hands. The sweat ran onto her fingers from her drenched skin.

"Unfortunately, yes. About six thousand dollars, and I won't be able to make it here until Monday afternoon at the earliest to replace it for you."

Bianca whispered lowly to herself, "Of course that's the

verdict. Seems to be my luck lately." She raised her eyes to Luke's, acknowledging his assessment and suggestion. "I guess I have no choice. Where do I sign to get this thing fixed?" Bianca asked, finally able to recoup her in-charge demeanor. His appeal was starting to wear off now that she knew all the details of her situation, but only a tiny bit. He was still sexy.

"Good news is, if you need to drink away your sorrows, you have plenty of vodka to drown them with." Luke shrugged. "I don't think storing it up in the blazing heat is such a good place though. You may want to move it downstairs where it's cooler—well, *usually* cooler, that is."

Bianca's face must have given away her confusion. "What are you talking about?" she asked.

"You know, the case of gallon vodka bottles you have stored upstairs. It was sitting right in front of the unit. I had to move it to get to the system. Was heavy as a boulder," Luke stated, wiping his brow.

"I still don't know what you're talking about. That's strange, I—. Never mind. I'll go up there and see. Must be something else. I don't even drink vodka."

"Well, you have plenty if you want to start now," Luke replied as he made his way to the door.

"What do I owe you?" Bianca asked, still rattled by the strange uncovering of booty in her attic.

"We'll settle up on Monday. But I'm sure it'll include a vodka drink." And with that, Luke winked and turned to go, closing the door to the garage behind him.

Bianca felt goosebumps on her skin. *Did he just ask me out for a drink?* Her high didn't last long though. She couldn't make it up the stairs fast enough to see what vodka treasure was lurking in the attic. Flinging open the door and flipping on the light, she saw it. Confused, she stepped slowly toward the brown cardboard container, lifting the flaps of the lid as if a snake might rise from the inside. Luke was right. Bottle after bottle of vodka sat tightly packed between cardboard dividers. Most disturbing was the number of vacant compartments. Bianca noticed a white piece of paper shoved down in one of the corners and pulled it out, revealing a receipt dated only three months prior. And the credit card used...Tom's.

Bianca's heart sank. *Why would he buy this much alcohol? And why vodka? He only drinks beer.* There had to be a good reason for him to buy it. But surely there was also as good of a reason for him to want to hide it. She had only gone into the attic a handful of times. She never needed to, never wanted to. Tom had done all the moving of holiday decorations, storing of old things they probably didn't need anymore, and apparently, hiding copious amounts of liquor.

Reaching in her back pocket for her phone, she texted Sadie.

B: Gonna need that guest bedroom after all. And probably for a few days. Oh, and a big glass of wine. I'll explain later.

S: That doesn't sound good. I'll be home from the pool in a few. Meet you there.

B: Bring Charlie with you. I need all the brainpower I can get for this puzzle.

S: Oh dear. Will do. But full disclosure, I know nothing about AC systems.

Bianca held the receipt tightly in her fist with an overwhelming gut feeling that this had something to do with her husband's abrupt departure. Her gut pointed to a skeleton in the closet—or in this case, attic. She wasn't sure how she was going to do it, but she was determined to find out the details.

CHAPTER FOURTEEN

Sadie

IT WAS CLOSE to four forty-five by the time all three friends made it to Sadie's back porch from the pool. Bianca's cry for an emergency intervention had alerted Sadie that this wouldn't be a quick conversation, so they decided it would be best to shower and plan for dinner together—which, with Bianca's move into her guest bedroom and Charlie's lack of culinary skills, became Sadie's task by default. In the low country, that time of day was known as teatime—or better yet, wine time. It was that golden hour right after daytime activities and just prior to prepping food for dinner. Sadie grabbed three stemless wine glasses from the butler's pantry, a chilled bottle of French rosé, and a wine opener, and headed to the wicker chairs that faced the western marsh. No need to bring a wine chiller. The three of them would split the bottle three ways right off the bat. There was only one thing Southern women loved more than a monogram, and that was cocktail hour.

"We're gonna need another one of those," Bianca stated, nodding her head to the wine bottle in Sadie's hand.

"That bad, huh?" Charlie asked. "Lukey must have delivered some shitty news."

"In more ways than one," Bianca confirmed, taking a hefty gulp of the pink liquid as she fell onto the blue cushion.

Sadie chuckled as she saw Bianca's chug. "Guess this means I'm not going for a run tonight."

"No. Tonight we can just talk to Levi *without* the run. I need you," Bianca demanded as she patted the cushioned seat next to her.

"Okay, spill the beans." Sadie sighed and followed her friend's command, plopping down next to her.

"Is there *any* good news? I always like to start with something positive first. Was Luke at least easy on the eyes?" Charlie asked.

"Actually, yes. Now that you mention it, let's start with that first. Luke is *not* how we pictured him. Well, he is, but much, much better. I must say, Charlie, I totally blew off your proposition, and I was mistaken. He was rugged, handsome, and very confident and direct, despite being a youngster." Bianca tapped her pointer finger to her temple and looked off dreamily into the distance, indicating deep thought into the proper Luke description.

"Yummy. That sounds like a delicious combo—young and commanding. Those young dudes have amazing rebounding ability..." Charlie trailed off in a blissful dreamy state.

"I can only imagine," Bianca chuckled. "But the blue collared man typically isn't my type."

"Anything can be your type for one night." Charlie winked and took her own large gulp of wine.

"Charlie, you never cease to amaze me. Is everything fair game in that boundless world of yours?" Bianca teased.

"Listen, I have standards. I'm no easy catch, but I don't believe in hard boundaries. I like looser ones...fluid... keeping my options open, ya know? It's like avoiding a new item on a restaurant menu. How do you know you aren't missing out on your favorite food if you never try it?" Charlie defended.

"And that's why we love you, dear." Sadie patted

Charlie's cheek with maternal adoration while Charlie beamed like a proud child.

"Don't encourage her," Bianca rebutted. "So *now* do I have permission to get to the bad part—or *parts?*"

"Proceed. We're all ears," Sadie confirmed, rolling her wine-free hand in a progressive motion.

"First off, my entire AC unit needs to be replaced, to the tune of six thousand dollars. And it won't be installed until Monday afternoon at the earliest. Sorry, Sadie. I'm here for a while," Bianca stated with sarcastic remorse. "But that's not the worst of it."

"Let me guess. You also have a rat infestation," Charlie joked.

Sadie snickered at Bianca's blatant dismissal of Charlie's antics as the apparently rattled Bianca pressed on.

"Luke also discovered an entire case of gallon bottles of vodka in the attic. And I don't drink vodka." Bianca stopped and stared at Sadie, and then at Charlie in silence, apparently waiting for a reaction.

"Well, I do," Charlie stated. "I'm happy to take it off your hands."

"That's not the point," Bianca reinforced with an agitated tone.

"That's odd. Maybe the previous owners accidentally left it up there?" Sadie quizzed.

"I wish. I found the receipt stuck down in the box. It was dated three months ago, and it was paid for with Tom's credit card. To my knowledge, my husband didn't drink vodka. Only beer."

"Were you guys planning a party or anything? Was it maybe a gift for his clients?" Charlie asked, obviously searching a possible explanation.

"No and no. If I was planning a party, you two would know it. And I would be appalled if this was a gift for his clients. This wasn't a good brand of vodka. It was the cheap stuff. Surely Tom wasn't drinking this without me knowing. Why would he feel the need to hide it from me?" Bianca asked.

"Who knows? His departure was so bizarre and abrupt, I wouldn't be shocked at any shady activity. Why don't you just ask him?" Charlie asked boldly, turning to Sadie for affirmation.

"That's an obvious option," Sadie reluctantly agreed, her mind now secretly spinning to the past.

"Thanks, but no thanks. Our only communication now is through our attorneys. And what makes you think he would tell me the truth? Honestly, maybe it's best I don't know the answer. I don't think I could handle any more revelations right now anyway," Bianca huffed.

Sadie's mind whirled, flashing back to two years ago, right before Levi's diagnosis. It had been a random Tuesday. Sadie couldn't even pinpoint what exact month it was, but she remembered the azaleas were in bloom, so it must have been spring. Levi had come home for lunch, which he frequently did to take advantage of her kitchen. When Levi left to head back to work, his truck battery was dead. To make matters worse, Sadie's car was at the shop being serviced, so not only did they not have a spare car, but no live battery to jumpstart Levi's truck.

"I'm going to see if Tom's home," Levi muttered, frustrated by the situation.

But more memorable than the inconvenience was Levi's reaction when he returned from across the sac: "Sadie, Tom was drunk," Levi said in confusion.

"Drunk? Are you sure? It's noon on a Tuesday. Surely he was just groggy or something. Maybe he was napping."

"Sadie, I've spent my fair share of time in frat houses and pubs. I know what drunk looks like. And this was drunk," Levi confirmed.

Sadie's eyebrows furrowed. "Okay, I won't argue that. But what exactly was he doing when you saw him?"

"He could barely hold his keys, which I took from him just to be on the safe side. I don't think he could have even backed the car out of the driveway safely. And he was slurring his words. Don't say anything to Bianca. I'm sure this was just a random occurrence. Maybe he just needed to blow off some steam. We all have our moments. I don't want people meddling in our business, so let's not meddle in theirs. I'm sure if there *is* a problem, Bianca knows about it. No need to make it public on our watch."

Sadie had agreed to keep her lips sealed. And honestly, she had almost forgotten about the incident entirely. Soon after, Levi had gotten his diagnosis, and the drama across the street became her last concern. But the memory now made sense. It was possible that this was more than just a one-time occurrence. But how would she tell Bianca? She had just said she didn't want to know any more. Plus, knowing Bianca, she would be mortified that Levi had seen Tom in such a state. It was water under the bridge now. Sadie decided to let the story lie until if and when she needed to divulge the information to her friend. But until then, for her friend's sanity, the secret needed to be buried with Levi.

By this time, the first round of wine pours had kicked Sadie into a tipsy mood. If a proper meal was to be served, food should be on the agenda next. Besides, any minute now, Max and Tad would be yelling from the game room upstairs asking when dinner would be ready. Growing boys and an afternoon of swimming made for big appetites. Sadie ushered her two friends to their regular posts in her kitchen. Bianca assumed her sous chef role, slicing and chopping and prepping with the skill of a surgeon. Charlie took her place at the sink, ready to wash veggies and clean the cooking paraphernalia as it came to her; and Sadie, well she did what she did best—create her delicious concoctions.

"Charlie, you haven't mentioned Gabe recently. How awkward has it been at work since the mini make-out session and his divulgence of the secret lady friend?" Sadie asked as she started preheating the oven. She had picked out some filets, fresh green beans, and squash from the refrigerator, as well as a large loaf of Italian bread from the pantry. She figured more wine would be consumed and some bread to soak it up would be smart.

"It hasn't necessarily been awkward, but it has *definitely* been more guarded. I guess you could say I've been all business—no small talk or kidding around like usual. I just can't believe that he didn't say anything to me about her." Charlie shrugged. Sadie handed her the vegetables to begin washing.

"You can be pretty forward and relentless. Maybe he was afraid of what level of competition it would take you to," Bianca stated matter-of-factly.

"Those are facts. I can be super competitive. But when it comes to competition with other women, it's degrading and useless. I don't beg. Or pout. If a male prospect can't see my value, I shouldn't have to point it out to him. Either he's too blind to see it, or not worthy of it. Neither indicate the characteristics of my soulmate," Charlie said confidently. "It's why I typically can move on from relationships easily. But this one stung a little more than usual, and I can only assume it's because we were friends first. I haven't ever really had romantic feelings for a male friend before, so it hurt on more than one level. But it's okay. Lesson learned. Don't fall for your guy friends," Charlie said with conviction.

Sadie was a little more than shocked. She had never seen her boundless friend draw a line in the sand. "Let us write this moment down. Charlotte Compton has a rule," Sadie stated, clapping her hands together in one loud slap.

"Let's not go that far. It's just an observation. I don't

have that many guy friends anyway. Just Dominic. And that situation is more than safe. It would take Cupid himself to strike us both simultaneously with launch missiles," Charlie corrected.

"Well, I know you're disappointed, sweetie. It was obvious you really valued your relationship. But don't let him jade you. I can't help but think you two wouldn't be the best fit anyway. He sounds very…automatic. And you, my dear, are the swirliest, most spontaneous person I know. Hopefully, you can still salvage your friendship," Sadie said with a comforting tone.

"Oh, I'll be fine. Do you have any idea how many crushes and relationships I've had go south on my dating resume? Tons. And let me tell you a secret… I've never died from a broken heart. And ironically, I've crawled away from each one, finding deeper love than I had before. I guess I just need to find *The One* the inspires me to call it quits." Charlie shrugged.

"Cheers to that. Because if people could die of a broken heart, I would have been in the coffin as of Tom's departure," Bianca concurred, raising her wine glass to Charlie's.

Sadie nodded. She surely would have died from a broken heart too. And some days she felt like she still might. Levi's death had pushed her to the edge of the cliff. Some days, she actually *did* feel dead inside. And if it weren't for Tad and Max, she would have all but crumbled.

Bianca and Charlie must have read her mind. She saw their loving eyes and smiled back at them. Raising her glass to theirs, she fought back tears and followed with a nod. She took one last long sip to finish off the first bottle of wine, thankful she had these two heartbreak survivors at her side.

Charlie's eyes drifted from hers to the front door as a knocking sound billowed into the kitchen. Sadie turned to see Kate through the glass, standing on the front porch.

SCARLETT ADAIRE

"Oh hell. The queen herself decided to grace us with her presence," Charlie said through a fake smile as she waved at Kate.

"Who?" Bianca asked.

"Kate. Better grab another bottle of wine. We're gonna need a refill to withstand this torture," Charlie answered, pointing for Bianca to get a chilled bottle from the fridge.

"Wonder what she wants? Were you expecting her?" Bianca quizzed as she followed Charlie's orders, grabbing another bottle of pink rosé from the refrigerator.

"No, I wasn't. Shhhh. I don't want her to hear you guys. And be nice to her," Sadie scolded as she left the kitchen. Walking to the front door, she could see Kate was dressed in her usual full-on Kate attire: a bright yellow shift dress with zebra high heels and large gold earrings. Her Louis Vuitton mini bag was draped crossbody-style across her torso while her gold aviator sunglasses rested on top of her head like a headband.

"Hey, Kate. I wasn't expecting you. So nice of you to stop by. Come in." Sadie quickly hugged her sister-in-law and guided her into the kitchen. "Charlie and Bianca and I are just prepping some dinner. Would you like a glass of wine?"

"Oh no. I can't. I just have a minute," Kate said as she waved quickly to Sadie's two friends. Sadie could see the look of concern plastered across Kate's face. "Could I speak to you privately for a moment?"

"Of course," Sadie responded, leading Kate to the screened porch. "Have a seat." Sadie pointed to the wicker chairs that she and her friends had just vacated a few minutes prior.

"No, thank you. This won't take but a moment." Kate stood facing her, nervously fidgeting with her purse strap. "I know Evan told you he didn't agree with the California trip."

Sadie nodded, not sure what to say.

"He said you seemed on board with the idea. Thank you for going to bat for me like you said you would." Kate forced a smile as her eyes dropped to the floor. "But I'm still going..." Kate trailed off.

"Oh. You are?" Sadie couldn't hide the shock in her voice.

"Yes. Evan and I had a huge argument last night. It didn't end well. We both said some things...that we'll probably never be able to unhear." Kate's eyes met hers in a locked stare.

Sadie could only imagine what vicious words had rolled off Kate's tongue. Kate was ruthless, especially when she had an agenda.

"Lainey and Ava won't be going. I'm here to ask you to please help Evan with them. They adore you. And please remind them that sometimes moms must follow their dreams too," Kate added with a pain in her voice Sadie had never witnessed before from her sister-in-law.

"Of course. Sure thing, Kate. It's only two months. I've been wanting to spend some time with them anyway. You know, catch up from the past year of being a little more than preoccupied," Sadie assured her.

"Thank you. I don't mean to hold you up," Kate said, looking toward the kitchen at Bianca and Charlie, who, much to Sadie's surprise, appeared to be doing a good job not being nosey.

Sadie escorted Kate to the front door, still speechless. The situation hadn't ended like she'd expected at all. Never in a million years had she though Kate would go to California despite her husband's disapproval. She wanted to call Evan to make sure he was okay, but now wasn't the time. He was probably smoldering hot. She would hear from him when he was ready to talk. Heading back to the kitchen, her expression must have said it all.

"What was that all about? Was she begging you to

throw one last Hail Mary to Evan for her?" Bianca asked with an annoyed tone.

"Don't think I need to. She's going anyway. *And* leaving the girls here with Evan," Sadie said wide-eyed.

"No fucking way. I didn't see that one coming," Charlie added, waving a large squash in the air.

"Now that I think about it, I'm really not all that shocked. Kate Carson is selfish enough to do something like this. We've just never seen her have to battle this hard," Bianca argued.

"Speaking of battle, she said she and Evan had a big fight last night. It doesn't sound good. She came to ask me to help with the Ava and Lainey for the summer," Sadie professed.

"It'll be good for them. They need your influence. The last thing this world needs is two more versions of Kate." Bianca shrugged.

"You and Evan co-parenting together. This should be an interesting summer for you guys," Charlie said, raising her brows insinuating drama.

"We'll make the most of it. And make some good memories, I hope." Sadie smiled. She couldn't help but be a little bit excited. If Kate wasn't going to see the value in the presence of her husband and daughters, she would more than gladly embrace it herself.

CHAPTER FIFTEEN

Charlie

THE WEEKEND HAD crept along. Charlie wanted nothing more than for Monday to roll around so she could finally see Dominic. She couldn't wait to show him *her* place, rather than it being *him* in the spotlight. Of course, his monopoly of attention wasn't on purpose. It wasn't that he wasn't interested in her life or her accomplishments. She was always happy enough to just be in his presence, but there was no competing with Dominic Houston. His world was just a brighter planet than Charlotte Compton's.

Charlie practically skipped into the office, bright red patent heels and all. Red was Dominic's favorite color, after his college alma mater. Even after he played for the Carolina Panthers for years, he still loved the Louisville fan base. And they loved him. His face was plastered all over the football stadium and alumni center. Local television ran constant commercials with his glowing smile hypnotizing the onlookers to buy this or that. But those gigs weren't about the money for Dominic—well, mostly. Charlie sensed that somehow, he was afraid that the city he loved so much might forget him. Out of sight, out of mind. Conversely, the salty rivals in Lexington were more than happy to forget he even existed. And for good reason. The Lexington Catholic High School all-star had chosen the in-state rival forty-five minutes down the road rather than his hometown University of Kentucky. The entire state of Kentucky had been in pure shock when he'd announced his signing selection. News reporters went wild. Fans went ballistic. The Wildcats had thought they were a shoe-in. Dominic claimed it was to be in a bigger city, but Charlie knew better. Dominic had always loathed the Southern-smothered city of Lexington. He'd craved something a little more urban. He was offered football scholarships to schools across the country. Several schools gave him every penny they legally could, and probably some they shouldn't have. No one looked that closely twenty years ago, so who knew what under-the-table extras he was baited with. But Dominic had made it clear he wanted to be near his friends and his family. Either way, he was still adamant to this day that he had made the right choice and continued to rub salt in the Wildcats' wounds any chance he could.

Charlie's inner giddiness thinking about the quarterback was uncontrollably spilling over to her work mode, as she noticed more stares and glances from her usually unamused coworkers. Gabe must have caught the same vibe. Charlie could tell he wanted to ask her why she was practically glowing, especially since she had been only slightly short of cold to him since his girlfriend reveal. It hadn't been necessarily purposeful on her behalf—she wasn't *trying* to make things uncomfortable—but he had drawn a hard line in the sand. And for Charlie, that meant game over. It was strictly business at this point, no gray-area friendship or flirty platonic romance. So, the fact that the typical Charlie pizzazz was back surely made Gabe inquisitive.

"You seem mighty chipper today. What's got you so peppy on a Monday morning? You're usually dragging with your emotional bag of Sunday scary leftovers with your extra-large coffee mug." Gabe prodded as Charlie grabbed her phone to see if by chance Dominic had texted. He had decided to cut the drive time down with a detour to Charleston on Sunday to visit an old teammate. She had taken a half day off from work so she could go home and freshen up, but she wasn't sure she would even make it that long before she combusted.

No messages yet. Dominic Houston was never ever on time, so she wasn't sure why she expected a peep from him for at least another hour since it was barely nine o'clock.

"Oh, um, yeah. I have company coming today," she mumbled as disappointment set in about the lack of texts. She tossed her phone onto her desk. Charlie glanced up to see Gabe eyeing her with brows furrowed, obviously gathering there was more to the story. "It's Dominic. Geez, you're nosey." Charlie smirked, trying to stifle the joy she'd felt letting his name roll off her lips.

"Oh. That's cool. Should have known it was someone important with that pep in your step," Gabe probed further with a raised eyebrow. "I still find it odd that we've been friends for nearly a year, and you never told me Dominic Houston was your best friend. It's just strange that it never came up," Gabe stated, part suspicious and part agitated.

"Oh. Wow. So now you know how it feels to be left out of a major detail of your so-called friend's life when you thought you knew just about everything about them. At least the big things anyway. Like a girlfriend, per se." Charlie couldn't help herself. He had teed up the home run and she wasn't about to choke.

Gabe's eyes darkened. She wasn't sure if it was from the jab, or the thought of her having another close male friend that made his mood change. Especially one of Dominic Houston's caliber.

"Anyway, he's staying with me tonight on his way to Jacksonville, so I'm leaving at lunch. I'm sure you can handle the rest of our agenda by yourself today."

"Of course. Who needs Charlotte Compton to finish launching the biggest back-to-school marketing campaign since Crayola was founded?" Gabe shook his head, annoyed, as he walked backwards toward her doorway, his arms raised in exasperation.

"I highly doubt this project is *that* big, and I doubt even more that you'll miss my sarcastic input," Charlie rebutted, hands on her hips.

Gabe stopped abruptly, his eyes narrowing. "Don't ever doubt for a second that I miss your input. And never doubt that I miss your sarcastic, push-me-to-the-point-of-crazy attitude. The past few days of cold-shoulder Charlie Compton haven't been fun. Listen, I know I should have been open about dating someone. I just didn't know how to tell you. And I didn't want to ruin our relationship. I'm sorry. I never meant to hurt you," Gabe said with so much sincerity that Charlie was slightly uncomfortable.

"Gabe, don't worry about it. I've been disappointed by men hundreds of times in my life. Do you really think I'm going to stay rattled for long by a man that didn't even have the courage to put his dick inside me?" Charlie asked with a sassy smile and a wink. She knew her typical inappropriate rebuttal would alert Gabe that she had indeed moved on from any heartache he may have caused her.

With perfect Dominic Houston timing, her phone lit up and vibrated on her desk. The smile that plastered across her face as she saw his name pop up signaled who the sender was.

"Guess not. Especially with Dominic Houston sleeping with you tonight. Have fun and behave yourself," Gabe said, shaking his head.

"It's not like that. *We're* not like that. But I most definitely will have fun. See ya tomorrow," she yelled as he walked out the door, then she scooped up her phone to see Dominic's words.

D: Heading your way. Better be excited to see me.
C: Excited is an understatement. Drive slowly. I'm sure you're in some pimped-out race-mobile ready to defy the speed of light.
D: Do my best. This Ferrari practically drives herself. I'm just along for the ride.
C: Tell her to keep you safe for me. Love you.
D: Love u.

Charlie's heart raced with nervous excitement when she heard the doorbell ring. *Finally, he's here! What in the world took him so long?* Dominic was forty-five minutes late, which for him, that was basically on time. But for Charlie, it was a gut-wrenching eternity. Racing to the door, not wanting to make him— or herself for that matter—wait any longer, she grasped the bronze doorknob to the gateway that separated her from her favorite guy. As she swung it open, her heart stopped, her breathing ceased.

There he was—Dominic. His intimidating face and stature didn't fool her one bit. The broad shoulders, hard brows, and extra-long appendages would ignite fear in anyone that crossed him in a back alley, but not Charlie. She knew his heart, his soft side.

The sight of her caused his fierce, piercing eyes and firm jaw to soften, eliciting a charming smile that would melt any woman's heart, especially hers. "Charlie," he whispered in a deep, low tone.

"Dom," she spoke through an exhale that she desperately needed after unconsciously holding her breath for way longer than she'd realized. Within seconds, she had her arms wrapped tightly around his neck and his arms were crushing around her waist as he lifted her up in a bear hug. She released one arm, sliding it to his face and smiled endearingly at her friend as she unapologetically took note of his every feature. His cheekbones were strong, his brow pronounced, and his chin fierce with its cute vertical crevice, all topped off with the most beautiful brown skin she had ever seen.

"You are a sight for sore eyes, mister," Charlie professed, placing a firm kiss onto that protruding cheekbone and rubbing his bald head.

Dominic's smile beamed as he buried his face into her neck. "Look at you, girl. Haven't changed a bit." Dominic pushed her back to arms' distance, eyeing her from foot to hair. "Now tell me why again some fancy ass white dude hasn't snatched you up?"

"Maybe I'm just un-snatchable?" Charlie smirked. "Now come on in before the paparazzi get us."

"Aw, I'm not worried about those jokers. You're in a gated community. I'm more worried about your neighbors wondering why you let a black dude into your white suburbia neighborhood." Dominic snickered as he entered the foyer and took a long look around.

"True. With that bright yellow Ferrari in the drive, they probably think you're a drug dealer or something. Or my pimp." Charlie laughed, spinning around with arms spread wide, proudly suggesting he take a look at her space.

"She only want me for my pimp juice…" he sang, quoting an all-too-familiar Nelly song from their high school days. "So, this is your crib. Charlotte Compton style. I like it. It's organic with a dash of Kentucky horse country," he added as he pointed to the large sketch of a mare above the white brick fireplace.

"Always gotta add a piece of home, right?"

"Yep. Once a Kentucky thoroughbred, always a Kentucky thoroughbred." Dominic winked as he made his way into the individual rooms.

Charlie smiled, following his footsteps in double time. She saw him peep into the guest room.

"This mine?" he quizzed.

"Yep. Sheets all set for ya. It's no millionaire's bed, but it'll do for you, I hope," Charlie confirmed as Dominic nodded in approval. Making his way to the master, he flipped on the lights.

"This where the magic happens?" he asked with a smirk, making his way to her nightstand, picking up a photo of Charlie and her parents.

"Yes. Well, when there's magic to be had. Been a little magic-less lately," Charlie muttered under her breath as she walked to his side.

"Oh no. There's a drought in Charlotte Compton's Disney World of Love?" He laughed as he sat the frame down and jumped back on her bed, spread eagle. "Then I guess it's cool for me to make myself at home here on your sheets and stretch my back. No one to get angry with me spreading my masculine pheromones in their territory," Dominic said, stretching. "That sure is a long-ass drive."

"It is. Why didn't you fly straight to Jacksonville? Not that I didn't want you to visit—I can't imagine living another day without your pheromones rubbed into my sheets—but I would've happily driven the hour and a half there to meet you. I would've even gotten you at the airport and brought you back here."

"Trust me. I would have much rather flown. I hate driving long distances. But I'm trading in the Ferrari for a new one, so I wanted to drive this one down one last time. I could have had it brought on a truck. Might have been smarter. Would have saved mileage on the car and my back," he confirmed as he winced in pain," but I wanted to spend a little more time with her before she gets a new home. It's like one last rodeo."

"Geez. It's just a car, Dominic." Charlie laughed as she snapped her fingers, motioning for him to lay down on the floor. He quickly jumped to her command. For years, after games and practices, she had walked barefoot on his back to massage it. Her small hands were no match for his extra-large body. She had needed something strong to dig deep into his massive muscles, so she went for the biggest tool she had: her full body weight.

"Yes! I knew you'd take good care of me, Charlie. You always do." Dominic almost belly-flopped onto the floor for his favorite muscle kneading.

"Anything for my pimp." She laughed, leaning onto the bed with her hands, walking wobbly across his broad ribs. "I'm not as small as I once was, or steady for that matter," she explained as she supported herself with her mattress.

"It's perfect," Dominic somehow pushed out with tons of extra air behind it. "Hope you washed those hammertoes before I got here." He chuckled breathlessly as she dug her bare feet into his back.

"Beggars need not be choosy. Keep it up and the service ends," she threatened.

"I love those hammertoes," he quickly replied sarcastically.

"Now that's more like it," she accepted as she saw a smooshed smile spread across the profile of his face. Charlie's heart filled with affection as her mind drifted back to all the years she'd spent wobbling like a drunk in a sobriety test on her friend's torso. She had wanted desperately to follow Dominic to Louisville for undergrad, but her parents were dead set on a pricey private school for her higher education. So, as a compromise, she'd applied to one of the best liberal arts universities in the country, which happened to be only half an hour away from Kentucky's Mr. Football. Week after week, she'd traveled to the big city to watch him play and hang out after his games. With his practice schedule and team restrictions, there wasn't much flexibility for him to visit her. And there was the fact that he didn't have a car. So that left Charlie doing most of the traveling. But, like the years that followed, she didn't mind, as long as she got to see him. Sure, there had always been onlookers and whispers, but neither seemed to mind. And that hadn't changed at all over the years either.

"So, we going out for dinner? I know you aren't the biggest cook," Dom asked as Charlie stepped onto the floor and reached her hand down to help lift him up to his feet.

"Excuse me! I can cook a few things. And as little time as I have you to myself, the last thing I want is to go somewhere for dinner and be mauled by fans during our meal. So, no, I'm doing the cooking tonight."

"Really? Okay. Do we need to order pizza for backup? You know I got a lot of real estate to feed." Dom eyed her as he rubbed his belly.

"I bought tons of chicken and baked potatoes and made a huge salad. I know what you like," Charlie said confidently.

"Yes. Yes, you do…" Dominic trailed off, his eyes softening and his voice lowering. Charlie watched as his gaze fell to her lips and realized he was insinuating more than just food.

Caught off-guard by his response, an awkward silence fell between the two of them as they stood beside her bed, staring at each other. Stumbling for words, she quickly grabbed his hand, pulling him toward the hallway once more. "You haven't seen the best part yet," Charlie professed as she took a relieving deep breath of air, her head swirling to understand his unexpected sentiment. She felt his palm get sweaty and couldn't help but think of how many footballs it had grasped.

He seemed eager to see her final destination as he short stepped behind her, laughing at her childlike excitement.

"Here. *This* is why I bought this house." Charlie beamed as she led him to the screened-in porch outfitted with a deep porch swing big enough that even the massive Dominic Houston and a few of his teammates could pile up on it. The room was cozy with pillows and blankets galore. A round unfinished wooden table held a small curation of her favorite potted plants and partially read books. Just beyond the screens were two large live oak trees giving much needed shade from the intense Savannah sunlight. A cool breeze blew off the marsh in the distance, causing the Spanish moss to billow like sheets on a clothesline.

"Wow. This is awesome. I can see why this was a selling point for you." Dominic stood with his hands on his hips, eyeing the view beyond the oaks.

"They don't have views like this in Kentucky, do they?" Charlie asked proudly as she plopped down on the soft cushion of the swing and patted the spot next to her.

"Nope. But the ones at home hold their own value," Dominic rebutted as he sat down beside her.

"Getting a little sentimental these days? You been back home in a while? Might do you good to rub your toes in some bluegrass. Speaking of feet, it's my turn." Charlie spun herself around and draped her calves across Dominic's legs.

"You actually want me to touch those nasty things?" He turned his nose up to her.

"You touch stinky dudes and their sweaty bodies for a living. My perfectly manicured feet should be a delicacy in your world," Charlie argued as she lifted her foot to his face.

"Gross." He slapped it away and then huffed. "Okay. You have a point." Dominic grabbed her size-nine foot with his strong hands and Charlie couldn't help but stare at the size of them. For years she had made fun of them, calling them his Mickey Mouse mittens because that's exactly what they looked like, besides the color. There wasn't a part on his body that wasn't genetically perfect for playing professional football—well, all the parts she knew of anyway.

"So, tell me more about this Charlie Compton love drought. Seems odd. I need more details."

"Damn, you are such a girl," Charlie snapped. "I wouldn't say it's a drought…just a misfire on my account."

"Misfire? Do explain," Dom urged as he leaned his ear toward her while somehow still keeping his massage rhythm.

"So, this guy I work with—" she began.

"Hold up. Work relationships are a horrible idea. You're right. Major misfire," he interrupted, shaking his head.

"Don't be so judgy-judgy now, mister. What do you know about dating co-workers? Been burned by some cheerleaders or something?" Charlie defended quickly.

"Now that's an entirely different category. Cheerleaders are more like work perks," he said with a sneaky smile.

"Go ahead. I didn't mean to interrupt."

Charlie quickly tried to close the subject. "You're gross. Never mind. Besides, it's for the best. He has your same philosophy: dating co-workers is a no-go."

"Wait. He turned *you* down? What a dumbass. Who would be stupid enough to turn down an opportunity with Charlotte Compton? Even if you *are* coworkers. Hell, I'd have fucked you at least once just to say that I had." Dominic shrugged.

Charlie was somewhat taken aback by Dominic's comment. He had never talked about her in sexual terms, *ever*. Surely, he was just making her feel better from having been deflated by Gabe. "Doesn't matter now. He missed the boat…" Charlie trailed off as Dominic moved to massaging her calves.

"Sounds like he doesn't deserve you anyway, chick. Bigger and better fish in the sea."

"So, what about you?" Charlie probed.

"Honestly, trying to find my way in this new life we

call retirement. I'm in my thirties and football has been my whole life. What the hell do I do now?"

"Relax. You deserve it," Charlie answered.

"That's not what I mean. What purpose do I have now? What is my next legacy to create?" Dominic asked but didn't seem to want an answer as much as reassurance.

Charlie could tell his heart was heavy. It all made sense to her now. She knew exactly what she needed to do—ignite his confidence. She had done it a million times; before big games, before the draft, and before he was *The* Dominic Houston. Sitting up, she leaned in toward him. Looking directly into his brown eyes, that for the first time ever seemed helpless. "You can check legacy-leaving off your to-do list. You have exuded more greatness in your three-plus decades than most do in a lifetime. What you do with the rest is frosting on the cake. Got it?" Charlie whispered with intention.

Dominic's eyes softened and he smiled at his friend. "You always know what to say. You've had my back since we were kids. I've never told you how much that means to me." His eyes drifted down to his hands. Turning his palms up and eyeing the light brown skin adorned with calluses and oversized knuckles from more broken and dislocated fingers than she could recount, he sighed heavily. "I gotta find something to keep these guys busy. Or…I'll go crazy."

She twisted her leg around toward him and shoved her foot in her face. "Here's a perfect place to start." Charlie laughed.

Rolling his eyes, he smiled and squeezed her foot tightly. Suddenly, she felt sorry for all those footballs that had been crushed by this grasp over the years. "I'm being serious, Charlie. You wanted to know why I didn't fly to Jacksonville. Well, here's your answer. I needed to see you. Get back to my roots. Be with the one person who I know loves me for me. I know you and that creative mind of yours will come up with something epic for me to spend the next chapter of my life doing—but no pressure." He laughed, trying to lighten the conversation. "Okay," she said compassionately as his plea struck a chord in her heart. "I'll see what I can do. But if I know anything about men, and we both know I do, I know that the first place to start to make them feel better is with their stomachs. Let's go eat." And with that, she grabbed his hand and squeezed it tightly, shuffling him to the kitchen.

CHAPTER SIXTEEN

Bianca

"UGH! HOW MUCH longer is this going to take? Not that I haven't loved every single minute of our sleepovers, but I'm ready to roll around in my own bed," Bianca huffed as she stared out the window of Sadie's front door. The Lowcountry Air van had been sitting in her driveway for three hours. "Surely to goodness, Luke is almost finished."

"Bianca, be patient. The poor guy is being nice by working late for you. He could've said he'd do it tomorrow morning," Sadie reminded her.

"I know. Maybe I should take him some water or something and check to see how things are going."

"I say leave the man alone and let him do his job if you want back in your house tonight. Besides, sounds like you may be a distraction to him." Sadie winked.

"Oh, geez. I don't think so. I'm sure he's flirty with every female client he meets. I'm just another impatient, rich old lady to him. Speaking of flirting, wonder how it's going over there at Charlie's with her 'friend.' That bright yellow Ferrari is blinding. My retinas are permanently seared. I've seen at least four people walk around the sac just to eye it. I'd love to hear the story circling the neighborhood gossip train right now." Bianca chuckled, thinking about all the Stepford wives and preppy husbands making their guesses about who the owner was and what was going on behind Charlotte Compton's closed doors. "Life isn't fair. Charlie has a Ferrari in her driveway driven by an NFL star, and I have a fucking AC van sitting in mine. Bet no one is talking about that."

"I'm sure she's enjoying having him here. Sounds like she adores him. And you're an oral surgeon for goodness sakes, Bianca. If you want a Ferrari sitting in your driveway, go buy one for yourself," Sadie rebuked.

"True." Bianca shrugged at the accurate statement and turned to head toward the kitchen. Grabbing a bottle of water from the fridge, she returned to see Sadie eyeing her suspiciously.

"You're going over there, aren't you? Don't be pissy if you don't get back in your house tonight."

"Oh hush. I'm being kind. And besides, I want to see if Luke has uncovered anymore attic 'surprises' for me. I won't be gone long. I don't want to melt." Bianca smiled coyly and marched the seventy-five yards across the sac to her front door. Twisting the knob and pushing the door open, she felt a surprising wave of cool air. *Ahhh. There is a God.*

A loud knocking sound echoed down the stairwell as she made her way to the bottom step. "Luke!" Bianca yelled. With no response, she figured he couldn't hear her due to the heavily insulated attic.

As she climbed the stairs and reached the open doorway to the attic, she could see him hovering over the shiny new AC unit, sweat dripping from the tip of his nose. His light blue T-shirt was drenched, two shades darker than it had been when she first saw him earlier in the day. With it pressed close to his skin, she could see the outline of the physique it was covering. His job's manual labor had to be the mainstay of his physical fitness, and it was serving him well. Tom surely hadn't looked like that. But he also never broke a sweat—well, except maybe to lift boxes of vodka into their attic.

"You doing okay?" Bianca asked timidly, so as not to startle him.

"Oh, hey. Yeah, just wrapping up here. Should be getting you cooled off in no time." He beamed, and Bianca couldn't help but notice how gorgeous his smile was. It was by no means perfect—it wasn't one-hundred-watts white or perfectly straight—but it was sincere and sexy.

Feeling herself blush, she quickly handed him the bottle of water she had come to deliver. "Here. Thought you might need this."

Nodding, he took the gift.

"Did you happen to find any more fun surprises up here? Your vodka find last time was quite the shocker." Bianca watched his forearms flex as he twisted open the top of the water bottle. Tipping his head back and chugging the clear liquid, Bianca was thankful he couldn't see her staring dreamily at his neck while his Adam's apple pumped fiercely to keep up with the flow.

"Wow. I sure needed that. Thank you." The plastic crackled as he crushed the empty bottle and shoved it in his cargo pocket. "To answer your question, no. I didn't find any more surprises. Well, except for this dead bird that looks like it's been here for a while. Must have gotten in somehow and not been able to find its way out. You may want to have someone check for any holes or openings. You don't want bats to find that secret passageway," Luke advised as he gathered up his tools and placed them in his toolbox.

"Bats? Great. Now that's exactly what a single woman wants to hear." Bianca shuddered at the thought of having to deal with that, and once again was overcome with anger at Tom for leaving her to have to deal with household things like this.

"I'm sure there aren't any now. I didn't see any signs of other critters. There's no need for panic. Let me show you how to work the new thermostat," Luke said as nodded toward the doorway.

Walking down the stairwell to the hallway thermostat, Bianca was pissed that she had been so quick to rush out of Sadie's house and not freshen up before bolting over to see the progress. She was certain that Luke was behind her with a perfect view of the top of her head as she descended the stairs in front of him. Her surgical cap always left her thin brunette hair looking as if she'd been wearing a ball cap all day. She could have at least fluffed it a little.

"I set it for you already. I hope that's okay. I know how cold you like it at your office, so I went ahead and set it on ice cream." Luke chuckled.

Bianca laughed because he was right. A hot surgeon was an angry surgeon. And no one wanted an angry surgeon. She felt a twinge of embarrassment that he had been to her office enough times to know how she kept the temperature, yet she had never noticed him—much less taken the time to thank him. "Thank you. For everything. For taking care of the office and my house. I owe you big." Bianca blushed, realizing that her words came out way more sincere than what a customer would typically say.

"No problem. Happy to help…" Luke trailed off just as Bianca heard the front door open unexpectedly without a knock.

"Bianca? You okay?" She heard coming from the foyer.

"Um, yes. Sure, Sadie, come on in," Bianca responded sarcastically to the familiar voice. She gave Sadie a what-the-hell glare that she hoped Luke couldn't see when her friend rounded the corner to them. "Sadie, this is Luke." Bianca's arms stretched out toward Luke, her palms up in presentation mode. "He is currently my hero."

"Well, he's currently my hero, too, if it means he gets your crazy ass out of my guest room. Nice to meet you."

Sadie waved and flashed a quick smile to the savior of the moment.

"Nice to meet you, too." Luke responded and an awkward silence of at least four seconds followed. "Okay then, I'm going to be on my way. Let me know if you need any help with that thermostat, Dr. Moretti." Luke threaded his way between the two women and headed toward the door.

Bianca shot Sadie a glare from hell once Luke's back was to them and raised her arms in WTF style.

Sadie shrugged and mouthed *sorry*.

"Oh, Luke! I need to pay you," Bianca yelled as she ran to catch him.

"No, that's okay. I'll send you the invoice in the mail this week. Besides, I know where to find you," Luke reassured her with a nod and wink as he loaded his tools into the back of his van.

Bianca thanked him and made her way back into the house with Sadie still standing at the base of the staircase like a scolded puppy.

"Seriously? *You* barged in here. What's going on?" Bianca asked as she breezed past Sadie and headed to her refrigerator to see what needed to be tossed out after being gone for a few days.

"Well, I got to thinking after you left that we don't know this man at all. He could be an ax murderer. I didn't want you here by yourself with some stranger. Sorry. I worry about you…" Sadie trailed off, and Bianca knew why her words stopped.

"What? You worry about what? About me being all alone? Is that what you were going to say?" Bianca asked testily while she scanned the shelves of the fridge, moving aside yogurts and cheeses to find the expired hamburger meat she remembered she had.

"Maybe. There's nothing wrong with being alone though. For all accounts, I'm alone too. And I'm super appreciative when Evan stops by to check on me. So, don't get all pissy, okay? I love you."

Bianca turned and tossed the package into the stainless bin. Sadie was right. A worried friend was a true friend. "I know. I love you too," Bianca said, her tone much calmer.

"And honestly, I wanted to see what this Luke guy looked like. He's a cutie," Sadie said with an added wink.

"I knew it! You and Charlie. So. Damn. Nosey. My divorce has barely started and you two have me knockin' boots with the first man that walks in my door. Literally. Unbelievable."

"Oh, B, chill out. It's all in good fun. That poor man wouldn't know how to handle your spicy ass anyway. He looks like a baby with a beard. And a sexy beard at that."

Bianca couldn't help but nod in agreement. "Yeah, I've been dreaming about that beard and where it could go on my skin," she admitted with a giggle. "But he's way too young. I would scar that poor man for life. Speaking of spicy, what do you say we go knock on Charlie's door next and put our eyeballs on this Mr. NFL?" Bianca said sneakily as she tied up the trash bag and opened the door to her garage. "Come on. I need to take this out anyway before it starts to stink."

As the two friends made their way to Charlie's after disposing of the bag of soiled groceries, Sadie peeked inside the Yellow Ferrari. "I can barely see anything in there, these windows are so dark," Sadie said as she cupped her hands around her eyes and leaned in toward the glass of the car.

"I think that's the point. He's famous. That's what famous people do. They buy flashy cars so you know someone important is inside, but they keep you curious by hiding their identity. It's all such an odd game," Bianca stated matter-of-factly.

Sadie nodded in enlightenment and wiped her nose

smudge marks from the glass. "Are you sure this is a good idea? I hate to interrupt her," Sadie asked as Bianca stepped onto Charlie's porch and rang the doorbell.

"Oh, so let me get this straight. It's okay for you to show up uninvited to *my* house and interrupt my conversation with Luke, but barging in on Charlie is inappropriate?" Bianca asked snarkily as she heard footsteps coming to the door. Bianca was almost blown away when she saw the massive human that opened the door. His face was nearly perfect, in a warrior sort of way. His skin, as brown as it was, shined brightly like it had been polished to a semi-gloss. The white T-shirt that adorned his upper body hugged every inch of his perfectly formed chest. The sleeves grasped the top of his bicep tightly, unable to stretch even the slightest bit over the bulging muscle. Bianca was sure he was watching her stare, which caused her words to stutter in an uncharacteristic nervousness. "Hi. Um, you must be Dominic."

"All day, every day. At least that's what they tell me," he replied in a confident voice. His bright white teeth revealed themselves in a perfectly sculpted grin.

"We hope we aren't interrupting anything," Sadie added from over Bianca's shoulder. "We wanted to stop by and—"

"—and be nosey?" Charlie appeared under Dominic's arm. As tall as she was with her barefoot five foot nine height, she still fit easily underneath his outstretched arm that rested on the door frame, well over six feet from the floor. Charlie flashed a proud smile as she introduced her old friend to them. "Well, come on in. We're finishing up dinner. Might as well have a glass of wine with us." Charlie beckoned them in.

Sadie nudged an elbow into Bianca's side as they watched Charlie perform in hostess mode, which they had rarely seen the likes of.

"Did you survive Charlie's meal?" Bianca asked, eyeing

the dirty plates piled in the sink. "We were worried you might go to bed hungry."

"I see they're also aware of your culinary reputation," Dominic said to Charlie, snickering as he helped grab wine glasses out of the cabinet. "I offered to take her to dinner or order pizza, but she insisted. I'm actually impressed. It was delicious." Dominic raised his hand to high five the brunt of the poking.

"The joke's on you guys. I've been hiding my cooking skills so that I don't have to put forth any effort. I save my talents for special events only. I like the element of surprise." Charlie stuck her tongue out playfully at Bianca.

"Surprised, we are. The next gazebo night is on you, sister," Sadie added.

"Gazebo night? Sounds fancy. Do tell," Dominic probed as he filled the two new glasses with red wine and topped off the two existing.

"It's nothing fancy. It's just our girl's night venue down by the water. We make hors d'oeuvres and cocktails every Thursday night and watch the sunset and analyze our lives—which lately, have been more than eventful," Charlie answered.

"Are boys allowed? Or is it girls only?" Dominic asked, obviously unaware of the recent departure of the only two men in their friendship circle. The room fell silent, and Bianca tried to cover up the awkward moment.

"Actually, we'd love to show a dude our sacred space. Let's take him down there, Charlie. Come on," Bianca replied, smiling at the large, oblivious human.

"Wow. I feel super special right now. Three beautiful ladies taking me to their secret lioness' den," Dominic said. He wrapped his arm around Charlie's neck in a headlock and mimicked a lion's roar.

"Great," Charlie replied, unamused. She appeared more like a little sister being bullied by her older brother than the super successful marketing guru that Bianca had

been privy to. It was endearing, seeing her in a new light.
"Now you really *will* look like a pimp," she muttered,
unraveling herself from his grasp and heading to put her
shoes on. "Well, let's go," she barked as she stared at the
three of them standing idly in the kitchen holding their
wine glasses.

Bianca nodded to Dominic and Sadie, and made her
way to the front door, opening it with a butler's bow. As
the four of them traipsed down the gravel path to the
white, wooden haven, Bianca couldn't help but notice
the difference in Charlie's demeanor. She was playful,
silly, and for a lack of a better term, comfortable. Bianca
watched closely as her typically smooth and sophisticated
friend skipped a double step beside the large figure that
appeared to be just as delighted in the moment.

"Ta-dahhh!" Charlie belted out as she leapt up the
steps of the gazebo, finishing the display off with a grand
finale twirl and curtsy.

"This is beautiful. Now I can see why you ladies keep
this place a secret," Dominic said as he gazed out over the
water. The marsh grass danced as the tide made its way
in and the sun had started its descent toward the horizon.
Bianca watched his eyes bounce around from one wave
crest to the next, obviously enamored by the view.

"Yeah. You rat us out, you're dead meat, mister. I'm
praying the paparazzi haven't followed us here," Charlie
said as she peeked her head around, pretending to look
for any stalkers.

"We've made a ton of great memories here—shed a lot
of tears, had a lot of laughs, and licked a lot of wounds,"
Sadie added as she wiped dust and bright yellow pollen
from the bench before taking a seat facing the water. The
time from March until May was prime pine pollen season. It covered any and all outdoor surfaces, including
their beautiful oasis.

Dominic smiled and raised his glass. "I would like to

propose a toast—to the best wound-licker I know, Charlotte Compton. Thank you so much for allowing me into your home, introducing me to your friends, and for always having my back. I love you, chick." Dominic tipped his glass to Charlie's, then made his way to the two onlookers who were in awe of his charm, as well as his open display of appreciation toward Charlie.

Charlie's face turned a bright shade of red, which Bianca had also never seen—well, not from embarrassment, but from anger, for sure. Charlie wasn't one to show any signs of weakness, and a bashful smile was completely uncharacteristic. Bianca stood amazed as Charlie fidgeted with the ring on her right hand nervously.

It didn't take long for the wine glasses to empty. Charlie seemed more than anxious to usher them all back to the sac. "I would love for us to stay here and chat all night, but I do have to work tomorrow and I'm sure Dominic is exhausted from his drive. We'd better be getting back," Charlie proclaimed as she grabbed Dominic by the arm. Her hand barely cupped half of his bicep, which flexed larger as he bent his arm up to escort his tall brunette friend down the steps back toward the sac. Dominic cupped his hand over hers and leaned into her with a smile.

While Bianca obeyed Charlie's orders for departure, she watched the two unassuming old friends. There was something between them that made her heart smile—something they probably didn't even sense. Maybe it was endearment, maybe it was comfort, or maybe it was both—but Bianca knew one thing for certain… it was love.

CHAPTER SEVENTEEN

Charlie

IT WAS HUMP day, thankfully. Charlie wasn't used to entertaining company, especially not on a work night. She had barely made it through Tuesday without needing a nap, and despite having gone to bed at a toddler hour the night before, she still felt like a huge double shot of espresso might be the only cure for her exhaustion.

She and Dominic had finished Monday evening by polishing off another bottle of wine on her couch and catching up on life. While Charlie knew a headache loomed, she didn't want the night to end, so she went toe-to-toe in alcohol consumption with someone double her size, which was never a smart thing to do. The corners of her lips unassumingly turned up at the thought of their evening while she stared mindlessly at her computer screen. There was something so comforting about having Dominic around. Obviously, he was protective. He was manly...alpha. But more than that, he was *good*. He was like her favorite weighted blanket, keeping her safe and secure. It sucked that he was always so far away. And famous. Charlie couldn't help but hope that now that he was retired from the NFL, maybe he would have time for more important things...*like her*.

"Now that's a smile. You seem to have perked up some today," Gabe taunted as he tossed a stack of stapled papers onto her desk, causing her to jump back and snap out of her thoughts.

Charlie glared at him from over the top of her glasses. He had been a prick since Dominic's visit, making things as difficult as they could be on her. Despite her exhaustion, she was elated. Her giddiness was palpable. But she was also tired and still recovering from a hangover, and by his efforts, she sensed his jealousy and determination to make her as miserable as possible. Charlie huffed at his snarky comment, grabbing the stack of papers reluctantly.

"Oh, I'm sorry. Was I interrupting something? Like maybe a dream vacation with the one and only Dominic Houston? I sure would hate to interrupt that. Let me know once you're fully present and ready to discuss this launch plan." Gabe shot her a sarcastic thumbs up and walked back to his office.

He wasn't wrong. She *was* thinking of Dominic. And more importantly, she was missing him terribly. Grabbing her phone, she typed in his name like she had at least twenty times in the last two days, pulling up his contact and opening their text history. She had scrolled through their words a hundred times, rereading every single letter that was there. It was nothing special, just their normal conversation and banter. But this time, as she went to close out the screen like she had so many times without typing any messages, she saw dots blinking.

D: Said goodbye to my sweet Ferrari without any tears. Flight back home was good. Home safe. Thanks again. So good to see you. Miss you already.

C: Yay! You must have ESP. I was about to make sure you hadn't caved and decided to keep her. Happy to get you to myself for once. Just like old times. Miss you too.

Charlie's heart sank. She was sure it would be another eternity before she could see Dominic again. More dots blinked and she was more than elated to learn that her current worry was unnecessary.

D: Say... I have an NFL gala coming up in a few weeks in New York. Do you want to go with me? It's formal. I know you like a reason to wear a fancy dress.

Charlie's heart skipped a beat. In all their years as friends, Dominic had never asked her to an event with him. He had plenty of Barbie dolls lined up to be his arm candy. She wanted to jump up and down on her desk, but somehow, she contained herself, knowing that Gabe was probably eyeing her closely to see if she was reviewing the launch packet yet. And nothing in that stack of papers warranted such a display of excitement.

C: Wow. A sidekick to Dominic Houston? I would be honored.

D: Great. And you and I both know you're more than my sidekick. Thanks for the pep talks the other night. I know I can be vulnerable around you and feel safe. You are no doubt a badass chick, but my favorite version of you is the softer side of Charlotte Compton. The one most others don't get to see. I'll email you the invitation for details. Can't wait. Love you.

C: You know I'm your biggest fan and loudest cheerleader. Always have been, always will be. Love you too.

Charlie's heart pounded in her chest, her mind spinning. *What will I wear? Where will we stay? Will we have separate rooms? Wait, is this a date? Ugh! Charlie, simmer the fuck down...* Her brain was unraveling, and she knew her two friends would have the same reaction. Charlie had never even considered Dominic as a "date." She shook her head at the weird thought. *Charlie, you're friends. You're going to this event as friends. Period. End of story*

Tossing her phone down onto her desk, she covered her face with both hands, and let out a loud sigh, not realizing Gabe stood in her doorway.

"That bad, huh? Guess I should start over," Gabe replied to Charlie's expression of angst.

"Oh, no. Sorry. I haven't had a chance to look yet. It's not you. I'm on it right now. I'm sure it's great." Charlie scrambled to get focused, grasping the stack of white papers and placing her glasses appropriately on the bridge of her nose. As she skimmed through the first page of the proposal, it took every bit of laser focus to keep her mind in the present and out of the future. Her eyes drifted up catching Gabe's expression that blatantly revealed his suspicious thoughts. She wasn't about to give up any information to him. After all, he was the king of omitting. It wasn't his business what she did in her personal life anymore. He had tossed out his privileges as her confidant when he'd decided to hide the fact that he had a girlfriend for who knew how many months. A twinge of sweet revenge filled her soul, and she couldn't help but revel in the fact that her life had gotten a lot more interesting than anything his world could conjure up. But he made the rules…not her. In that moment, however, she was thankful for them. Had she been able to convince him to bend, she wouldn't have been available to attend this event with Dominic, which was by far more appealing than hanging out and talking about marketing. She smiled, thankful for unanswered prayers.

CHAPTER EIGHTEEN

Bianca

"COWHORNS," BIANCA MUTTERED as she retracted the cheek of an anesthetized and sedated patient. Her assistant obliged per usual, on point, placing the metal torture device firmly in the palm of her boss's right hand. Bianca's gaze was fixed firmly, never wavering from the intended target: a pesky lower molar that had seen its day. With her grip tightly around the forceps, she pressed firmly left and right, completing a procedure she had performed thousands of times. Sweat beads on her forehead and foggy magnification loupes indicated that her surgical gear was indeed a full-body humidor. She couldn't help but grin behind her surgical mask, remembering Luke's comment on how frigid she kept her office. The moment itself was verification as to why her thermostat stayed well below normal comfort range.

Her mind quickly shifted to his smile. It was perfect. Especially with his red-tinged beard as a frame. There was something about him that she was drawn to. Maybe it was his simplicity. His down-to-earth persona. His commanding demeanor. Being a surgeon, she had always looked to date someone like herself: professional, educated, polished, and well, wealthy. It wasn't that she thought she was too good for someone like Luke. She just didn't know anyone like him. How would she? She had grown up with a physician father, lived in a high-end suburban neighborhood, gone to school at the most elite universities, and settled in a country club neighborhood. But she had followed all the rules with Tom and look where it had gotten her. What would be the harm in just a simple date? Her dad and grandma weren't around anymore to wave their judging fingers at her selection in men. Her heart sank in discouragement. *I guess it doesn't really matter anyway. I'll probably never see him again...*

"Dr. Moretti," Jane whispered from the doorway of the operatory, "Luke from Lowcountry Air is here to drop off the invoice for the work he did at your house. He asked to speak with you, but I'll let him know you're in surgery. I can write him a check if you'd like."

Bianca's heart skipped a beat. Luke could have just as easily mailed her an invoice, but he had chosen to drop it off. There was no way she was letting him out of her office without seeing him this time, especially after the numerous times he had graced the facility unnoticed by her. And now, she knew what company she would be missing out on.

"Thanks, Jane, but I'm finishing up. Will you please ask him to wait in my office? I'll be with him in a few minutes." Bianca was beyond grateful for Jane taking care of her every need. She had gotten more than proficient at diverting unannounced visitors, like sales reps and lab technicians who always managed to pop in at the worst times. But this impromptu visitor was different. Bianca stripped off her surgical attire down to her scrubs. She had undoubtedly dropped a few pounds since Tom's departure. Her appetite had taken a major hit, despite the temptation of Sadie's delicious leftovers that she frequently brought by. Bianca coveted Sadie's love language, food, which was hers as well. But even Bianca's all-time favorite Sadie Compton dish, chicken pot pie, had lost a little of its luster recently.

Bianca checked her makeup, which she had always felt was pointless with her daily donning of masks, fluffed her hair after being mushed into her surgical cap, and headed briskly into her office. She didn't want to seem too excited to see him, so she decided to make her typical "I'm a really busy oral surgeon, and you're being graced by the ten minutes of attention I'm about to give you, so let's make this quick" entrance into her office. As she rounded the doorway, she was caught by surprise. He wasn't in his work attire, despite it being a Wednesday afternoon. The board shorts and long-sleeved rash guard alluded to an afternoon of play. Luke stood reading the accolades and diplomas mounted perfectly in black frames with white mats she had painstakingly hung on the wall. In that moment, she was almost embarrassed at her display of narcissism as Luke's eyes drifted to each one.

"Hey, there," Bianca chirped as she made her way past him to her desk, pulling out her checkbook from the drawer. "I was wondering when you were going to come repo my AC unit since I hadn't paid you yet."

"I said I knew where to find you," he replied, still eyeing her accomplishments. "And as always, it's Antarctica in here." He chuckled, rubbing his hands together and shoving them down into his pockets.

"Ironically, I was laughing during surgery a few minutes ago while sweat rolled down my forehead, thinking about how you called out my frigid temperature preferences. I guess it's my age and the multiple layers of PPE that make my core ignite into an inferno." Bianca handed him the check.

"I like your age," Luke responded without skipping a beat.

"Is that so? Do you even know my age?" Bianca rebutted, slightly taken off guard by his boldness.

"I know enough," Luke replied with more confidence than Bianca thought he deserved.

"Are you off today?" she asked as she pointed to his shorts, trying to change the subject.

"Yes. Decided to hit the waves. And now I'm even more thankful I did. I can thaw out at the beach after I leave here."

"That sounds fun. I am sure it's well deserved. Thank you again for rescuing me from the fires of hell. I'm loving my new ice box." Bianca chuckled.

"Any time. It has a pretty good warranty, so I don't think you'll need me for several years," Luke responded as he headed to the doorway of her office.

"There's always maintenance," Bianca rebutted, shocking even herself at the forward justification for another meeting. Luke must have taken it as a sign, spurring a moment of courage.

Suddenly he stopped, as if he had forgotten something. Bianca almost bumped straight into his back, trying to stop her momentum as she followed behind him. They both laughed at the awkward moment. Turning to her, he said in a suggestive tone, "I really would like to take you for a drink if you ever get the time. I know you're super busy. And I promise to buy you something other than vodka." Luke smiled. "You have my number."

Bianca was speechless. It had been years since she had been on a date. Seven to be exact. The thought of it made her stomach flip with nervous jitters, so she smiled and nodded, trying her best to keep her composure. She figured the best thing to do was to channel her inner Charlie Compton and press the boundaries of her pre-inflicted and previously dictated dating ideals. If nothing else, he seemed like good company. And she had to start somewhere...

"That sounds fantastic," Bianca said, a tiny bit too excited.

"Great," Luke said with a sexy smile.

And just like that, she had hopped back on the horse, fearless of the fall.

CHAPTER NINETEEN

Sadie

SADIE STARED AT the calendar chock-full of base-ball practices, end-of-school-year events, and social obligations that hung secured to the refrigerator with an oversized magnet in the shape of a basketball. Despite the mess of handwriting and highlighted days, today was glaring right back at her: May fifteenth. What should have been a celebration for her husband's forty-second birthday, was instead a cruel reminder of how quickly life could change. Of course, Sadie was bound and determined to make the day great and memorable for her sons. She had planned a special dinner with Levi's favorite meal as the entrée: sea scallops and vegetables on the grill. Sadie was thankful that the meal prep was simple because trying to hold her concentration long enough for an extravagant recipe on a day like today wasn't a task for the faint of heart. Birthday cake and ice cream would be served, a happy birthday song would be sung, candles would be blown out, and cherished stories would be told. Yes, today would be Levi's, despite him being gone.

Evan had offered to bring old photos of him and Levi to show Tad and Max. Sadie knew the pictures and stories were as much of a comfort to Evan's broken heart as it was his professed role-model agenda. Sadie had invited Kate and the girls as well, but in typical fashion, they had prior obligations. Kate, of course, had texted with her deepest regrets for not being able to make it, but with the upcoming California trip, there *'simply wasn't enough hours in the day'*. Sadie wasn't disappointed. She knew her capacity to put on a happy hostess front would be minimal. She also knew that her ability to bite her tongue when Kate drew the focus from honoring Levi's birthday to her own flash and lights would also be absent.

Sadie could only assume that the storm was still brewing between the couple anyhow, and that Evan wanted space away from the turmoil. She was happy to be a safe haven for him, and she hoped he would divulge more details of their altercation.

Sadie rubbed her finger over the old family photo hanging next to the calendar. What she would give for one more night in Levi's arms. As much as she missed his voice, his presence, and his love, she missed his touch the most. His arms were covered in a flannel shirt in the photo, but she could still see his skin, tan, and freckles from too much time spent fishing and golfing with too little sunscreen. And she could smell his scent.

She couldn't help but wonder if she would ever be held again. She couldn't imagine being intimate with someone other than Levi. She closed her eyes and took a deep breath, dreaming of how he had made her melt with the slightest kiss on her neck. How his strong hands would grasp her waist, pulling her in close to him as he squeezed her tight up against his chest. She longed for his hands—callused from doing all things manly—to brush the hair from her face, cupping it in the sweetest hold while planting the warmest kiss on her lips.

He had been her hero, her lover, her protector. There was no way in this world she would ever find that again. And even if she did, she didn't know if she could ever get past the guilt of being in someone else's arms. So, she had decided the day that he died, that this would be her new reality. She would live vicariously through memories until she was reunited with him in Heaven. He was the love of her life, her soulmate, and she was blessed to have found him. She knew some people never did. So, that was the cross she must bear—loneliness.

Sadie snapped herself back into reality. She was getting good at that skill. Since Levi's death, it was so easy to get lost in her thoughts of the past, and in turn, of what her future would look like. Opening the refrigerator door, she pulled out all the necessary ingredients for Levi's birthday dinner. She had gotten a later start than she had planned. The day had gotten away from her. She had found herself wandering off in thought about Levi more times than she could count. Every little thing triggered her memories of him—random emails from retailers had happy birthday wishes to him; two birthday postcards came in the mail from the sporting goods store and the dentist; and, of course, her phone calendar had sent alerts reminding her of "Hubby's birthday," that as painful as they were, she couldn't bear to delete. The magnitude of the day—or the pain, for that matter—was inescapable.

"Hey, lady," came a familiar voice from the living room. It was Evan.

Ugh. She sighed. *I'm such a jerk.* She had gotten so caught up in her own emotions, she had forgotten to check in today. Certainly, this day was just as hard for him. Mustering up the best smile she could, she flashed a sweet, welcoming grin to the taller, more aged version of her late husband.

"Evan! Hey, there. You're early. I didn't expect you for another hour or so." Sadie watched him set the most pristine cake box with a bright pink ribbon onto the counter. It had to be Levi's favorite inside there—chocolate cake with chocolate frosting. Next came two pints of Ben & Jerry's vanilla ice cream plopped upon the counter. Levi had never wavered on his birthday cake request, and Evan claimed that he couldn't remember a birthday celebrated for his brother without those two things. Other requests had come and gone—pizza, fajitas, and even the scallops and vegetables that were on the menu that evening—but the dessert selection had stayed the same. This year, Evan had offered to take care of the cake and ice cream for her. One less errand made a world of difference to her stress level.

Max and Tad must have heard Evan arrive. Their feet stomped like a stampede as they raced downstairs to greet him. Hugs and a few high fives passed from both nephews to their beloved uncle.

"Uncle E, did you catch that Braves game last night? It went into extra innings! Mom let us stay up to watch it 'til the end!" Max yelped.

"Sure did, buddy. But nothing beats the old-school Braves of the '90s that your dad and I used to watch: Dale Murphy, Tom Glavine, and David Justice. Need I say more? And that was pretty cool of your mom to let you stay up that late on a school night. Your grandma would have never let Levi and I do that. You guys are lucky to have such an awesome mom…and uncle." Evan winked at Sadie as she smiled and shook her head at his comment, signifying that he was being too kind and full of himself all in the same breath. He followed up with a playful jab to Tad's arm and a ruffle to Max's full head of auburn brown curly locks. "Speaking of your dad, I brought over some old pictures that I found of us fishing when we were kids." Evan picked up the old, orange-tinted photos that had faded from the original hues. His eyes twinkled as he stared at the two young boys in the images, dressed in cut-off jean shorts, socks with horizontal stripes pulled up way too high, trucker hats with brand names no one could recall anymore, and fishing poles with hooked fish held by proud anglers.

"Look at Dad's hair. It's so curly." Tad chuckled as he leaned over his uncle's arm.

"Now you see where Max gets his," Sadie chimed in.
"What kind of fish is that?" Max asked.
"That one's a redfish. You can tell by the black round spot near its tail. There are tons of those around here. We'll catch some this summer for sure," Evan stated matter-of-factly.
"When do we get to go fishing? Do we have to wait until Aunt Kate leaves?" Max asked innocently, obviously not one bit sensitive to his aunt's departure.
Evan's brows furrowed, but he just chuckled at his nephew's excitement and innocent rudeness. "How did you know Aunt Kate was leaving?"
She most certainly hadn't mentioned it to them, but Sadie's heart skipped a beat wondering if she had accidentally let the news slip. She was typically Fort Knox when it came to private personal matters.
"We heard Mom and Mrs. Bianca and Ms. Charlie talking about it when they were over the other night after Aunt Kate stopped by," Max replied confidently.
Sadie's face turned a bright shade of red. Maybe she and her counterparts had had a bit too much wine to notice their volume—or the eavesdroppers.
"A-ha," Evan said with an enlightened tone, nodding. "We can go fishing very soon. Aunt Kate leaves in a few weeks anyway. Don't worry. We have all summer to fish and golf and do whatever your mom allows us to do."
They all three eyed Sadie as she carried a platter of raw food toward the back door, heading to the grill. "Geez, Evan. No pressure there," Sadie huffed. "As long as you take care of your chores and your summer reading assignments, I couldn't care less how many fishing hours or golfing rounds you three partake in."
"You heard her, boys. We're free birds this summer!" Evan fist bumped the two smiling boys as they jumped up and down, unable to contain their excitement.
Sadie pushed her way through the back door, hoping

to escape the conversation. She needed to get out of the room and compose herself. She was certain Evan would be prying as soon as he could as to what she knew. She had never been one to gossip. She was a secret keeper—maybe to a fault—but Kate had popped in unexpectedly when her friends were there, and that wasn't under her control. And in her defense, Sadie had tried her best to stay neutral, which in her mind, meant free and clear of the entire topic as much as possible. After all, the last she supposedly knew, Evan had informed her he had vetoed the idea. Obviously, her source of intel was Kate, and she could only imagine Evan's curiosity as to his wife's side of the debate.

The old fishing stories, combined with making plans for the next two months' worth of excursions, continued through dinner. Sadie was thankful to have something to focus on other than the huge gaping hole in her heart. As she lit the double chocolate cake with candles that spelled Levi, she fought back tears. But when it came time to close their eyes and make a wish right before all four of them blew out the candles, there was no way to keep her eyelids from expressing tears that had been barely contained. A salty stream gushed down her cheeks and she broke into a million pieces.

"Mom. Are you okay?" Tad asked tenderly, moving his way to her side to comfort her.

"Yes, baby. I am." Sadie nodded, grabbing her dinner napkin to wipe her face.

"Did you make a wish for Dad to come back?" Max asked innocently.

"No, sweetie. I know that isn't possible. I wished for something else. Something very important. I can't tell you, or it won't come true. It's a secret." Sadie smiled and winked at them. She watched as Evan's gaze landed on hers. She couldn't help but wonder what his wish was. He was so kind, yet so stoic. The ultimate caregiver. And once again, she wondered what his heart yearned for. The cake was cut and eaten in near silence. There just weren't any words she could come up with besides commenting on how delicious it was.

"This has been such a great day. Thank you, Evan, for bringing the dessert. Boys, it's time for showers and bed. I let you stay up late last night to watch the Braves game, so tonight is going to be an early turn in, okay?"

"Yes, ma'am," they replied in unison, giving their mom a kiss on the cheek and Evan a hug.

"I'll be up to tuck you in after I finish the dishes," Sadie said, shooing them up the stairs. The room was silent. Evan helped her clear the table and load the dishwasher, obviously dancing around her and the elephant in the room.

"Spill the beans, Sadie. What did Kate tell you?" Evan finally muttered, catching Sadie off-guard as he pinned his long arm to the pantry door above her shoulder, trapping her between it and his tall frame.

"What do you mean?" Sadie gasped in a knee-jerk reaction. His question alone was enough to rattle her, but his bold posture did way more than throw her off. She didn't mean to be deceptive or illusive, but she hadn't been this close to a man since before Levi's death. Her heart pounded in her chest. Her mind chalked it up to the conversation, but her heart argued otherwise.

"You know what I mean, Sadie. It's obvious she got to you. I know you don't share secrets, but it's me. And I need to know what she told you." Evan was firm and equally convincing as he hovered over.

"She told me you two had a huge fight, and that she's going to California anyway…without the girls," Sadie said quickly in one breath.

"That all?" Evan pried, his eyes beaming a laser into hers.

"Uh-huh. And she asked for me to help you with Lainey and Ava," Sadie added.

"And...?" Evan said with raised eyebrows.

"And she wants me to let the girls know that sometimes moms have dreams to live out too," Sadie whispered gently, hoping the words came out soft enough to keep from gouging Evan's heart.

Evan's head dropped, shaking in disbelief. Lowering his arm back down by his side, he stepped back, easing off his territorial hold on Sadie's location.

"You okay?" Sadie asked tenderly.

"Do I have a choice?" Evan responded with a sarcastic huff. "I lost my best friend and brother. Now I'm losing my wife," Evan said matter-of-factly. "Oh, hell. Who am I kidding? I lost her a long time ago. Our marriage has been dead for years. Now it's just a formality, I guess."

Sadie was confused. Kate hadn't alluded to any sort of separation, but Evan's side of the story did. "Formality?" Sadie questioned.

"Yeah. I told her it was me or California. If she left, then that was her answer."

Sadie's face no doubt did more than a proper job of showing her surprise.

Evan continued. "I'm assuming she conveniently left that part out."

"Yes," Sadie replied in shock with an exaggerated nod. She couldn't believe it. Kate Carson was leaving behind a gem of a husband and two daughters. If she could have stretched her arm long enough to reach the high horse Kate was riding, she would have slapped her clear off it. "I am so sorry, Evan. I had no clue. I surely would have tried to convince her otherwise had I known that part," Sadie said with sincerity.

"It wouldn't have mattered. Kate made her decision. And in all honesty, I'm not even sad about it," Evan said with the indifference of a man that was tired of fighting.

"Mommmm," Sadie heard Max's voice ringing from upstairs.

"Shit. Sorry, E. Give me a few minutes," Sadie said, excusing herself to tuck the boys in like she had promised. Her mind whirled while she hurried through the motions of prayers, kisses, and nighttime *I love yous.*

Sadie tiptoed down her staircase, eyeing Evan sitting quietly on the gray suede couch, flipping through the channels. As she rounded the edge of the sofa, she caught a glimpse of the sadness in his eyes. It was pitiful seeing someone so heartbroken. She wondered what she must look like after her outburst of emotion at dinner. Her eyes had to be a puffy mess and her nose a bright shade of raw. She was certain the last year had aged her well past the thirty-seven-year mark that she should be portraying.

Evan's eyes never left the television screen, but his hand patted the cushion beside him, motioning her to take a seat next to him. She smiled at his gesture, and obliged his request, without the slightest bit of thought—until she sat down. In one natural swift movement, his arm raised, and she tucked herself tightly under his wing innately. She felt his face land softly on the top of her head, while her cheek pressed firmly into his chest, his heartbeat audible.

"You okay?" he asked, using his free hand to pat her thigh.

"Are you?" she responded.

"I asked first," Evan retorted.

"If I say yes, will you believe me?" Sadie replied, trying to wrap her head around the fact that she felt an overwhelming sense of calm in his arms.

"No," Evan replied softly, and chuckled.

"Then why did you ask a question you already know the answer to?" Sadie asked quietly.

"Because sometimes, if I can convince myself to say out loud that I'm okay, I can trick my heart into believing that I am. I figured you could utilize that tactic after today. Can I ask another question?" Evan pried.

"Sure. Do you know the answer to that one too?"

"Probably. What did you wish for tonight when you blew Levi's candles out?"

Sadie stayed silent for a few seconds, trying to gather the words. She wasn't sure if she could say them without breaking down. "I really want the wish to come true. Should I still tell you?"

"I'm no miracle worker or magician, but if there's something I can help with to make your wishes come true, then I say take a chance on telling me." Evan's words were sincere. Although she wasn't quite convinced he could help her, she felt safe enough to divulge, since they seemed to be in the confession mood, after all.

"My wish was that Tad and Max would know what true love looks like. Levi was such a good husband. I want *them* to be good husbands. I want *them* to pick good wives. I want *them* to have love like we loved. If they don't have that right there in front of them, I'm afraid they'll forget. I can't wish Levi back to life, but I *can* wish for his boys to grow up to be the kind of man he was," Sadie replied, her voice cracking with tears.

Evan kissed the top of her head, and in a big brother squeeze, reassured her. She felt her body tingle and quickly shifted the subject.

"What about you? What was your wish?" she asked sincerely.

Evan paused as Sadie quietly waited for his reveal. "About the same as yours…" He trailed off. Somehow, she knew that was only partially true, but had the sense not to pry deeper. The moment was heavy enough.

Pushing herself away from him slowly, she looked bashfully down at her hands that rested on his thigh, wondering what someone would think if they saw the two of them tangled up on the couch. "I'm super exhausted. I need to go to bed," Sadie said softly, hoping not to offend Evan, but desperately needing to process all her emotions.

"Running me off, eh? I understand." Evan stood from the couch and headed to the door. "You know I'm always here for you guys."

Sadie nodded and thanked him again, bidding him good night. "Ditto, E. We'll get through all this together."

"I know," he confirmed with a wink.

Her mind raced as she made her way to her soft white sheets. She couldn't help but think back to how eerily safe she'd felt in Evan's arms. Convincing herself that this was only natural, since he was a clone of Levi, she snuggled deep under her covers, thankful that the dreaded day of Levi's birth was almost behind her.

CHAPTER TWENTY

Charlie

NOW THAT THE cat was out of the bag on her cooking capabilities, Charlie had been nominated to bring the hors d'oeuvres for tonight's gazebo night. Caprese salad seemed easy enough. It didn't require a stove, the prep was simple, and it carried with it a fancy flare. Charlie filled three individual glass containers with the contents and topped each off with fresh cracked pepper.

"Voilà, bitches," she muttered proudly to herself as she smiled, thinking of how impressed her two friends would be at her presentation. She also knew they may be a slight bit angry that she had so successfully hidden her talents from them for the simple fact that she just didn't like cooking. Period. It was too hard doing it for one, and had always reminded her that, in fact, she was alone.

Charlie packed the containers carefully in her backpack cooler and slid her cell phone into the side pocket. The screen showed a missed text from Dominic. Since his visit, they had been communicating quite a bit more than they normally did. She wasn't sure if it was because he had more time on his hands with retirement, or because of the upcoming event in New York. Either way, she was glad to have his attention.

D: Hi. What's on the agenda for tonight? Heading to that sweet spot?

C: Yep. Just packing up some caprese salads. Guess who got nominated to bring food? My incognito talents have been uncovered thanks to your big mouth.

D: Aw. You mad at me? You're cute when you're mad. You get this vein that pops out in your forehead. It's a warning sign that the snake is about to strike.

C: Cute? Never heard that before. Scary, yes. What's on the schedule for you? Hot date?

D: Nah. My suave days are over. Too much drama. Besides, I have the hottest date ever coming up in a couple of weeks.

Charlie's eyebrows about raised off her forehead. She had noticed Dominic's messages had been particularly flirty since his visit, leading her to secretly wonder about his intentions upon asking her to the gala: friends, friends with benefits, actual date, or whatever other combination of the previous might be possible. She had convinced herself they were just two old friends, and that Dominic had obviously been in a sentimental mood since his retirement and decided to take "old faithful." After all, she had never really thought of him in a romantic sort of way. It had never even been a consideration. And after the fallout with Gabe, she couldn't imagine wanting to cross the line with a friend ever again, even if the opportunity presented itself. She and Dominic had been close for decades.

Everyone knew that adding intimacy to a friendship could only go one of two ways: really good or really bad. She and Gabe had just proven that. And to boot, neither she nor Dominic historically had a very good record with dating relationships in general, which made taking a swing on each other anything but a good idea. Even though she had never been known for having dating limitations, this one might be her only exception. She needed Dominic. She wasn't about to lose him over a romp in the sheets, no matter how sexy he was. Either way, she didn't want to damage his ego. And he was probably just being his flirty self anyway. It was just throwing her off that the flirting was directed at her for the first time ever. If Dominic had feelings for her, why would he have waited so long to tell her? He could have done it years ago.

C: *Hot date? Ha! I guess as hot as two old friends can be. Don't tell me THE Dominic Houston is slowing down on the world of women. He has a reputation to uphold. I only hope I don't throw salt in that epic game of yours.*

D: *You're just now worried about throwing salt in my dating game? You've been doing that since high school. Every chick I've ever been with has been jealous of you.*

C: *I'm not sure why. I'm not your type.*

D: *Why would you say that? Charlotte Compton is every man's type.*

C: *My boobs aren't fake enough, my eyelashes not long enough, and my ass not round enough. Oh, and my drama not interesting enough.*

D: *Geez. You think that's my type? You're making me look pretty shallow.*

C: *I see what I see. And I see the clock striking 6:30. Gotta go feed the wolves.*

D: *Ha! Okay. Have fun. Tell them I said hi. And don't get too drunk. You've gotta work tomorrow.*

C: *Thanks, Dad.*

He was right. She did have to work tomorrow. She was only going to have one glass of wine...so she planned. But the three friends hadn't seen each other in two weeks. Sadie had been busy with all that came with May and the end–of–school events like field days and teachers' gifts. Bianca had been swamped gathering all her financial documents that were due for her divorce proceedings and with the wave of teenagers that had waited until school was out to get their wisdom teeth extracted before heading to college in the fall. Charlie had been busy too. She and Gabe only had June left before the

Moms' Back-to-School launch in July. They had been pulling long days and late hours trying to bring the marketing event into fruition. All these life events had made this evening's gazebo night a much-needed gathering for the three of them. Charlie wasn't sure who would unload the most stress, but she was certain there wouldn't be a silent moment.

Nearing the gazebo with her backpack cooler in tow, Charlie could already hear the chatter of two familiar voices.

"Un-fucking-believable," she heard Bianca chant as she stepped into the sacred space.

"I know. She's a piece of work. You know I try to never badmouth her, but this time, she deserves it," Sadie said in a condemning voice.

"I have a theory. In life, there are givers and there are takers. That bitch is one hundred percent a taker," Bianca stated matter-of-factly, waving a pointed finger in the air.

"Obviously I missed something terribly important. Do tell," Charlie said, pulling out the perfectly packed caprese salads from the cooler and proudly serving them to her friends.

"Kate and Evan are Splitsville. Must be in the air or something," Bianca responded bitterly.

"What? I'm so lost," Charlie said, baffled.

"Evan gave Kate an ultimatum. She conveniently left that part out when she stopped by when you guys were there," Sadie clarified.

"He said, 'me or California,' and that dumbass picked California," Bianca added, taking a big gulp of wine and shaking her head in disbelief.

"Evan told me this morning that he saw Kate's registration paperwork for her acting class lying on top of her packed bags. Guess what."

"What?" Charlie asked on cue.

"She registered for the class in her maiden name: Kate

Cox. When Evan asked her about it, she claimed that she didn't want her married name anymore now that they're separating. She wanted to get back to her roots, and it has a better ring to it than Kate Carson, which she said sounds more like a stay-at-home mom than an actress." "News flash! She *is* a stay-at-home mom," Bianca exclaimed.

"She also said she wants to protect Lainey and Ava from the whirlwind of her new identity. But she isn't worried about deserting her teenage daughters and the effect that will have on them? She's basically full of shit and makes no sense." Sadie shook her head in disbelief.

"Wow. Of all the selfish, shitty things that narcissistic creature has done, this whole situation takes the cake. How did Evan react?" Charlie asked.

"He seemed hurt, obviously, and angry. I think he wanted me to take up for her like I always do, and somehow create a justification. But I couldn't this time. She's lost her only ally." Sadie held her hand up, signaling a profession of truth.

"Agreed. You've always taken up for her. I know I was a little selfish in not taking Tom's last name as per southern standards, but I was already a practicing surgeon when we met. And I'm an Italian from Philly. People expect something like that from me. So, I get a pass. In my defense, everyone already knew me as Dr. Moretti. And giving my doctorate's degree and years of education surname to a man that didn't earn it seemed unsettling. And at this moment, I'm more than happy I didn't change my name after what he did to me," Bianca huffed.

"Your situation is different, B. If I were to ever get married, I would for sure change my name. If I'm marrying them, then I should be proud to take their name. What about you, Sadie? Do you ever think you would change your name if you were to remarry?" Charlie asked gently.

Sadie's eyebrows raised in shock. "The thought never

crossed my mind. I don't think I'll ever remarry. There's no way I could ever replace Levi. But if I did, I wouldn't change my name. First of all, for the boys' sake. I want us all to have the same last name. And secondly, to honor Levi. He was my husband. My true love. Being blessed enough to find that again is highly unlikely, but if so, the guy would have to know his place in my heart. I doubt there's any man alive that would agree to being second place." Sadie shrugged, taking a long, drawn-out sip of her wine.

"I agree. You and Levi had something very special and rare. I hope to find that someday. But, sweetie, don't ever rule out a second chance. Your love for someone else doesn't have to replace Levi. Do you remember what you said when you got pregnant with Max? You wondered how you could ever love another baby as much as you did Tad. But when you had Max, your love for Tad wasn't diminished. Your heart grew double in size. Who knows? Maybe that's true for marriages too," Bianca said endearingly.

Charlie could see the pain in Sadie's eyes. She knew the best thing was to change the subject. "Not to be insensitive, but have you gone out for drinks with that AC guy yet, Bianca? I'm sure he's wondering why you haven't texted him for drinks. He *has* asked you twice. Now you're being just plain rude."

Bianca's demeanor changed to annoyed. "I'm not being rude, Charlie. I happen to be going through a shitty divorce right now. I've been up to my eyeballs in business and building appraisals so that Tom can attempt to take half of our possessions in this legal battle. Adding another flame to the blazing fire isn't exactly my definition of fun. Plus, he is way too young for me," Bianca defended.

"It's just a drink," Sadie responded, pouring more wine into Bianca's empty glass.

"You two. Always tag-teaming me," Bianca huffed.

"Wait a minute. The last time I checked, it was you two that tag teamed *me*, busting into my house so you could get your peepers on Dominic," Charlie stated, flabbergasted.

"Facts. Speaking of…have you picked out your attire for this big, fancy New York City weekend yet? I bet you two do it, so make sure to pack pretty panties." Bianca chuckled, high fiving Sadie.

"We most certainly will not 'do it.' We're friends. I would never cross that line with him and jeopardize that," Charlie defended, clinging onto her recently created solo boundary.

"Give me a break. Charlotte Compton has never had any 'rules' when it comes to men. Why suddenly the hard line in the sand? The way you two acted the other night, you might as well have been fucking for years. It was the happiest I have ever seen you around a man—or around anyone, for that matter. Your chemistry was palpable. Are you staying in the same room?" Bianca asked with a snarky tone.

"Yes."

"They're doing it," Sadie agreed under her breath as she lifted the fork of balsamic-soaked mozzarella cheese to her mouth.

"Ugh. Okay. Yes, he is sexy. Yes, I love him. Yes, I enjoy every second of being in his presence. However, I *need* him. And he *needs* me. If we cross that line, there's no going back. No future partners for *either* of us will ever trust our friendship. It isn't worth it to me. I love what we have. It's enough. Period. Hence, the newly formed hard boundary." Charlie fought back the urge to tell them about their pseudo-flirty texts as of late. She felt guilty for not divulging the truth, but she didn't want to fan the flames. She was having a hard enough time sorting through her own thoughts about him. There was no denying she was attracted to him. And her friends were right—they *did* have amazing chemistry. That was obvious to anyone that had known them over the decades. But they had both proudly shrugged off any questions or accusations with an honest, "Nope. Just friends."

"I bet you two would have amazing sex..." Bianca trailed off, apparently in a dreamy state. "And you would be filthy rich."

"I couldn't care less about his money. I loved him before all that. Before he was *The* Dominic Houston. I loved the poor black guy from the 'hood with the cool kicks and the weird swag. I loved the guy that loved me—the white chick that marched to the beat of her very own drum. The girl that couldn't give two shits about what all the pretentious vultures in their high school thought," Charlie quickly snapped, defending her intentions. "And who the hell are you to preach about going out of bounds? You can't get past your Italian daddy's ingrained checklist of what your dating criteria should be. How about you take a dose of your own medicine, doc?" Charlie chugged the last bit of wine in her glass. She knew she had sworn herself to one drink, but she suddenly needed another. She had just taunted the Italian, which meant a stand-off was about to ensue.

Bianca's face turned dark. She had struck a chord. Maybe too tight of one. She suddenly wished she could retract that last blow. Sometimes she couldn't help herself. She didn't know what it was, but Bianca had a way of pulling out her vicious tongue. Maybe it was the fact that they were two alpha females, or maybe it was that initial sense of competition that had fueled their friendship in the first place, but either way, she should've toned it down a notch. Bianca's skin wasn't thick enough for Charlie's truth serum at the moment.

Sadie appeared to sense the standoff. "Geez. Chill out. Just go have a good time. You've been working so hard lately. You deserve a great weekend of being pampered by a sexy man, even if he *is* just a friend. Speaking of friends, how is it going with Gabe? Have you salvaged your friendship?" Sadie asked.

"I guess. We didn't have a choice. We've been working together non-stop these past few weeks. It's been strictly business. There wouldn't be time for any flirting or bickering anyway, even if we wanted to," Charlie replied, starting to feel tipsy from the wine. She hadn't drunk anything since Dominic's visit. She had sworn off hangovers after that night. And she had needed laser focus at work. As a result, the alcoholic buzz was kicking in faster than normal. She responded to her wave of remorse from her previous jab at Bianca. "Hey, B, I'm sorry about what I said about your checklist. You do you, okay? Date whoever you want whenever you're ready," Charlie said in an encouraging tone.

Bianca's eyes never left her glass. "It's cool. No biggie," Bianca answered nonchalantly.

"Charlie's right, B. You do what feels right to you, when it feels right. We just want to see you happy again. That's all," Sadie reassured her.

"How do you do it?" Bianca asked sincerely, raising her head to Sadie and then turning to Charlie.

"Do what?" Sadie asked.

"How do you get over a broken heart? Sadie, you lost the love of your life. I don't know how you get out of bed every day. And Charlie, you never seem to let any man get to you for more than a blink in time. How do you let someone in and then bounce back, seemingly unscathed?" Bianca asked genuinely.

"I'm not the one to ask, sweetie. I'm not even close to over my broken heart. I default to Charlie," Sadie said, tipping her glass to her.

"I guess I'm just used to it. You just believe that something else out there is better for you. And in the meantime, until he comes along, you live a life full of adventure," Charlie added with a smile.

"Adventure...hum...Maybe you're right," Bianca concurred as she sat up straight and puffed out her chest proudly. "Ladies, meet your new friend—Bianca Moretti. 'The antithesis of predictability'."

Charlie smiled at her spicy friend. She knew old habits died hard, but for Bianca Moretti, it was a start. She couldn't wait to see what her rule-follower friend considered adventurous.

The three friends finished their drinks and made their way back down the gravel path to the sac. Charlie was enjoying her carefree buzz swaying through her front door. Dropping her pieces of clothing one by one on the way to her bedroom, she crawled in and dragged her limbs over the soft, cool sheets.

As soon as she laid down, a dim light popped up on her phone resting on the bedside table. It was Dominic.

D: You had more than one glass, didn't you?

C: None of your business. Checking in on me or something?

D: Maybe.

C: I'm safe and sound. Snuggled into my favorite place. My bed.

D: Sounds amazing. Wish I was there with you.

C: I wish you were too.

She responded without even a second thought. Immediately, her hand cupped her mouth as she watched Dominic respond without missing a beat.

D: I can't wait for New York. Is it okay if we don't leave the room? Well, except for the gala.

Charlie's pulse quickened as her core tightened from the electricity that his words incited. She tried to play it cool, determined not to read too much into his words. Texting had a way of muddling the intentional meaning of a conversation.

C: You know me. I'm easy to please. Just feed me and I'm

happy.

D: I promise to please you. And feed you. And do other unspeakable things to you.

Charlie's eyes were in full focus, reading and rereading his every word. She hadn't a clue how to respond to that. There was no denying his intent. As much game as she thought she had, suddenly she felt like an amateur trying to come up with the next thing to say. She had met her match. And more than anything, she was starting to doubt her own recent rules on friends and sex. After all, she had just told Bianca to live a life of adventure. Maybe she should stick to her original playbook.

C: Unspeakable things? Like what?

She couldn't help but ask, appearing to play dumb yet hanging on those damn flashing dots.

D: I said unspeakable. Guess you'll have to wait and see.

C: Hmmm… Okay, fine. Be elusive. I'm closing my eyes. Big day at work tomorrow.

D: Good night. Love you.

C: Love you too.

Charlie tossed her phone onto her bed. *Holy shit. Did we just sext? Ugggh. This is all so weird. So…complicated.*

She closed her eyes and promised herself to rethink all this in the morning…with a completely sober mind.

CHAPTER TWENTY-ONE

Bianca

SHE COULDN'T BELIEVE she was actually doing this. Bianca scanned the room for any familiar faces. Luckily, she didn't see any. She had purposely picked a place on Tybee Island, at least twenty miles from her neighborhood, to meet Luke for drinks. North Beach Grill was an inconspicuous place, typically filled with mostly tourists. The likelihood of her running into any friends, patients, or coworkers would be minimized. Plus, it was a simple atmosphere...and she needed simple. She had relayed to Sadie and Charlie exactly where she would be. She didn't know Luke from a hole in the ground, after all. And you couldn't be too safe these days.

"There you are," a voice said from behind her.

Whipping her head around quickly to see the body that matched the familiar voice, she was immediately impressed with the view. Luke was dressed in baggy gray utility shorts that stopped above his knees, brown leather flip flops, and an old, weathered Van Morrison T-shirt. She suddenly felt overdressed in her Lilly Pulitzer beach-style shift dress and gold Tory Burch slides. In her uppity neighborhood, her attire would have been considered borderline underdressed. But here, with him, she felt pretentious. And old. The complete dichotomy of their apparel made Bianca's heart sink. This was her worst fear realized: their lack of anything in common. What in the world was she thinking agreeing to this? Her father's patriarchal words rang loudly in her mind. Nothing in their lives was alike: job, education, nor obviously style. There was an innate reaction to bail out, run for the door. She could kill Charlie and Sadie for bullying her into this.

"Wow. You look nice," Luke said as his eyes scanned her from heat to foot. Bianca couldn't help but blush at his compliment. It had been a long time since she had been looked at by a man that way. Years of marriage had a way of putting a damper on lust.

"I figured scrubs were a little inappropriate," she responded, downplaying his compliment, and praying that her face wasn't the burning shade of fire red that it felt like it was. "You look nice too," Bianca replied in return. She wasn't lying. He was sexy as hell with his relaxed style and neatly trimmed beard with a hint of red whiskers in it. She also couldn't help but notice the crow's feet wrinkles that appeared as he squinted from the sunset, which were the only signs of aging on his face. She hadn't asked his age yet, but he couldn't be a day over thirty.

"I wouldn't say nice. Comfortable would be more like it. Since I moved to the beach, my wardrobe has slowly gotten more relaxed. There's really never a need to dress up when it's the sand and sea every day," Luke replied, flashing a sexy smile.

"Oh, so you live out here? You hadn't mentioned that before," Bianca asked.

"Yep. I moved to Tybee about three years ago. Decided it was time to put my life in the slow lane. A beach shack and a surfboard are exactly what I needed. I'm in the scorching heat all day, crawling around in attics and fixing broken AC units, so it's nice to come home and jump in the ocean and cool off after a long day at work," Luke explained. "So, what do you want to drink? I'm guessing not vodka." He chuckled, waving to the server for his attention.

"I usually drink wine, but here at the beach, I'll take a fruity drink. Miami Vice?"

"Good choice. I'll do that too. I usually do beer, but that sounds good." Greeting the server with a high five, it was soon apparent that they knew each other. "Hey, man. How goes it? Been busy today?" Luke asked the tall, skinny man with sweaty temples and tired eyes.

"Naw, not really. I look like shit today because we stayed out too late last night at Huc-A-Poo's. I think I'm sweating out all the beer I had. You missed it, bro. Where were you?" the server asked.

"I had an early start this morning, so I didn't wanna be out all night. I had a job in Statesboro I had to be at by six a.m. Plus, I had an important date tonight with this pretty lady. Josh, do you know Dr. Moretti?" Luke extended his hand as he introduced Bianca to the server, whose name was presumably Josh.

Josh shook his head, his eyebrows raised high as he looked at Luke, obviously impressed with the company.

"Please, call me Bianca. Nice to meet you." Bianca was now overwhelmingly uncomfortable. Her "date" had just called her "doctor."

"What can I get you two to drink, *Dr. Moretti*?" Josh asked with a fancy tone.

"A Miami Vice, please," she replied with a forced smile. She needed that drink. And fast.

"Make that two, buddy. And put a floater of dark rum on top for both," Luke commanded with a wink.

"I got you, bro. Coming right up." Josh gave Bianca a thumbs up and turned to place the order. She couldn't help but feel like she was back in college on a date with a frat boy trying to get her drunk enough to lower the threshold on all her rules and inhibitions. But by the third delivery of Miami Vice with those delicious extra dark rum floaters, she didn't care. The conversation had waxed and waned from work to hobbies and finally to past relationships. Luke seemed to tiptoe around his dating history, which Bianca assumed meant he had not had many serious relationships. She had him pegged as a lifelong bachelor, a free-spirited surfer dude, from the small bits of information he had afforded her. On the flip side, he knew more about the current dying state of her marriage than any service mechanic should ever know.

"So, do you mind me asking what happened with you and your husband?" Luke asked cautiously.

"If I knew, I would tell you. Honestly, I know about as much as you do. One day we were cooking burgers and planning a family, the next, he was moving out while I was at work with no warning. There's a piece to this puzzle that I don't have, but someday I will. I'm just trying to get the courage to ask him all the details. I've got to be ready for the blow. I'm working on my armor at the moment, still recovering from his first TKO punch." Bianca stared down at the third glass of red and white concoction that was melting into one pink slush. "How about you?"

"Man. Compared to your Lifetime story, my world is lame." Luke chuckled, but Bianca was surprised at his genuine empathy for her situation. "I'll tell you this. I have loved. And I have lost." Luke's eyes went soft. She didn't pry—she knew better—but seeing him vulnerable made him her equal in this capacity, even if it was just on this one level. After all, she was a big ball of heartache too. "But I'm here with you right now. So that makes me the luckiest guy in the world. Never did I think you would say yes to a date with me."

She smiled softly at him. She was just as surprised with herself too, but she didn't want to seem arrogant. "Why would you say that?" she asked, playing dumb.

"Seriously, Bianca. Come on. You're a doctor, you're

beautiful, and you're rich. I'm just a poor old beach bum that fixes air conditioners."

"I wouldn't call you "old." Speaking of, how old are you?" Bianca took the window of opening in the conversation to find out what had been gnawing at her since she met him.

"What does it matter?" Luke replied quickly.

"It doesn't. As long as you're legal to drink," Bianca laughed pointing to the empty glass that sat in front of them.

"Well, if you must know, I'm 25." Bianca nearly choked on her own spit. He was a kid. She was a decade older than him. And she had lived...school, businesses, marriage, homeownership...Luke must have read her mind.

"Age is just a number, Bianca."

"It's way more than a number. It's a direct correlation of what you know about life. It's hobbies and experiences and life lessons."

"Yeah, that's true. But the last time I looked at my watch you and I had been sitting here for two hours without a second's lapse in conversation. So, we must have something to talk about."

Bianca smiled. He was right. And she had enjoyed every minute. "Well, just don't ask me my age then," she said with a chuckle.

"Don't worry. My momma raised me right. I learned at a young age to never ask a woman her age or weight. Besides, I already know how old you are," Luke said with a hint of cockiness.

"Oh, you do? How so?" Bianca asked with a suspicious tone and raised eyebrows.

"I saw your college graduation diploma hanging in your office. I did the math. I might not be exact, but I'm sure I'm pretty close."

Bianca shook her head in amazement. She knew that damn wall of accolades was going to bite her in the ass one day. But she was impressed with his detective work, and more importantly his attention to detail, which happened to be directed at her. Maybe Charlie was right. For the first time since Tom's departure, her heart felt unbroken. Whether it was the fruity drinks or the new connection with Luke, she was at ease for the first time. Bianca smiled a real smile as she felt her guard drop. Luke must have sensed it.

"Let's get out of here. I'm two blocks away. Walking distance. Come on." Grabbing her hand, he waved to Josh. "Put it on my tab," he said as he led Bianca across the wooden floor planks of the beach deck. Bianca didn't argue. They held hands and quickly paced the two blocks toward the small beach bungalow that sat on the corner. It was cute and charming, like Luke. The porch light shined bright as they climbed the tabby shell steps to the front entrance. Rattling his keys, Luke opened the door to the quaint space.

It was a bachelor pad, no doubt. Mismatched pieces of furniture somehow came together to become more eclectic and styled than she would have imagined. There were no milk carton end tables or lava lamps, thank goodness. His taste reminded her of a boat captain that had found his way into an antiques shop. Old life preservers hung over the Savannah brick fireplace with driftwood bookshelves flanking either side. Two surfboards stood tall, leaning into the far corner of the room. A weathered leather couch with terry cotton-covered navy-blue pillows sat pushed against the far wall. Luke motioned her to take a seat. She obliged as she walked across a faded, old oriental rug that had seen its share of sand and saltwater feet.

"I'll grab us some drinks. I must admit, my bar stash is limited. I rarely ever drink here. I'm usually out at one of the local dive bars. Do you drink beer?" he asked.

At this point in her drunken state, beer sounded perfect. "Sure. I'll take whatever you have," Bianca replied, suddenly feeling way more comfortable with him than she had intended. As he handed her the brown glass bottle, she couldn't help but notice his hands. They were so callused, especially for his age. She couldn't imagine the hours they had spent working and mending any mechanical situation gone awry. Between his crow's feet and the calluses, she was hanging on to every detail that made him appear older than he was, trying to convince that voice in her head that it didn't matter.

Luke tipped his beer bottle to hers and lifted it to his lips for a drink, not taking his eyes off her. "You are so gorgeous," he said after taking a deep swallow of his beer.

"How many women have you said that to?" Bianca asked as she matched his gulp and eye contact.

"Not as many as you'd think. I'm glad to get a date with you before the entire town knows that you're on the market. Otherwise, I wouldn't have a chance." Luke smiled and leaned in to take her drink. Sitting it on the dark wood coffee table, he grabbed the back of her neck tightly underneath the low ponytail she had crafted while sitting out in the humid air earlier in the evening. He was strong…and commanding… and she liked it. It was the first time ever in her life she let someone take charge of her. His eyes stayed locked on hers and as he moved closer his lips softly rested on hers. His tongue pressed deep into her mouth as she felt her pulse quicken. The excitement was beyond measure. Never in a million years had she ever thought she would kiss another man, much less one like Luke. She felt herself melt into his arms that were now wrapped tightly around her.

She smiled as he pulled away from her lips, her eyes staying tightly closed in fascination. It may have been the best kiss she had ever had. At least that she could remember.

"I'll take that as compliment."

"Uh-huh," she whispered as she let her eyes slowly open. Her hands reached to cup his beard, her fingers resting on the soft lines of crow's feet that framed his green eyes. Pulling him back to her, she kissed his neck, noting his earthy scent of patchouli combined with salty air. Before she knew it, she could feel the coolness of the leather couch on her back. With her Lilly Pulitzer dress hiked up, Luke pressed himself on top of her, between her thighs. The weight of his body on hers sent chills down her spine. She melted as his hand slipped between her legs and into her pink lace panties. Letting out a deep sigh, her heart raced faster than it had in years. The excitement was exhilarating. Charlie was fucking right: she could feel her heart healing with every intense beat. She could get used to this life of adventure.

Bianca watched Luke raise up and pull off the well-worn T-shirt over his head with ease, revealing a trim chest adorned with an artistically detailed grim reaper tattoo covering his right pec muscle. Being the sheltered progeny that she was, Luke was the first man she had been with that had even had a tattoo, much less one as dark as this one. But her instinctual red flags waved in vain as she reached to unbutton the cargo shorts that separated their skin. Raising her arms above her head, he slipped her shift dress off with ease. He buried his head in her chest and slipped his fingers under the cup of her bra, extracting her breast from the hot pink lace bra that had secured it. She felt the warmth of his breath land on her skin and her body gushed with heat.

His hands skipped to her hair and cupped the back of her head. Pulling her in close to his skin, he sat up, lifting her with him and guiding her leg across his lap to straddle him. Bianca sighed as she felt him move inside of her. Leaning back and pressing her hands firmly onto his thighs, she raised her chest up toward the sky, opening her heart and closing off her limits. She needed him.

She needed his desire and his touch to reawaken the pleasureful senses that Tom had stripped from her; she needed his protective masculine aura to make her heart feel safe. Somehow, Luke had broken past the roadblock that abandonment had created, and she wasn't angry. As they moved slowly together, she knew he couldn't be her forever, but he was most certainly her right now.

CHAPTER TWENTY-TWO

Sadie

KATE WAS GONE. And Evan's spirit appeared finally at ease. To be more specific, he was happier than she had ever seen him. Sadie had taken it upon herself to see that Lainey and Ava had plenty of activities to occupy their time with their mom being clear across the country. Evan didn't think it was the right time to tell them about the separation just yet. He had claimed he needed some time to let them cleanse from Kate's toxic aura. It was no shock that Kate hadn't had the guts to tell them either. After all, nothing was ever her wrongdoing, and she most certainly would never deliver the story in truth. Inevitably she would be back, ready to inflict her holier than thou justification as to why her dreams and aspirations were more important than the vows she'd made to her husband. Until then, Evan had voiced he had three months to reprogram his teenage daughters back to factory setting, one depleted of cares of social status and material highs. Evan had asked Sadie and the boys to join him and the girls on his boat for a quick fishing trip. Sadie was never much of a fan of fishing, but knowing that Evan might need companionship, she agreed to go.

"Did you pack the sandwiches yet?" Evan asked as he lifted the cooler onto the countertop.

"No, not yet. I was going to let you put the water bottles in first. No one likes a smushed sandwich," she replied, handing him the stack of aluminum foil-wrapped food to put in the cooler.

"Oh man. You know how we Carson boys like it. Nothing tastes better than a cold ham sandwich on white bread that's been wrapped in aluminum foil and eaten in the hot sun." Evan beamed as he grabbed them.

"It's the only way Levi would eat them. Your mother spoiled you boys rotten." Sadie laughed at the thought of how much she catered to them.

"You have no room to speak, missy. You've filled her shoes nicely. As a matter of fact, I think you have her beat. We're way more spoiled now by you than Mom." Evan laughed as he leaned into her side, wrapping his arm around her shoulders in a playful squeeze. "Why do you think I hang around here so much?"

"I was hoping it was for the company. Now I'm thinking it's for the food," Sadie poked, giving him a hard pat on his gut.

"It's both. I promise," Evan said, exaggerating a gasp for air from the hit. They both laughed as the boys came running into the kitchen.

"Let's go, Mom. What's taking so long?" Tad asked, grabbing the beach towels from the countertop.

"Yeah. Come on. I have all the fishing poles loaded in the back of your truck just like you asked, Uncle Evan," Max said proudly.

"On our way. Just finishing the coolers. Mom and I will be there in a second. Go ahead and get in the truck," Evan responded in his fatherly tone as his tall, lanky daughters followed their cousins down the hallway to the garage. Sadie loved seeing him in that role. And luckily, she would get to see it all day today firsthand.

The ride to the marina wasn't very far. Evan kept his boat at the Savannah Yacht Club about fifteen minutes from her house. The drive was gorgeous as they passed over bridges and down causeways that sliced right through paradise. Marshlands and waterways flanked the route, and Sadie basked in happiness at how full her soul was. Evan had the radio cranked loud, playing country music that blared out of the speakers, trying to mask the voices of the kids in the backseat singing every word to every song. Sadie glanced at Evan and his profile revealed half of a smile. His heart was full too. She closed her eyes and thanked God for this moment of bliss and prayed that someday, these would outweigh the times of sadness.

After about three hours of baiting hooks and casting reels, everyone had had enough of the scorching South Georgia sun. The Savannah heat in May was no joke, and Sadie longed for some relief from the harsh rays. She was quickly reminded of why she had rarely accompanied Levi on his fishing trips. The food and water had all been devoured by the parched anglers, and the shrimp bait had been depleted. Sadie smiled as she eyed the two boys nodding off in the back seat of Evan's truck as they drove back through their route. Their sunburned faces dotted with little brown freckles revealed the massive display of Irish genetics they inherited from Levi and Evan's mother's side of the family. Despite layers and layers of high-strength sunblock, they always came home with pinker cheeks than Sadie wished them to have.

Evan had rolled the windows down on his truck and the breeze felt amazing on her warm skin. The radio was on silent, so only the whipping sound of the wind rang in her ears. Sadie felt Evan's hand slide on top of hers as it rested on the console. Giving it a tight squeeze, he smiled at her. Her heart skipped a beat and her pulse quickened, then her gut sank as the weight of her innate reaction became apparent in her mind. She couldn't move. She let his hand stay right where it was. It felt so good. So safe. *Damnit, Sadie, this can't be good. What would Levi think? You know good and well that Evan's just being kind to you. He's like your brother for goodness' sakes. Don't be ridiculous.*

It would never work between you two. What would people say? What would the kids think? Dear God, get me home. Sadie's mind raced with thoughts, but her body stayed still. It was a skill she had mastered over the past two years since Levi's diagnosis.

When they got home, it was all she could do to get the truck unloaded and the kids settled. She had intended to invite Evan and the girls to stay for dinner, but she needed to be alone. She needed time to clear her mind and process the day. Instead, she politely excused herself and dressed quickly for her coveted evening run. Evan was still piddling around in the kitchen when she came out and grabbed her phone and earbuds.

"I thought you said you were dying of heat stroke on the boat. And now you are going for a run?" Evan asked, his eyebrows raised suspiciously.

"Yeah. I need to clear my mind. Hey, thanks again for today. Keep me posted on how things go the next few days with the girls. I'm here if you need me," Sadie replied as she made her way to the door. She hated to be rude and hoped she wasn't hurting Evan's feelings.

"I needed today too. Helped me clear my mind…and remember what it's like to enjoy someone's company." Evan smiled gently at her, and she was suddenly aware that his gesture in the truck wasn't at all innocent. There they were, two lonely, brokenhearted souls. She stared hard at his eyes, trying to find anything to say. She knew it, he knew it. Their hearts were magnets, drawn into the safety of each other.

"I, um, I need to go run. You understand, right?" Sadie mumbled nervously.

"Yep. Gotcha," Evan replied as he made his way to the door. Sadie waited until his truck had gotten out of sight before she took off, feet pounding the pavement faster than her normal pace. With each step, a new thought zoomed in and out of her mind, from guilt to relief, and anger to hope. Her body was a bucket full of emotions piling up faster than she could sift through. Mile after mile only added more confusion.

Collapsing back onto her pavers, as she always did, her weight seemed heavier than usual. Probably from all the extra emotions she had acquired. As she lay staring at the night sky that wasn't quite fully dark yet, she was overcome with anger. Why did Levi have to die? Why was she even having to deal with this situation? If he were alive, all would be normal. She and Evan would be in-laws and friends at most. But now, she was faced with feelings she never imagined she would have. Despite her anger, she knew her heart deserved love. But surely it could come from an easier, less complicated source.

Her mind drifted back to his touch. Her heart leaped, remembering how good his hand felt resting on hers, and how safe she felt with his arms around her the other evening on the couch after Levi's birthday dinner. There was no doubt that she and Evan had some talking that needed to occur. Otherwise, it could only get more awkward. Evan was level-headed and smart and had his family's best interest at heart. He would know how to handle this. She needed to be honest with him and follow his lead like she had always done with Levi, and all would be okay.

CHAPTER TWENTY-THREE

Charlie

CHARLIE'S BED LOOKED like a war zone with piles of potential outfits strung across it. She had taken the day off work, which Gabe's workaholic ass wasn't too happy about considering their upcoming launch, but they had been working their fingers to the bone. With all the recent late nights, early mornings, and lunches they had worked through, taking the day off to fly to New York to see Dominic was well earned and much deserved. She hadn't finished her coffee yet before she got a call from Dominic.

"Hi! Cannot wait to see you. Whatcha doing?" she heard his voice ringing in her ear.

"Trying to figure out what to pack. You know me, I'll most certainly fail the airline luggage weight limit," Charlie confessed as she stared at the mound of clothes on her bed.

"Yeah. You're a ridiculous over-packer. But most importantly, make sure to pack your best bra and panties set." His voice lowered into a sexy tone.

"Checked that off the list first. But those tiny things aren't the weight culprit. My shoes and dresses are."

"You always look amazing. Doesn't matter what you bring, it's going to take me two seconds to get you out of it," Dominic replied with per usual confidence in his voice.

"Go eat your Wheaties. You're gonna need them," Charlie playfully punted back to him.

Their flirty banter had gone to an entirely different level over the past few weeks. Charlie had finally wrapped her head around the idea that she and Dominic were most certainly stepping outside of their friendship box. She had decided to chalk her friendship/romance failure with Gabe up to divine intervention and take a page from her own playbook: just go for it. She was a sucker for a game-winning last-minute shot, and maybe this was theirs. Maybe it was finally their time, and all these years they had spent loving each other as friends had been the foundation of their future. She wanted to pinch herself. What would it be like when they kissed? Sure, they had kissed on the cheek and held hands for years, but not like this.

"Have I ever told you how much I love your style and am in awe of your boss-level skills and just overall adore you?" Dominic quizzed in a sweet, soft tone. "Just FYI. Let it be known, I am clearly a huge Charlotte Compton fan."

"Nothing compares to my fan level for you. And by the way, is this not the most random thing ever?" she asked as she paced nervously back and forth across the rug on her bedroom floor. It hadn't been that long ago Dominic was sprawled out on it face first as she wobble-walked on his back. It was the last time she had seen him, and this next visit was about to have an entirely different feel to it. "It is for me. Don't get me wrong, I love it. I guess I just wonder why now though, after all these years, are we doing this?" Charlie couldn't help but ask the question that had been lingering in her mind. Now seemed as good as any to have the conversation. She was certain that once she was in his presence, all clear-thinking abilities would be out the door.

"It is and it isn't," he said through a chuckle. "It's the

perfect storm of unexpected outcomes and timing. It seems improbable and random, but at the same time, the connection and chemistry we've had from day one of our friendship makes it not. But I love it too. I love that we can be open and honest and unfiltered and vulnerable with each other with a foundation as friends. I love that I know you have my best interests at heart, and I can trust you with my life. I love that we understand each other and can help fulfill needs for each other mentally, emotionally, strategically, and physically with genuine love, care, appreciation, admiration, and attraction for each other. I know that no matter what happens between us, we will always love and care for each other, and be close, whether that's as friends or something more. In the meantime, I adore and appreciate you and I can't wait to have amazing, uninhibited sex with you."

Charlie felt a lump swell in her throat and her core melt into the floor. She had never in thirty-five years of life felt that loved. Of all the relationships she'd ever been in, no one had ever said words to her with that level of honesty. She wanted to bottle up this feeling and keep it forever. Her heart pounded as she responded.

"Dom, I feel the exact same way. As scared as I am about stepping beyond our friendship to this level of intimacy, I trust you wholly. I know you wouldn't hurt me for anything. And I know we haven't come to this point in our relationship without thinking through this a thousand times. More importantly, I know if we don't do this, we'll always wonder "what if.""

"You're right. I would never ever hurt you. Not in a million years," he added.

"I love you. I gotta go or I'm going to be late. I'll text when I get to the airport."

"Love you too. We can finish this conversation up in person."

Charlie tossed her phone into the pile of clothes on her

bed and cupped her face in her hands. She laughed to herself in disbelief and shook her head. She would have never predicted this, not in a million years.

There was a knock at her door as she ran her fingers through her hair in deep thought, pondering the situation more. It wasn't even nine a.m. yet. Who could be knocking?

As she opened her front door, she saw the culprit. "Wow. Look what the cat dragged in. Someone decided to crawl out from underneath that boy toy she's been playing with non-stop," Charlie said sarcastically as she waved Bianca into her house.

"Oh whatever, Charlie. You're the one who told me to go have some fun. I'm just doing as you said," she defended playfully as she followed Charlie to her bedroom. "I wanted to stop by before I left for work to tell you good luck this weekend with Dominic. I won't be home before you leave for your flight. Are you nervous?"

"That's an understatement. I'm about as nervous about being *with* Dominic as I am being *seen with* Dominic. Supposedly this gala is airing live on ESPN, and I'm not a fan of being on national television," Charlie admitted. "I've spent years flying under the Dominic Houston radar, and I sadly think that's about to end."

"Well, it looks like you have plenty of outfit options to choose from. Geez. Is that your entire wardrobe on your bed?" Bianca laughed, eyeing the pile of dresses and clothes.

"Almost. I still have some time to sift through the rest of my closet for any missed pieces." Charlie laughed as she lifted a long red dress. "I think I've decided on this one for the event tomorrow night." The gown was gorgeous. She had gotten it on impulse at Nordstrom a few years back. She hadn't had a clue where she would wear it, but she knew when she did, it would be an important event. Turns out her psychic abilities had been spot-on.

"Looks like a winner to me. I'll make sure Sadie and I watch for you on TV. It's not every day our bestie gets to be the date to one fine-ass NFL star. Has he said anything about you staying in the same room together? Seems like he might have some intentions besides a friendly date." Bianca's eyebrows raised up and down, indicating excitement.

"Maybe," Charlie stated confidently as she lifted a sexy red bra and lace panties, dangling them in Bianca's face. "I'm packing these in case." She figured she might as well at least hint that this trip was more than platonic, even though she hadn't divulged the details of her recent steamy conversations to her friends. She didn't want to spring a complete surprise onto her and Sadie when she got back, so she figured a clue wouldn't hurt. Besides, her recent conversations with Dominic had been pretty straight forward as to what was going to occur, and Charlie was starting to get more and more confident in the idea of her and Dominic as a couple.

"What? I knew it. I want every single detail when you get back. Do you understand?"

"Yes, ma'am." Charlie nodded with a smile, flinging the red lace set into her suitcase.

"Have you thought this through? Once you cross this line, there's no going back. You're great friends but remember to be gentle with each other. Tread lightly. This isn't some random person. This is your best friend," Bianca advised in a motherly tone.

"I knew it—these past few weeks with you and Luke have all been a façade. Here I was, thinking I'd finally gotten through to you, but here she is, rearing her ugly head again…Bianca, the queen of cautious." Charlie snickered.

"That's different. He's a fling. It's for fun. Luke's a great guy, but he most definitely serves a purpose—he's a Band-Aid…" Bianca's words trailed off as she glanced down at her phone.

"Does he know he's a Band-Aid?" Charlie asked, peering at Bianca over her nose.

"I'm sure I'm just another notch in his belt. Speaking of bandage, I've got to run. That's the office calling me about a patient in pain. Listen, be careful and send lots of pictures. You're going to have the best time," Bianca reassured her, kissing her cheek and quickly bolting out the front door.

Charlie skipped to the shower, turning the hot water on full blast. She had a lot of maintenance to do: painting her nails, shaving her legs, and making sure her lady parts were pristinely groomed. This was her most important date yet. She needed to be impeccable. She *wanted* to be impeccable. After all, he was the most impeccable man she knew. There wasn't a thing she didn't love about him. He deserved the best and that's what she would give him: Charlotte Compton, Platinum Style.

The steam from the shower left the air so thick she could barely see past her nose. Charlie wiped the condensation from the mirror and stared at herself. Today was special, and she wanted to remember what she looked like before her life changed this weekend. She would never be the same. It wasn't every day you fell in love with your best friend.

After feverishly going over her entire body with a fine-toothed comb in the shower, she turned the water off and stepped out onto the white terry floor mat. She bent over, twisting her hair into a towel. Making her way back to her bedroom, she saw she had a missed text from Dominic.

D: I have a random idea…

C: Go ahead with said random thought…but remember, I'm trying to get all prettied up for you and I don't want to miss my flight, so make it quick, mister.

D: Ha ha. Facts. Okay, I'll get to the point. Usually when two people become intimate, it takes some time to learn about

their preferences, likes, dislikes, etc. Most people don't have the advantage of being as comfortable, knowing, trusting, unfiltered, and vulnerable as we are with each other. Let's take advantage of that...I want to know all your hot spots. I want to please you without the hinderance of a learning curve.
C: Typical Dominic Houston. Always a game plan. Always seeking the win. I can promise you there isn't one thing you can do wrong. But since you asked, I will tell you. 1) Chemistry: I like looking at someone across the room, meeting eyes, and seeing sparks. 2) Feeling irresistible 3) An alpha male: I am in boss-mode all day long. I like a dominant partner. I have a feeling you'll have no problems with this. You're the biggest alpha male I know. 4) But my biggest turn on is being connected. And we have that in spades.
D: Got it. Easy. Currently drawing up plays for the playbook. Now hurry your ass up.

———◆———

Charlie's mind was mush. She could barely concentrate on anything. Somehow, she managed to get dressed, packed, and to the airport, but she was certain she had forgotten something. As long as she had her ID and her gown, she could buy the rest.

The flight from Savannah to LaGuardia was an easy two-hour direct trip. Thankfully, the flight had food and beverage services. After a Woodford Reserve and Coke, Charlie's heart rate started to finally slow to its normal pace. She stared out at the bright white clouds as the airplane wings sliced through them with ease. Once this plane landed, her life would be different. And she was ready for that. She was ready to be with *her person.* Ironically, he had been there all along—and in true Dominic Houston fashion, late as usual.

CHAPTER TWENTY-FOUR

Sadie

SADIE'S ARMS WERE loaded down with grocery bags as she scurried through the garage, trying to make it all the way to her kitchen without dumping the contents onto the floor. Even after decades of grocery shopping, she still hated this part the most: unpacking. Times like these made her think of Levi. He had always told her to text him when she left the grocery store, and he would be watching for her to help unload the car. As soon as her fingers touched the garage door opener, she would see his face appear from behind it. He was so thoughtful. She loved that she never had to ask for help. He was already there.

Sadie heard someone shuffling behind her. For a second, she was startled, wondering who the intruder was, until she saw Evan.

"Oh, hey. You scared me for a second," Sadie admitted breathlessly, partly from carrying groceries and partly from his surprise appearance.

"I'm sorry. I pulled up as you were heading inside. I saw you had your arms full, so I was trying to hurry and give you a hand," Evan explained as he took some bags from her allowing her to open the door into the house with the newly freed grasp. She started to unpack the bags and place them in their proper places in the pantry.

"You're a lifesaver, E. Thanks. The boys are with friends

tonight, so I'm shorthanded of usual helpers. Are Lainey and Ava with you?"

"No. They're sleeping over with friends too. They had had enough of Dad, I think," Evan said with a chuckle. "I took them to the fishing store with me today. That reminds me, I gotta get something from my truck. I'll be right back," Evan said as he headed back out through the garage. He returned carrying two new tackle boxes and placed them on the counter, one blue and one yellow. "They're for Max and Tad. Their very own tackle boxes. I put together the essentials for them. I thought they could fish in the lagoons out here in the neighborhood this summer while I'm at work if they get bored or want to practice."

"That's so sweet. How thoughtful. They will love that. They'll be back tomorrow sometime. I'll be sure and give those to them then. Say, do you want to stay for dinner?" Sadie asked. "I'm about to make some fajitas. Nothing fancy, but I'm sure you could use a homecooked meal with Kate being gone." She figured now was as good of a time as any to discuss the elephant in the room.

"I'd love that. And you and I both know that I never got homecooked meals even when Kate was home." Evan chuckled as he helped her finish unloading the bags.

Sadie nodded in agreement. "How's it going in California? Heard from Kate?"

"Not a peep. Don't know and don't care. Ava and Lainey have texted and Face Timed her. She told them she's so busy she hasn't had much time to do anything but recite lines and rehearse. In her words, she's 'finally living her dreams,'" Evan said, shrugging his shoulders.

"Everyone deserves to live their dreams, I guess," Sadie said with a smile. Turning to stock the refrigerator, her mind raced. She couldn't help but wonder how anyone could have dreams that didn't include someone as great as Evan right by their side. He must have read her mind and her soul. She sensed him behind her.

Wrapping his arms tightly around her, he squeezed her close and her whole body melted. He leaned close enough that she could smell his cologne. "You are right. They do..." Evan whispered in a deep, seductive voice. She felt his hands move from her shoulders to her waist, gripping the front of her hips and igniting a blast of excitement between them. Without hesitation, she grabbed the back of his hands and squeezed them firmly, pressing her backside deeper into him and nestled the back of her head onto his chest. Her heart pounded as he ran his lips across the side of her neck slowly, causing cold chills to speed down her spine. Turning to face him, his eyes met hers as if to ask for permission for what was about to occur.

Sadie's gaze landed on his lips. "Please. Please don't make me tell you no. Because I really don't want to," Sadie whispered.

"I won't tell you no if you don't tell me no either," Evan whispered in return.

Sadie closed her eyes and tears dumped down her face. Evan cupped her cheeks, using his thumbs to wipe both streams away as he leaned in and passionately placed his mouth to hers. Pulling him in as close as she could to her tingling body, she could barely breathe. He felt so good.

He pulled away as if in slow motion, still with his hands holding her face. "I'm not him. And I never expect to be. I can't take his place, but I can love you like he did." Evan's eyes filled with tears and his head dropped. His arms wrapped around her, they just stood there in the kitchen, holding each other in a tight grip.

Without a word being spoken, she guided Evan to the couch. Something stopped her from taking him to her bed. It was her sacred space still, and she wasn't ready for that yet, but she wanted to be near him, to feel his skin next to hers. Raising her arms, she pulled her navy tank and bra off, revealing her breasts. Evan followed suit, unbuckling his brown leather belt and tossing it to the seat next to him. His body was a nice shade of brown, thanks to his recent boating trips, highlighting the few gray hairs on his firm chest. That was undoubtably a Carson trait: fit torsos without even the slightest bit of effort. She had already seen the genetic characteristic expressed in Max and Tad.

Evan crawled on top of her, engulfing her in a tight hold. This was the safest she had felt since Levi was diagnosed with cancer. She didn't want to let him go. His hips pressed firmly into hers, and she felt him hard against her as she wrapped her legs even tighter around him.

"Are you okay?" she heard him ask softly in her ear.

She couldn't answer. The lump in her throat was burning too fiercely to respond. She pulled far enough away so that she met his gaze and nodded in consent.

Evan pushed upright, but only long enough to complete the process of undressing, both himself and her. As he entered inside her with a steady, deliberate pace, she knew she was safe. She needed him. And he needed her. He wasn't Levi, and she knew that, but he was Evan, and in his own way, he was the best she had ever had.

CHAPTER TWENTY-FIVE

Bianca

"DAMNIT!" THE STRAP of Bianca's overnight bag slipped off her shoulder nearly causing her to drop the pizza box and the six pack of Corona Lights she was toting up to Luke's front door. He must have heard her yell because he flung the door open in a rush to see what the commotion was about.

"Geez, Bianca! You scared me to death. I would have helped you carry all of this in, you know," Luke responded in an annoyed and partly relieved tone. Thankfully there was no more damage on the line than a pizza in disarray and maybe a few broken beer bottles. She handed him the pizza box and stepped into his house with a large sigh, dropping her oversized leather tote just inside the door and sitting the beers on the floor beside the coffee table.

"I know. I thought I had it all under control. Obviously not," she said reluctantly.

"You always think you have everything under control, Bianca. You don't have to carry all the weight on your own. I'm here to help you." Luke's firm attitude with her was one of the things she loved about him. He wasn't one bit intimidated by her. And it was even more odd in her mind that she took his direct attitude coming from someone barely over the drinking age. Usually, a man trying to tell her what to do just made her push back

harder. But something about Luke was different. She was
sort of getting used to this thing called chivalry.

"I know. And I appreciate that. Really. I do. I just have a
lot of...baggage," Bianca responded alluding to the met-
aphorical aspect of her situation. Luke apparently caught
her underlying sentiment. Making his way over to her,
he wrapped his arms over her shoulders and nestled his
nose against hers. The whiskers around his lips tickled as
he kissed her chin… and then her cheek… and finally
her lips.

"And I have two hands. Perfect for carrying all your
"baggage,"" Luke responded softly. Bianca's heart melted.
For as firm as he was with her, he was just as soft. It
was a combo she had never experienced before. Like the
perfect salty sweet snack. "Speaking of packing bags, you
know I can just as easily come to your place. You don't
have to always come here."

Bianca's eyes darted to the floor. She hadn't the heart to
tell him she just wasn't ready for that yet. And she hadn't
a clue when, in fact, she would be. For starters, Tom's side
of the bed was still all but warm. She wasn't ready yet
to have another man in that space. Then there was the
social factor. Having Luke's work van in the driveway
would spark gossip. And as much as she didn't care what
everyone in her neighborhood thought, she just wasn't
sure she was ready for the barrage of questions. Hell, she
didn't even know what she and Luke were: dating, boy-
friend/girlfriend, or fling of the moment. Those were
labels she wasn't ready to siphon through with all the
different rules and categorizations. More importantly, she
just hadn't been able to fully get past his age. Just as soon
as she would seem to forget it, something would remind
her. Whether it be a movie quote or song reference that
he didn't know, there was always a tiny reminder that she
had a decade on him. And that bothered her.

"I like coming here. It's my little getaway," she quickly

responded. It wasn't a lie. She did love spending time with him at the beach. And his eclectic beach shack had grown on her.

"Good. I like you being here. But what do you say I take you downtown to a nice dinner tomorrow night? We never go out, except for little dive places here on Tybee. I want to treat you the way you deserve to be treated," Luke said sweetly.

Bianca's mind raced with excuses. She wasn't ready for that either. For heaven's sake, the fancy dinners she was accustomed to would surely set Luke back a quarter of what his monthly rent was. And honestly, she had had her share of fancy dinners over her thirty-five years. She was just fine eating pizza on the couch and drinking a beer with him. Thankfully, she didn't have to make up a reason to turn him down. "I have plans already for tomorrow. I am going to Sadie's house to watch ESPN." Bianca watched Luke's face contort into a questioning furrow. "I know. I hate sports. It's a long story." Bianca didn't have the energy to get into Charlie's love life or social status for that matter. She had talked to patients all day and simply just wanted to snuggle up next to Luke. "Come on. Let's eat and relax. I'm sure you've had a long day too." Bianca pulled Luke down onto the couch next to her, opening the pizza box that he had sat on the coffee table.

"This is great pizza. Thank you for bringing it. But the offer still stands for a nice dinner," Luke said between bites. He must have sensed Bianca's diversion from a response. "Bianca, what are we anyway?"

Bianca's face flushed. "What do you mean?" She played dumb hoping to buy some time to come up with a response.

"You know what I mean," Luke responded firmly. Bianca watched his jaw clench. She could see the muscles flexing even through his thick beard.

"What do you want us to be?" she quickly tossed the ball back into his side of the court.

"I asked first, but since you're being weird about it, I'll tell you. I want *you*. We click. And on so many levels. I love your heart, your mind, your sexy body, and even your bossy ass attitude," Luke stated with conviction. Bianca already knew all of that. She could tell how he felt. She just wasn't ready to give them a title. This whole living a life of adventure was still new.

"I like you. A lot. I love that I can be myself around you. I can let my guard down. I don't have to be the powerful and strong Bianca Moretti that everyone expects me to be all the time. But..." She trailed off trying to choose her words wisely so as to not hurt him.

"But what? Is it my age? My career?" Luke finished her sentence.

"Yes," Bianca huffed. She could see Luke's eyes roll and his bare feet fidget over the oriental rug below them. "And the fact that I'm still so scared. Luke, please, just let this all happen organically. If you push me too hard, I'm going to run. Not that I want to, but I'm just a broken mess." Her sincere words rolled off her tongue with ease because it was the truth. She was a pile of smashed pieces of whatever it was Tom had left behind.

"Okay. I understand. I won't ask again. For now," he said with a soft smile.

"For now." Bianca nodded in agreement. "Let's just enjoy the moment."

Cupping her face in his hands, he leaned in to whisper into her ear. "Oh, we are most definitely going to enjoy this moment." Bianca felt her thighs tingle with excitement. There was no denying the power he had over her. She was deduced to a giddy schoolgirl with his slightest touch. Bianca sat breathless, still reeling from his lingering words in her ear as Luke stood from the couch. She felt his arms scoop down under her thighs as he lifted her up and over his shoulder. There were perks to being with a twenty-five-year-old: no aching joints, hip pains, or bad backs. And the recovery time from one steamy romp in the sheets to the next was unbelievable, turning most nights into marathon sessions. It was way different than what she had experienced with Tom over the last few years, which was typically a half-ass effort on his part. She had forgotten how much fun making love could be, especially when you have nothing to lose. Her heart was already rock bottom. It had nowhere to go but up. As Luke tossed her onto his bed, clad with mismatched sheets and a quilt that had had its fair share of wallowing, she couldn't help but smile. He was fun. And she loved how carefree he made her feel. As he crawled on top of her, his beard tickling her torso between tiny pecks from his soft lips, she finally felt his worn denim jeans between her thighs. He slid his arms firmly underneath her, and she caved, tucking herself safely into him. It was a feeling that was so unfamiliar, but one she was becoming addicted to…surrender.

CHAPTER TWENTY-SIX

Charlie

THE USUAL BLACK Cadillac Escalade with blacked-out windows pulled up to the arrivals area outside baggage claim. Dominic was the typical superstar with the anything-but-incognito incognito transportation. Out hopped the driver, who opened the door and motioned for Charlie to crawl into the third-row seat. She was greeted with the biggest smile plastered across a familiar face. She was sure her smile was just as big.

Scooting in next to him, she immediately planted a kiss on his lips. She had been planning their greeting the entire flight and figured it was better to face the nervous jitters head-on.

"Hi." Dominic repeated his usual greeting but with a surprised tone and his eyebrows raised.

Charlie laughed. She knew it was bold and forward, but so was she, and he knew that about her already.

"I thought you said you liked for the man to be in control of the romance." Dominic smiled, leaning in for another quick peck on the lips.

"You know me. I'm not great at holding back my emotions. And I'm also not great at being hungry. What's the plan for dinner?" Charlie asked. Her lips were still wet from his kiss. And despite it being their first, it seemed eerily natural, like they had done it a million times before.

"Charlie, you're always hungry. I came prepared. I

brought snacks." Dominic opened a large Yeti cooler full of champagne and charcuterie. "I already arranged for room service. I want to be alone with you tonight, and if we go out for dinner, we won't have any privacy. Hope that's okay."

Charlie nodded in agreement. She was well aware of the attention he drew in a crowd. Autographs, pictures, and handshakes seemed to take precedence over any company he may be in. Fans were ruthless.

Dominic popped open the bottle of Veuve and poured them each a glass. Raising his vessel, he whispered, "To my favorite human. Thanks for always being by my side. I adore you, Charlotte Compton."

Charlie tapped her glass to his. "To the coolest, sexiest, smartest, funniest man I know. I love everything about you, Dominic Houston." Her eyes never left his as they both took a long sip of champagne. This was real. And it felt amazing.

"Got somewhere to take you first." Dominic smiled, clearly hiding a surprise.

"And where would that be?" Charlie sounded like a kid waiting for a big reveal.

"It's a secret. Focus on that champagne, dear."

Dear... That sounded good coming from his mouth. Charlie watched as they left the city limits and crossed over into New Jersey. She had been here once before, to MetLife Stadium. Dominic's first game as a starting quarterback had been there, years ago. He had invited her, and as much as she hated cold weather, she agreed. Even with a seat in the fancy heated box, she remembered how frigid that November day was.

As the Escalade made its way toward the vacant stadium parking lot, Charlie wondered why he was bringing her there. They entered the players' tunnel and two facility staff members escorted them to the field, leaving her and Dominic alone in the empty, eerily quiet stadium. She had been on football fields with him many times before, but always during games, where the crowds were loud, and the music and cheerleading rang in her ears. She never understood how any of the players ever heard plays being called. Dominic said they had "alternative measures" for those circumstances. But that wasn't a problem now. The bowl shape of the stadium blocked out all the surrounding noise.

Dominic held her hand as he led her to the fourteen-yard line. Turning to her, he stopped and smiled. "Do you know what this is?" he asked.

"A football field?" Charlie responded confused, not quite sure where he was going with the question.

"No shit, Sherlock. Let me be a little clearer. Do you know why I brought you here?" he asked in a more determined tone.

"I'm assuming because this was where you had your start in the NFL," Charlie stated proudly.

"Yes. But even more specifically, this is the exact spot where I stood when I threw my first touchdown pass as a professional quarterback. It was the second quarter. We were in the red zone, and I was as nervous as hell. I remember looking up to the boxes, knowing you were there cheering me on. My whole body calmed. And on the next down, I threw a laser pass to the end zone. The crowd went wild, and all I could think about was how thankful I was for you." Dominic leaned in and kissed Charlie's lips firmly, pressing his tongue deep into her mouth.

She pulled him in closer, wrapping her arms around his shoulders and quickly realizing that as long limbed as she was, they weren't long enough to wrap fully around his broad shoulders. She slid her arms up around his neck, on her tiptoes, as he lifted her and swung her around still locked in a tight kiss.

Placing her safely back on the ground, he brushed the

strands of hair from her face. "I wanted this to be the spot where we first kissed, but you beat me to it when you laid one on me in the car." Dominic laughed through his words.

"Gotta be quick, Mr. Houston, or someone will beat you to the goal line," Charlie replied, knowing that he was always a fan of her football analogies. This was one hundred percent the most romantic thing anyone had ever done for her. She loved seeing this side of her best friend. Now she knew why women fell hard and fast for him. Not only was he gorgeous and successful, but he was romantic and thoughtful. Maybe all the years she'd spent giving him suggestions for his dates with girlfriends had come full circle, and now she was reaping the rewards. She couldn't begin to count the hours she'd spent as his therapist when his relationships when south. Or how many times she'd given him suggestions for that special girl for her birthday or Valentine's Day. It wasn't in vain. He was her greatest love-project.

"I also would like to undress you on the fifty-yard line, but something tells me that move might make headlines." Dominic chuckled as he led her back to the Escalade, but not before running his hand under her dress and grabbing her backside under the pink lace panties she had selected for the day. "Plus, this is a big ole' echo bowl and we don't want all of New York City hearing your screams."

Charlie's core was on fire, and it wasn't from the champagne. Dominic's confidence sent him to the next level of sexy. Charlie had always loved an alpha male—not a cocky meathead, but a man with swag. One who felt confident in his skin—and, more importantly, confident in his skills with women. Whether he was nervous underneath or not, Charlie couldn't tell. But that was his job. Stay calm amidst the storm. That was why he was one of the greatest quarterbacks of all time. No one, not even the biggest linemen, could rattle Dominic Houston.

His hand rested on her leg the entire way back into the city while they polished off the bottle of champagne and charcuterie plate in between kisses and smiles. She loved his hands. They were her favorite part of his body—well, of those she had seen so far. As big as his body was, his hands looked like they were stuck on like Mr. Potato Head parts that had gotten in the wrong box, one intended for a giant.

The driver pulled slowly up to the back entrance of the Ritz-Carlton. Men dressed in tuxes scurried to get them to the elevator and up to the Royal Suite. Charlie had seen inside more than her share of Ritz-Carltons throughout Dominic's career, but this was breathtaking. The room was modern and classy, with white and black furniture that framed the panoramic view of Central Park. Charlie had never seen what the fuss was all about with New York City—it seemed too big and too busy—but this suite was gorgeous and way over the top.

"Dominic, this is beautiful. But it's so big. We don't need all this space," Charlie stated in awe as she wandered through the rooms from the large living space to the dining room outfitted with a table large enough for ten people. "Who are you planning on being here? The entire NFL?" She laughed as she made her way into one of two bedrooms. "Do we have separate bedrooms?" she asked sarcastically.

"Only the best for you, boss," Dominic answered with a proud grin. "In all honesty, I booked the hotel when I first asked you to come with me. I didn't know if I'd have the guts to let you know my intentions before you got here, and I also didn't know if you felt the same. But I wanted you here either way. And yes, we may have a few people over for drinks after the gala tomorrow night—an afterparty, if you will. Depends on how we feel." Dominic made his way over to her as she stared out the expansive window at the city lights. Nestling up behind her, he whispered in her ear, "Thanks for coming."

"Thanks for inviting me," she replied, turning to him. Her fingers traced his collarbone that stood strong under his white shirt. His style was all his own. Usually dressed in some sort of athleisure, with a brand-new set of sneakers, he always looked cooler than anyone else in the room. No one else would have ever been able to pull off his look. And that made him even sexier.

"Why don't you go snuggle in the bed and get undressed. I have a few things to take care of quickly, and I don't want to be interrupted once I have you naked all to myself," Dominic commanded as he nodded to the master bedroom.

Charlie smiled, her belly suddenly full of butterflies as she obeyed his request. *So, this is it. This is the moment my best friend and I turn into lovers. Shit.*

Charlie kicked her wedges haphazardly to the side and pulled her dress up and over her head, revealing a hot pink set of lace bra and panties. She usually wasn't a fan of pink, but she felt sexy in this set, and she was ready to channel all the ultra-feminine vibes she could muster up. Charlie slipped under the crisp, cool, white sheets, letting her palms stroke the soft cotton that separated her from the mattress. She wondered what Dominic was doing, and then she realized as she heard music coming from the next room. Sade billowed out softly from the speakers as he rounded the corner to the room.

"Sorry. I didn't mean to make you wait, but I wanted to get our dinner ordered. I can't have you getting hangry on me. And I made a special playlist for us that I think you'll like," he admitted as he pulled back the sheets that covered her partially naked body. "I thought I said to get naked," he asked playfully as he crawled on all fours, stopping to hover over her. His mouth went straight to her stomach, which was rising with her now fast-paced breathing.

"I can't just hand myself to you. You do need to work a little bit," Charlie replied between heavy breaths.

His nose traced her ribs one by one as his hand grabbed her backside in a firm grip, creating a wave of pleasure. "There isn't an inch of you I don't want to touch," he whispered, his mouth hovering over her breasts. The feel of his breath on her skin made goosebumps raise over her entire body.

"Dominic, are you one hundred percent sure you want to do this?" Charlie asked sincerely. "Once we cross this line, there's no going back." Her thumb traced his brows. They were her second favorite part of his body, especially from this new angle from underneath him. They furrowed hard, revealing his concern at her question. He looked so sexy with the weight of gravity pulling on his muscles. She glanced down, her eyes moving from his neck past his chest down to his groin. She realized she may have a new favorite part of his body as she caught a glimpse of his erection.

"Of course. You?" he asked sincerely, pausing and linking eyes with her.

Charlie nodded with a soft smile.

"*We* are different. *Our* story is different. No matter what happens, I will always love you. You know that, right?" Dominic reassured her, placing a purposeful kiss on to her lips.

Charlie believed him. Sliding her hands down over her hips, she hooked her thumbs under the thin strings of her panties, peeling them off and tossing them purposefully to the ground beside the bed. Dominic's face transformed from concern into an approving sexy smile as he watched her deliberate actions. Charlie's palm traced slowly over his firm abs, down to his groin. Grabbing him with intention, he took her cue, pressing close to her. The heavy weight of his large body melted onto hers. Skin to skin for the first time, she couldn't believe how perfect it felt. Not much foreplay was needed. He had been working on that with his recent messages, creating a slow simmer of anticipation that was ready to be acted upon. He thrust into her with ease. Breathless, she rested her mouth on his jawline as he moved slowly but strongly on top of her. Stings of electricity pulsed through her body with every movement of his, their souls swirling in a perfect dance.

Charlie had made a lot of love in her lifetime, but none like this. Her soul had found its match in Dominic Houston.

CHAPTER TWENTY-SEVEN

Sadie

SADIE'S EYES POPPED open and shot over to the warm body lying next to her. For a second, she thought she may have been dreaming. But no. There he was. In the flesh—and only flesh. A man that she had known for decades. He was family, a friend, an uncle to her children, and now her lover. Never in her wildest dreams did she think this would be a moment she would experience, waking up next to Evan.

Her heart sank with the weight of confusing emotions flooding her conscience. And to boot, the fact that his truck had sat in her driveway all night might have more than one neighbor talking. Thank goodness Charlie was in New York and Bianca was probably with Luke somewhere, buried under some covers. Max and Tad wouldn't be home from their sleepover until well after lunch, so hopefully her overnight rendezvous with Evan would go unnoticed.

Evan must have sensed her internal restlessness. Rolling over with sleepy eyes, he smiled gently, allowing her anxiety to ease off a bit. "Morning," he whispered, placing a gentle kiss on her lips. Sadie's heart beat faster as his hand stroked her cheek. "You okay?" he asked gently.

"I don't know," Sadie confessed as a lump filled her throat. "I don't think I even remember what okay feels like anymore. Are you okay?" Sadie assumed his mind was as much of a blended mess as hers.

"I'm great. Haven't been this great in years," he confessed with a broadening smile on his face.

"What about Kate? Evan, what have we done? What about Levi? What would he say?" Sadie rambled, covering her face with her hands as she rolled helplessly onto her back.

Evan raised up onto his elbow, leaning over her. "Sadie," he said with a firm tone.

She didn't respond. She couldn't.

"Sadie, look at me," he commanded, pulling her hands back. She gazed up to see his handsome face. His green eyes were stern but caring. "First and foremost, Levi is gone. He's not coming back. Period. You deserve love and happiness. There isn't a wife in the world who loved and cared for her husband more than you did. It's one of the reasons I love you so much," Evan confessed.

Sadie's heart melted. *I love you.* Those words sounded so good to her ears.

"Secondly, Kate and I are done. We have been for years. You know it and I know it. It's been a slow, but sure death of a marriage. I've grieved it for longer than you know. She left. She made her choice. And that's that." Evan slipped his hand under her nightgown, his hand resting on her breastbone above her heart. "This, Sadie Carson, is what I love. You and your beautiful soul. There isn't a man on this earth who is going to love you more than Levi did. But I can promise you I will make a very close second if you give me a chance."

Sadie was emotionally paralyzed. She knew every word he said was true. Tears streamed down her cheeks as she nodded, confirming his words. "I love you too, Evan," she whispered. "It's a lot to wrap my head around. Can you be patient with me? Give me some time to process all of this?"

"Of course. I'm not going anywhere. I've always been here, and don't plan on that changing. Even if you decide I'm not what you want." Evan smiled and kissed her softly. He rolled out from under the sheets, and she watched as he dressed in his clothes from the previous day. "Better get home before the neighbors start talking." He laughed as he buttoned his shirt. "I fully expect Bianca to be calling you any moment."

"We should be safe. She's been crashing with her boy-toy on Tybee, and Charlie is living the high life in New York with her friend Dominic. She went to some NFL event with him."

"Dominic?" Evan asked.

"Dominic Houston. You've probably heard of him."

"Dominic Houston? The NFL quarterback? How the hell does she know him?" Evan asked, obviously impressed.

"Knows him from high school. Bianca's coming over tonight to watch the event on ESPN with me. We're hoping to catch a glimpse of her. She claims they're just 'friends,' but I bet she crosses that fine line this weekend. You know Charlie—she has very few boundaries when it comes to men." Sadie chuckled, rolling her eyes at her friend's zest for life.

"Yeah. We all have lines that we never imagined we'd cross, don't we?" Evan asked rhetorically. Sadie nodded, knowing he was implying their current situation. "I'm no expert at life, but what I *have* found is that sometimes, if you leap across the line, it makes the next step not so scary. Just go for it. Don't overthink it." He walked to the edge of the bed where Sadie still lay. Sitting down beside her, his hand cupped her face. "The other night on Levi's birthday, do you know what I wished for when we blew out the candles?"

Sadie shook her head, prodding him to go on.

"This. This right here with you."

Sadie smiled. They had no doubt leaped across the line last night. She hoped he was right. Her guilt was trying to get the best of her. If they were going to do this, she would need to come clean: to Levi, to her kids, to her friends, and to herself. The weight was already too heavy. She had always been the confidant, the one people turned to with their secrets. And she kept them safe and secure. But this was different. This was her secret, and if she was going to finally fly, it was time to offload some weight.

CHAPTER TWENTY-EIGHT

Charlie

CHARLIE BATTED HER eyes a few times to clear up the blurry view. The room was still dark from the blackout drapes that meticulously sealed off any sunlight that might have tried to creep in through the seams. She reached for her phone that lay charging on the nightstand next to her. Nine fifteen a.m. That wasn't too late. She had assumed it was later than that with the horrible night's sleep she had gotten. She had found it extremely hard to sleep next to a man she was so attracted to. Her entire body had tingled with electricity most of the night from pleasure. It had been a solid hour after their lovemaking session before her heart rate returned to normal. She hadn't wanted to close her eyes. She'd wanted to keep Dominic in her view forever.

She wasn't surprised that Dominic wasn't next to her. She was certain he'd already left for his standard morning workout. Nothing had changed since high school. She remembered even after long nights out partying, he would still be up and gone before she or anyone else had moved a muscle. He claimed that was what separated the pros from the rest of the crop. "You can rest when you're dead," she could hear him say.

Her stomach rumbled with hunger pangs. She had burned off more than a few calories last night with their frolic in the sheets. Reaching for the switch on the bedside lamp, she saw a piece of paper fall to the floor. Charlie noticed the handwriting right away.

Good morning, beautiful. I figured you needed your rest. You were quite the boss last night. Breakfast is waiting for you on the balcony. I'll be back shortly to take great care of you. Can't wait to enjoy my beloved Charlotte Compton.
XOXOXO,
DH

Charlie's heart skipped a beat. A love note from Dominic. She held it tightly in her hands. From signed yearbooks to autographed footballs, she had seen his handwriting hundreds of times, but not like this. Not these kinds of words, and definitely not addressed to her.

Charlie's feet hit the floor with a little more pep in their step than usual. Grabbing the plush white robe that lay draped over a blue velvet chaise lounge that they had broken in quite well the night before, she wrapped it tightly around her and tied the waist. She grabbed the handles of the two pocket doors that separated her from the main living space and slid them open dramatically just like she had seen in so many movies with fancy apartments. The bright sunshine nearly blinded her, making her wince, as she tried to make out the entrance to the balcony. She needed food ASAP.

The balcony was breathtaking. A small wrought iron table flanked with two white-cushioned chairs sat underneath a covered patio. Bright green ivy vines crept up on either side, creating the perfect private setting, but still accentuating the view of the city. The table was set for a queen—and a hungry queen at that. From pastries and hard-boiled eggs to fruit and waffles, there was enough food to feed an army. Charlie sat down and poured herself a cup of coffee from the carafe. She wanted to pinch herself. She snapped a picture with her phone and sent it to Dominic.

C:*You are too much. Thank you.*

D: *Nothing's too much for you. Plus, I know how crabby you get when you don't eat.*

C: *Truth. But you know I'm not like all your other girls. I don't care one thing about being fancy. A protein bar and coffee would have sufficed.*

D: *I know. Simple. And that's what I love about you. Well, one of the things...*

C:*Are you coming back soon? Did you eat?*

D: *I'm finishing up my workout. I have a few loose ends to tie up. There are shops all around here. Go have some fun and I'll meet you around lunch.*

C: *I didn't come here to shop. I came here to see you.*

D:*And I am so glad you did. But being a pro athlete has its perks and its pitfalls...*

C: *Boy, do I know that. The story never changes. Okay, I'll entertain myself. Just a tiny girl all alone in a big 'ole city.*

D: *I promise I'll make it up to you...*

C: *Uh-huh..*

D: *Love you.*

C: *Love u.*

Charlie couldn't resist sending the same picture to Sadie and Bianca. She didn't want to seem like she was bragging, but by God, she had never been spoiled like this before. Not that her other lovers hadn't been kind and thoughtful, but this was on the verge of *Pretty Woman* status. Her phone buzzed immediately. It was Bianca.

"Un-fucking-believable. Where are you? The Ritz or something?" came an overly exaggerated Philly accent out of her phone.

"Yes. As a matter of fact, I am. And it is *un-fucking-believable*," Charlie mocked.

"I hate you," Bianca replied sarcastically.

"No, you don't." Charlie laughed.

"You're right. I don't. So, how's it going? Did he hit it yet?" Bianca asked crudely.

"Geez. Way to beat around the bush."

"Hehe."

"Yes. He *beat around my bush*, you gross pervert. And it was amazing. Better than I ever dreamed. I couldn't even sleep last night. It was all I could do not to wake him up for another round. Lord have mercy!" Charlie yelped in her Kentucky twang.

"I'm not sure whether to congratulate you or tell you I'm sorry," Bianca huffed.

"What do you mean?" Charlie quizzed.

"Well, I'm sorry you missed out on years of amazing sex that you *could* have been having all this time. But congratulations on the longest session of foreplay in the history of lovers," Bianca stated sarcastically.

"Listen, everything happens as it should. If we hadn't been friends all these years, I doubt the sex would have been as good. It was so weird—I mean *reaaallly* weird at first. I was so nervous. Me, Charlie Compton, nervous with a dude. Can you believe it?"

"That's definitely a first," Bianca muttered. "What's next? Marriage, kids, a big house on a hill?"

"Not so fast. I'm thinking breakfast is next. As crazy as I am about him, this is all very new, knowing him this way. We still have a ton to figure out," Charlie replied, stuffing a big strawberry into her mouth. "Okay, gotta run. I'm starving. Make sure to watch for me tonight on TV."

"I wouldn't miss your debut for the world. Sadie and I'll be watching every second. What dress did you decide on?" Bianca asked.

"The long red one with the mermaid bottom," Charlie confirmed. Suddenly, the table full of calories looked like the cause of a potentially bloated belly. She needed to look her best in the form-fitting dress tonight.

"Good choice. I like that one," Bianca confirmed.

"Is Sadie home? She hasn't responded yet," Charlie asked.

"Not sure," Bianca quickly answered.

"You're not home, are you? Shacking up with Lukey, eh?" Charlie giggled.

"No, I'm not home. And yes, I'm lying in Luke's bed right now. He's gone out to catch a morning surf. I'm here staring at old, framed posters, mismatched furniture, and his guitar leaning in the corner, trying to remind myself that I'm not waking up in a dorm room," Bianca chuckled.

"Oh, well. He's not your future husband. Just have some fun, and be safe," Charlie reassured her.

"Not all of us can wind up with our best friend who also happens to be an NFL millionaire. What's it like living a fairy tale?" Bianca said snidely.

"I wouldn't know. I'm currently stuck on the phone with my salty friend," Charlie said as she took a long sip of coffee.

"Okay, bye," Bianca said through a chuckle.

"Bye, B." Charlie ended the call and looked around. Bianca was right. She was living her fairy tale. And with that, she took a bite out of the biggest chocolate-covered donut she had ever seen. After all, in fairy tales, there was no such thing as calories.

CHAPTER TWENTY-NINE

Charlie

CHARLIE RUSHED INTO the bathroom to freshen up. After walking the streets of New York City for three hours while Dominic finished up whatever "work" he needed to get done, she needed a little touch up before seeing her handsome date. And even with as far north as she was on the globe, let it be known that she was still capable of producing a good sweat. It was summertime, after all, and even though the humidity wasn't remotely close to a typical Savannah day, it was still hot. Dominic had texted that he was almost back to the room, and Charlie wanted to look her best—but not too good, like she was trying too hard. It was all so strange. Dominic had seen her at her worst: hungover, sick, post-workout, and just plain Sunday slouchy. She never cared before. She hadn't been trying to impress him. But things were different now. *Very different.*

Charlie heard the door open and the rubber of his oversized tennis shoes making their way toward her. Her heart skipped a beat and she quickly swiped deodorant under her arms. Thankfully she was wearing a tank-style dress, so she had easy access to reapply. She had just sat the deodorant down on the counter when she saw him round the corner to the granite clad room. Instinctually, she fluffed her hair, pretending to fix a few strands that had gone astray.

"Hi," Dominic greeted. "Whatcha doing?" he asked, pressing up behind her.

Charlie had to catch her breath as just the sight of him made her chest heave. "Oh, trying to rope this mess of hair. With this heat, it's turned into a bird's nest."

"I like your bird's nest," he whispered into her ear as his hands wrapped around her waist and traced her thighs. Charlie could feel her body heat rising with every second of his touch.

"I was about to hop into the shower and start getting ready. We need to leave in a couple hours, right?" Charlie barely got the words out through heavy breathing.

"Yeah. Something like that," Dominic muttered as he slid his hand up the back of Charlie's thigh under her dress, pushing it up around her waist. Charlie couldn't take her eyes off the mirror. She couldn't believe what she was seeing: her own reflection tangled up with Dominic.

She leaned forward against the black-and-white-swirled granite of the vanity onto her elbows, pressing her backside firmly into him. She could feel him hard up against her. His large hand traced the length of her spine up to her neck and then, spreading his fingers wide, palmed her scalp with his large grasp. Squeezing tightly, pulling all the strands into his firm grip, he bent down over her, using his hold to tip her head back, bringing her ear within an inch of his mouth.

"I love you, Charlie," he whispered.

Charlie went numb. She wasn't sure how her legs were still holding her upright. She was certain she was only still standing from the support of Dominic's arm wrapped firmly under her waist. That same arm untangled from her thigh and with one smooth move, slid her black panties down to the floor with his athletic shorts in a close second place next to them. Her own body blocked the full-frontal view that she had of him in the mirror. She wanted so badly to turn and look at him, but she was no match for the tight grasp he still had on her hair. Charlie moaned as she felt him press into her. With one firm slap of his hand against her backside, she felt her whole body tense.

Charlie watched as Dominic took control of her. Her hands and forearms pressed tightly onto the cold stone and her eyes watered from the pleasure that skirted the borderline of pain. Finally releasing his grip on her scalp, his fingers traced between the front of her thighs, edging them both to climax. Charlie's hand slapped the mirror hard as her fingers traced down the glass, causing a squeaking vibration reminiscent of an off-key string instrument. Charlie caught a glimpse of the proud grin that made its way across Dominic's face before it buried itself lovingly into the back of her neck.

"Touchdown," Charlie whispered with a giggle behind it.

"I'm retired." He snickered.

"You still got it, baby." Charlie stood and turned to face him, kissing his lips. Calling him *baby* rolled off her tongue with ease. She smiled and headed to the shower, turning it on full blast.

"Mind if I join you?" Dominic asked as he grabbed two towels from the chrome rack.

"You just want me to wash your back, don't you?" Charlie snickered.

"Maybe," Dominic admitted playfully.

"Let me grab my scrunchie. Don't get my hair wet, though. I washed it this morning," Charlie commanded as she twisted her hair into a messy bun.

Dominic rolled his eyes. "Let me grab my scrunchie? That seriously is the whitest white chick thing you've ever said."

"Newsflash. I *am* a white chick," Charlie stated through a laugh.

"Yeah. But don't tell anyone. You are the coolest white chick I know." Dominic flashed a flirtatious grin as he dipped his bald head under the water. Charlie watched as his dark skin glistened under the shower. He was gorgeous. He always had been. She had just never really seen him in that way. As their conversation turned from sultry to silly, Charlie quickly realized how many checkmarks their relationship checked off for her. She couldn't imagine falling any harder than she just had. There would never be anyone to fill those great big shoes of Dominic Houston.

CHAPTER THIRTY

Sadie

HER MIND HAD been a caged animal all day. Sadie was tired of holding secrets—her own *and* everyone else's. She wasn't sure what had come over her. The only thing she could guess was that her romp in the sheets with Evan had stirred up a fire that she'd thought was long gone. Since Levi's diagnosis, she had successfully bottled up every emotion she had, good and bad, afraid to let anything seep out for fear of an avalanche. The ball was rolling now, and quickly, with no clue as to its projected path or potential target. She needed a plan for damage control.

"Did you ever talk to Charlie?" Bianca asked, setting two bottles of Veuve onto Sadie's counter.

Sadie eyed the expensive choice of beverage with raised eyebrows.

"What?" Bianca asked. "I figured if Charlie was going to be all fancy and famous, we should be drinking fancy champagne too."

"Good choice. I love Veuve. I'm also glad your salary paid for it." Sadie chuckled, placing the two wine glasses back into the cabinet and swapping them out for champagne flutes. "To answer your first question, yes, I texted Charlie. I wasn't feeling too well when I woke up, so I stayed in bed longer than usual, which is why I responded a little late." Sadie hated lying, but she wasn't yet ready to confess that she'd had a visitor that morning. She was still hammering out the details on that confession plan. "Good. I know this is a big deal for her. When I talked to her this morning, she was nervous, but super excited. That chick was floating on cloud nine. Sounds like Dominic's just as proficient in the sheets as he is the football field." Bianca snickered. "I sure hope this works out for them. I can't imagine what their relationship will look like if it doesn't. Once you cross the line, you can't go back."

Sadie's heart dropped. She couldn't help but think about the line she'd so recklessly crossed last night with Evan. Bianca was right. Things would never be the same, no matter what. "They're grown-ups. And they love each other on multiple levels. I'm sure they'll figure out what their relationship needs to look like." She knew she was really implying her own situation. Evan's words had been on repeat in her mind all day, so they easily rolled off her tongue to Bianca. "Sometimes, you just have to leap across the line."

Sadie could see the perplexed look on Bianca's face as she responded. "Okay, Shakespeare. What the hell does that mean?"

Sadie chuckled, realizing that it probably didn't make as much sense out of context as it had to her earlier when Evan had so eloquently stated it. "If you act impulsively, on pure instinct and gut, you override the anxiety and nervousness that comes with overthinking a risk. It's like getting into a freezing cold swimming pool. If you just stick your toe in, you may never actually get in. And then you miss the experience. But jumping in feet first, that's when the real magic happens. It's exhilarating and refreshing."

Bianca just stared at her blankly. "Wow. That's deep. I need a drink after that one."

Sadie sighed. She wished she could talk to her friend

about last night. Her explanation would make more sense to Bianca. But now wasn't the time. The conversation would take up the whole evening and right now was Charlie's moment. "It's about time to turn on the television. I'm so excited. I hope they show Charlie." Sadie attempted to escape her own thoughts. She grabbed both bottles of champagne and the flutes and headed to the couch. Both women curled up on opposite ends, leaning into the armrests. Despite the blazing Savannah heat, they grabbed thin blankets and curled up like two dormmates watching an episode of *Friends*.

Sadie noticed Bianca wiggling around on the cushion uncomfortably. Max or Tad must have left a toy on the couch. Probably an unassuming matchbox car or nerf gun paraphernalia. Bianca soon revealed the culprit underneath her—a man's brown leather belt.

"What the..." Bianca trailed off as she lifted the incriminating evidence high in the air, dangling like a caught snake.

Sadie gasped. It was Evan's belt. Sadie quickly concocted a lie. "Oh, goodness. I hope Evan doesn't need that. He changed here after work last night and sat his clothes there in a pile. He must have forgotten it."

"Well, the buckle poked me in the ass." Bianca huffed, tossing it onto the coffee table. "I thought you said the boys were at a friend's house last night. Why was Evan here?"

"He was on his way to the gym and stopped by to see the boys. He didn't know they weren't here. He changed into workout clothes before he left," Sadie replied. She could feel her face turning a shade of crimson. One lie was leading to the next. This was all so overwhelming. She quickly changed the subject to divert attention from the belt. "So, how's it going with Luke? You sure have been shacking up with him on Tybee a lot recently."

"Meh. It's going. You and I both know what it is: a

fling." Bianca lifted her champagne flute as she raised her shoulders in a nonchalant shrug.

"Maybe. But do you like him? Do you talk or do you just screw?" Sadie chuckled.

"Honestly, he *is* really nice, and we have a ton of fun together. But we are just so far apart in where we are in life. He likes mechanics, surfing, and the Grateful Dead. I like blood, guts, and Huey Lewis," Bianca said through a laugh.

"Why don't you bring him over one night so we can spend some time with him?" Sadie asked genuinely.

"No freaking way," Bianca quickly replied. "I'm fine going to Tybee and spending time with him there. I'm already topic enough in this neighborhood with Tom's strange and abrupt departure. I don't need another reason to attract attention," Bianca stated firmly.

There it was. Another skeleton. The weight of it felt even heavier. She had to find a way to tell Bianca about Levi's encounter with drunk Tom. Whether Bianca thought she was strong enough to hear the truth or not, Sadie wasn't strong enough to carry the secret anymore.

"Who cares what anyone else thinks, Bianca?" Sadie barked a little too harshly. It was happening. She was about to erupt. *Now isn't the time, Sadie. Calm down. We have a friend to watch on TV that is about to have the brightest moment of her life.* True confessions would have to wait.

"I know. You're right. But for now, I need simple. I don't have the energy to defend myself. Maybe when I'm a little more healed, I can handle a battle, but I'm too wounded still."

"Hey! It's on!" Sadie quickly shifted her view to the red carpet and sequined dresses on the screen as she turned the volume up. Sadie listened as the host announced an array of current and past NFL stars.

Bianca's eyes were glued to the program, obviously waiting for any glimpse of a familiar red dress and brunette hair. "There she is!" Bianca exclaimed, almost spilling her champagne. "That's her to the left of the man they're interviewing."

"That's Tom Brady," Sadie laughed through her words. "I do actually know that player. He's hot and my sons idolize him."

"Charlie looks gorgeous. Oh, I bet she's freaking out being around all those famous people."

"She can hold her own. Charlie always seems to trump everyone in her display of confidence. I doubt even this can rattle her game face. And she has Dominic," Sadie added.

The two bottles of champagne were almost polished off by the time the awards presentation started. By that time, Max and Tad had joined them on the couch and were giving play-by-plays of who the award recipients were and why they were so cool. Finally, the hosts rattled off an award honoring the Offensive Player of the Decade, and Dominic was the winner. The camera panned directly to him and Charlie.

"Oh, my goodness. Look at them. They look like movie stars," Bianca gasped. "And look at Dominic. Could he get any closer to Charlie?"

The camera showed Dominic's arm wrapped tightly around the shoulders of their beautiful brunette in the red gown, his other hand resting on her thigh. As the host finished up his long speech about Dominic's contribution to the NFL, he finally called Dominic up to the stage. Dominic leaned over and whispered something in Charlie's ear. Sadie watched as a big smile bloomed across her friend's face, blown up even more by the large television screen.

"So cool, Mom! Ms. Charlie is so lucky," Tad exclaimed as they watched Dominic make his way to the podium and microphone.

Sadie nodded in agreement. "Shhh. Let's listen to his speech." Sadie tried to calm the chatter in the room.

"Thank you so very much," Dominic began, his voice echoing out of the microphone. "What an honor it is to receive this award. I must admit, with as many awards as I've received, this one means a ton. It's not easy to stay at the top of the game the older you get and the more your bones hurt." The sound of laughter rang from the audience. "I could thank a million people, and you know who you are, but tonight, I want to focus on one person—*my* person. Charlotte Compton."

"Holy shit," Bianca gasped.

"B!" Sadie said in a reprimanding tone as her eyes got big and she nodded to the boys.

"Oh, sorry," Bianca apologized.

"Mom, come on. We hear way worse than that at school," Tad said with annoyance.

"Really?" Sadie asked.

"Shhh," Bianca commanded as she grabbed the remote from the coffee table and turned the volume on blast.

"...many of you may have seen her around at my games over the duration of my career. I'm sure you've wondered who the gorgeous brunette was." Dominic pointed to Charlie sitting in the crowd. The camera panned to her. With her bright smile and beaming brown eyes, she looked like a movie star. "This is my best friend. We met in high school. She was the cheerleader and homecoming queen, Miss Popular. I was the poor black kid on scholarship at a private school because of my strong arm and quick legs. She could have easily turned her nose up to me, but she never has. She's been there through it all—my wins *and* my losses. So, I just want you to know, Charlie, that I love you. I'm proud of you. I'm impressed by you. I'm inspired by you. You are a special being, Charlotte Compton. Thank you for everything."

Sadie's heart melted. As she slowly looked across the

room at Bianca, their wide eyes met and both women stared at each other, their mouths dropping open.

"That was seriously the most romantic thing I've ever witnessed," Bianca said. "If she doesn't marry that man, I'll kill her."

"Right?! And she said he had never expressed wanting to date her. She must be blind as a bat or in major denial," Sadie added.

Their faces turned back to the screen in time to see the image of Dominic returning to his seat with a large crystal trophy in his hand. He leaned over and kissed Charlie's lips in a borderline inappropriate kiss for a sports channel. Sadie grinned as Charlie's eyes met Dominic's and she was able to read the lips of her friend: *I love you too.*

"I'm texting her." Bianca grabbed her phone frantically and started tapping her fingers faster than lightning.

"She isn't going to respond. She's a bit preoccupied right now, B." Sadie laughed as Bianca's eyes never left her phone screen, completely ignoring her comment. Sadie saw her own phone screen light up on the side table next to her. Grabbing it, she saw a text from Evan.

E: How does it feel to be friends with a superstar? Saw Charlie's epic debut. Bet the paparazzi will be swarming your street soon trying to catch a glimpse of the life of Charlotte Compton.

S: Great. There goes the neighborhood. By the way, you left your belt on the couch. Should have seen me scrambling to explain that to Bianca when she sat on it.

E: Oops. Sorry. Not used to having to cover my tracks.

S: Me either. Guess that's a good thing… I told her you changed here before going to the gym, so if it comes up, that's the story. And I feel terrible lying, so we have to figure this out.

E: Figure what out? I know what I want.

S: Is this a good idea? It seems so hard.

E: Nothing in life that's worth having is easy.

"Who are you texting over there? Looks super seri-ous," Bianca asked, suspicion in her tone.

"Just Evan. He saw the speech. Nothing serious," Sadie replied innocently. Bianca was right though. The text thread was one hundred percent serious. She hated lying once again.

Taking a big sip of what was left of the champagne in her glass, Sadie sat her phone down and smiled at her boys. She wondered what they would think of her and Uncle Evan. He was already a great father figure to them and the closest thing to their dad. They adored him. But it all seemed so soon, so complicated. Sadie brushed the auburn hair from Tad's eyes and smiled. She had big things to handle. And the two most important were sitting next to her while the third stared at her phone screen in vain, waiting for a response from their newly famous friend.

CHAPTER THIRTY-ONE

Bianca

SUNDAY SCARIES WERE the worst. They carried their own sense of dread, but since Tom's departure, they had taken on a whole new level of gloom. Sundays had always been their day. No matter the situation, an invitation to anything that didn't entail time together with him was a hard "no." And it was the day of the week that included sex—no excuses. With jobs and stress and life in general, time for intimacy had a way of making its way to the bottom of the list. Fertility treatments had also had a way of putting a damper on anything romantic. But Sundays were different. They were the one day of the week Bianca devoted to her husband—period. That had been her grandmother's wedding advice, and she had stuck to it. Now, it was an exceptionally empty day she had to fill.

Bianca wallowed around in the sheets of her bed. For a second, she missed Luke's company. She hadn't slept in her bed very much recently, and now she remembered why. It was damn lonely. She reached for her phone that was charging on her nightstand beside her. Still no response from Charlie. *She's probably still tangled up with Dominic in the sheets*, she huffed to herself. Her fingers hesitantly tapped on Luke's contact.

Whatcha doin'? she typed with a slight hesitation. She wasn't even in the mood to talk to anyone. But she figured a quick check-in might lift her spirits.

L: Nothing. Just thinking about you.

Bianca snickered at his playboy reply. She knew his game. He was great with words. It felt good to have someone want her, even if she knew it would never, *could never* last.

B: Sounds entertaining. I'm laying here in my bed.

L: Want some company?

Bianca's panic response kicked high into gear. She had so far kept Luke a safe distance from her world. And she planned on keeping it that way for the time being.

B: Would love that, she lied. *But I'm heading into the office in a bit to do payroll. Was thinking I would head to you afterward.*

She *had* planned on doing just that, so she was truthful in that sense.

L: Sounds good. Just let me know when you get to the office. I may go to the beach and catch some waves.

B: K. Will do.

Bianca rolled onto her back and stared at the ceiling. She hated that she was so weak right now. She hated that she needed to fill the void. And she hated that Tom had put her in this position. *How could I have missed the signs? Was I so busy with my career and preoccupied with trying to have a baby that I just missed something?*

Bianca looked at the one place on her phone she had been avoiding: Tom's contact. She went to the text messages first. It was a strand of normal things: dinner, plans, grocery lists, and *I love you*s. Nothing at all abnormal. Then she went to the photos. Scrolling back through her favorites all the way back to the beginning, nothing looked off. Then she did it. She pulled up his phone number. Her thumb hovered over the call button for what seemed to be an eternity. She wanted so badly to call him. To ask him what the hell happened. But she couldn't do it. Something was stopping her. *Maybe deep* *down, I really don't want to know. If I don't know what pulled him away, then I can't be held accountable for it.* Her stomach churned with anxiety. She would have to face it at some point.

She let out a huge sigh and sat up hesitantly, dropping her feet onto the floor. Her phone pinged. She figured it was Luke, but to her surprise, it was Charlie.

C: *Sorry just now responding. Been a whirlwind. Yes, I was totally shocked. I can't believe he said all that on national TV. My phone has been blowing up with texts from people I haven't seen or heard from in years. And the cameras won't get out of my face. I don't know how Dom has done this all these years.*

B: *Stardom. It's not for the weak, Charlie. You can handle it though. Was starting to think it had already gone to your head since you hadn't responded.*

C: *Yeah, right. We had some people over to the hotel room after the event. It was crazy busy. Saw Sadie texted too.*

B: *Yeah, we watched with the boys. They think you're the coolest now. I've been demoted. I guess blood and guts surgery is no match for celebrity sport status.*

C: *Haaa. Well, I still think you're the coolest. I'll be back late tonight. Catch up this week? Will I see you or are you gonna be at Luke's every night?*

B: *Funny. I plan on being here at least on Thursday for gazebo night. Something tells me we'll have a ton to talk about.*

C: *Can't wait. TTYL.*

Bianca smiled. She was happy to see her friend find happiness. In a way, she had always felt sorry for Charlie. It wasn't for a lack of dates or interest in her—she was an amazing catch—but romance had just never worked out for her. Bianca had marveled at her ability to bounce back quickly from a broken heart.

Maybe she needed to channel that skill of hers too and force herself out of the bed. But first, she found a grain of courage. She was going to do it. She was going to ask

Tom to come clean—why had he left and why the hell were there empty vodka bottles in their attic? Her finger quickly went to her favorites. Her hand shook as she tapped his name. Slowly lifting the phone to her ear, she held her breath waiting to hear his voice. But much to her surprise, the number was disconnected. She dialed it again, thinking there was some mistake. But once again, there was an error message. Worry mixed with anger welled up inside of her. She pulled up her inbox and sent an email directly to him. Within seconds, it bounced back with a postmaster delivery failure.

Bianca's head grew horns. He had not only left her, but now he had deleted her completely. And their divorce wasn't even final yet. That was the last straw—but it was completely what she needed: anger to compel her to revenge status. If Tom wasn't going to play by the rules, then by God, she wasn't either.

Bianca marched her fancy ass to the shower, cranked up her music, and decided life was too short to follow all the rules.

———◆———

Bianca rushed into her empty office, still running on high throttle from Tom's antics. It seemed so quiet after hours. Without the sound of voices and instruments, it was eerie. Bianca had spent more than enough time alone in her office, typing notes, paying bills, and running a business. She wasn't going to be there long—just long enough to make sure payroll was finished. She was moving at the speed of light to get to Tybee, but she remembered Luke's request for her to text him when she got there, so she did. She didn't wait for his response. She figured the quicker she did the work, the sooner she would be done. And she was right. In no time she had finalized inputting the last calculation. She was surprised when she heard a knock on the front door. She figured it was a patient that had seen her car parked out front. Probably a dry socket needing tending to. Peeping her head around the corner to see who would be standing at the glass front door, she was surprised to see Luke.

"Hey, what are you doing here?" Bianca asked as she opened the door and locked it behind him.

"In the neighborhood and decided to stop by," he chuckled. Bianca knew he was lying. But it didn't matter. "I texted you back and told you I was on my way here." Bianca gave a look of apology for not checking his response. "No worries. Actually, if you want to know the truth, I've been dreaming of what it would be like to have you ride me in one of those dental chairs of yours," he whispered as he pulled her in close next to him.

Bianca's core tingled with excitement. It wasn't the first time a man had suggested a little hanky-panky in her office. Tom had begged for years to get her to have sex with him there. But something had never let her do it. Literally. She wasn't sure if it was her need to keep the separation of work and home, or her guilty conscious over professionalism that made her balk, but either way, she had never let her guard down enough to let it happen. Until then. She was done with rules as of this morning. If she was going to get over her heartbreak, she was going to do as Charlie said, by living a life of adventure.

Grabbing Luke by the hand, she led him to the back operatory. The excitement was more than she could handle as a large grin plastered across her face. Bianca relished the thought of getting back at Tom in some long shot way like this. Small victories.

"Sit there," Bianca commanded, pointing to the gray leather chair that sat in the center of the room. The seat was usually filled with some poor soul about to have their wisdom teeth removed, but this time, there was about to be a man feeling anything but pain.

"Yes, ma'am." Luke chuckled as he sat down on the sterile surface. Straddling him, Bianca pressed down hard onto him. She must admit, the design of the chair was perfect. Reaching around and adjusting the height so her feet met the floor perfectly, they both laughed at the setting. "Now this is customization," Luke said. "Lean me back a little, doc."

Bianca obliged and started unbuttoning his extremely worn denim shirt. Exposing his chest, she ran her fingers down the front of his body, over the Grimm Reaper tattoo that only Luke could pull off. The dimmed lights cast a sexy glow onto his tan skin. Luke followed suit, lifting Bianca's black maxi dress above her head and tossing it onto the floor. Bianca couldn't help but hope the cleaning crew had been as diligent as they were supposed to be with sanitizing the floors, knowing the bodily fluids and debris that covered them daily. Her attention was quickly diverted back to Luke as he pulled her in close to him and his now-exposed manhood that he had uncovered from his cargo shorts. Raising up and down on him, Bianca gasped at his touch. This wasn't what she'd dreamed her Sundays would ever look like, but she sure was enjoying it. Luke's hands grasped her backside firmly and she was taken aback when he abruptly jumped up and let out a shout.

"Oh, shit!" he exclaimed, staring wide-eyed at the doorway. Instinctually, Bianca turned, bare breasts and all, to see Jane, just as mortified.

"Oh, my goodness, Dr. Moretti. I am so, so, so sorry. I um— I um—" Jane tried to cover her eyes and turn around as Bianca scrambled for her clothes. Having her office manager catch her fucking the twenty-five-year-old AC guy was beyond mortifying. "Um, I'll talk to you tomorrow," Jane muttered as she scurried off toward the front of the office.

"Shit! Shit! Shit!" Bianca chanted as she chased her down the hall, pulling her dress over her naked body. "Jane, wait!"

Jane stopped and turned to Bianca, unable to make eye contact. "I am *so* sorry. I saw your car here, and the Low-country Air van, and thought there was a problem with the air conditioning again. I thought maybe there was something I needed to take care of. I had no idea…" Jane trailed off.

"I know. It's okay. I'm the one who should apologize. I shouldn't have done this…here. I don't know what I was thinking," Bianca said with remorse. Suddenly her life of adventure didn't seem so fun. "Please don't say anything to the other girls. I'm humiliated."

Jane nodded quickly. "Dr. Moretti, you own this building. You can do whatever the hell you want here. I'm no judge. And to be honest, I'm glad to see you moving on from Tom. You deserve better." Jane finally looked Bianca in the eyes. Her heart leaped at Jane's kind words and encouragement. She was so thankful to have her. "Now get back to what you were doing. My lips are sealed." Jane winked as she turned to leave.

Bianca smiled and re-locked the door behind Jane as she left. Down the hall, she found Luke fully dressed, sitting with his face buried in his hands. He must have heard her footsteps. He never moved, but the words, "I'm so sorry," made their way out from between his fingers.

"It's okay. I feel sorry for *her*. Doubt she'll ever get *that* image out of her head." Bianca laughed. "Luke, seriously, it's fine." She sat down beside him, wrapping her arm around his shoulders and giving it a squeeze.

"It's not. It's all my fault. Please don't be mad at me," Luke pleaded.

"She told me to finish what I was doing."

"There's no way I could get a chub right now. I don't care how many Viagras someone gave me. My fella has been traumatized. I've been caught many times in my years, but none like this."

They both laughed, finally making light of the situation.

"Let's go have some drinks. I think we could both use them. And I promise to finish you off...somewhere very private and safe," Luke suggested, wiping Bianca's smeared lipstick from her face.

"Luke, is it okay if we call it a day? I think I just need some time alone." Bianca hated to desert him after such a traumatizing moment, but the weight of the day was starting to get heavier in her mind.

His expression dropped, but he obliged her request. They locked up, said an awkward goodbye, and climbed into their respective vehicles. She sat in her car, watching as Luke drove away before dropping her face down onto her steering wheel. "What the fuck? Great. Bright move, Moretti. Bright fucking move."

Living a life of adventure was going to be something she needed to ease into, slowly and carefully. This attempt had totally backfired.

CHAPTER THIRTY-TWO

Charlie

FOCUS WASN'T HER strong suit at the moment. Charlie's mind kept drifting back to Dominic—in bed, in the shower, on the chaise lounge, and everywhere in between. His touch had consumed her and wrapped its grip around her like a constrictor, paralyzing her from anything other than dreaming about him. She hadn't washed her hair since she'd gotten back from New York. The strands still smelled like his cologne, and the scent was intoxicating. Charlie hadn't fallen this hard in her life.

"Charlie." A voice shook her from daydreaming. "There have been at least three reporters at the front desk asking to speak with you. Could you please do something about this? It's very distracting," Gabe announced with an agitated tone.

"What? That's odd. What do they want?" Charlie muttered innocently.

"Don't play dumb. We all saw Dominic's speech. It's been on every highlight reel in the sports industry. I'm sure they want to know more about his girlfriend." Gabe rolled his eyes and turned to leave.

"Hold on," Charlie called from her desk. "Stop right there, Gabe," she commanded as he stopped in his tracks. Despite the annoyance plastered on his face, he did as she asked. "Thank you," she responded. "And shut the door. We need to talk."

"About what?" he muttered, closing the door.

"About us," she responded firmly.

"What about us?"

"You have been nothing short of an asshole these past few weeks. What is *wrong* with you?" Charlie demanded.

Gabe shrugged. "Nothing. I have no idea what you're talking about."

"Yes, you do," Charlie argued. She knew she'd been a little short with him right after their fallout, but she had honestly forgiven him and tried to make every effort to recoup their friendship. She had moved on quickly with Dominic's romantic appearance in her life.

"I figured you have *him* now, so you don't need me to confide in about anything other than work anymore," he answered.

"Oh, I see what this is about. You're jealous, aren't you?" Charlie gasped, slapping her hand onto her desk loudly.

"You're crazy. And completely off the mark. I'm not jealous at all. I'm happy for you," Gabe defended, crossing his arms tightly over his chest.

Charlie stood from her desk and rounded the corner, sitting on it just the way she had the night she'd had her bare ass planted on the cool surface and his hands between her thighs. Gabe stared at her without a flinch.

"You liked it, didn't you? Me chasing you. The flirting. The late night texts. The chemistry. But unfortunately, you're the victim of your own self-inflicted rules. I couldn't compete with what is innate within your stubborn being. And thankfully, now I don't have to worry about that. The universe presented me with something so far beyond my wildest dreams. And the funny part is, I actually get it now. I *get* why you have boundaries. I never really had any rules to play by when it came to love but having to decide whether to take the leap with my best friend was the closest thing to a boundary that I've ever faced. Luckily for me, I made the decision to jump across that line, two feet in. And I don't regret it one bit." Charlie smirked. In a way, she felt sorry for Gabe. How would he ever find love like hers and Dominic's if he wasn't ever willing to take risks? But that wasn't her problem now.

"Yeah, well, good for you. Maybe someday I'll be more of a *daredevil*. But until then, could you please handle the front desk situation like I asked?" Gabe headed to the door, slamming it behind him.

"Great. Now this should be fun to deal with for the rest of my career here," Charlie muttered to herself as she reached for her phone to enlist Dominic's advice.

C: *Any tips on handling reporters? They're bombarding the front desk wanting to speak to me.*

D: *Sorry, babe. Comes with the territory. You're tough. You can handle them.*

C: *I'm not worried about me as much as my coworkers. Will it always be like this?*

D: *Nah. It'll calm down soon. I'm retired now. They'll forget about me in a week. Everyone is still buzzing from the gala, that's all.*

C: *Next time, write me a love note, okay? Don't profess your love in front of millions.*

D: *Ah, don't be so salty. You deserve the best. And an epic profession of my love is exactly what you're worthy of.*

C: *Nothing is ever simple with you, is it? Go big or go home. Typical Dominic Houston…*

D: *Modesty isn't my strong suit.*

C: *Okay. Gotta go try and smooth this shit out with my coworkers.*

D: *Geez. Okay. Talk to you tonight.*

C: *Love u.*

D: *Love u more.*

C: *Always the one up…*

D: *Always. But it's true.*

Charlie tucked her phone into her pants pocket and headed down the elevator to address the current situation. Gabe wasn't exaggerating. As the elevator doors opened, she was blinded by camera flashes and waves of strangers from the front windows of her building. Charlie glanced at Simone, the sweet lady sitting behind the tall mahogany wood desk. Charlie felt horrible for putting her in such a commotion.

"Simone, I am *so* very sorry. I'll try to take care of this. This all should die down soon," Charlie said.

"What in the world?" Simone huffed. "They're vultures."

Charlie's heart sank. She wasn't sure she was ready for all this attention. She was just a girl from Kentucky after all. This fame stuff wasn't in her repertoire. She had seen the mob plenty of times but had never addressed them on her own without Dominic. They had never cared much about her without him around—until now.

She made her way confidently to the front entrance, unbolting the front door that Simone had used as her barrier.

"Hi, everyone. I'm sure you're here to find out more about me and Dominic. I'm flattered that you're interested, but if you would please grant my place of work some privacy, I would really appreciate it," Charlie said in her most grateful pleading voice.

"Ms. Compton, can you elaborate on your relationship with Mr. Houston?" a reporter asked, shoving a microphone almost in her mouth.

Charlie flinched, not expecting such a bold attack. "Um, yes. We are old friends, and our relationship status is very new," she said with a slight stutter.

"What exactly is that status?" came another question from a different voice.

The mob was closing in on her and she looked back at Simone in desperation. "That's a private matter. Please respect that," Charlie pleaded as she made her way back to the doors of the building. She was starting to panic. This was way more than she had signed up for.

"So, you are saying you're friends with benefits?" came another call from the crowd.

Charlie's insides burned at the comment. How dare they make assumptions, especially one as insulting to her love for Dominic as a flaky hookup between old friends? Her eyes widened, her head spinning around to seek the culprit as the snakes of Medusa crawled from her skull. "Excuse me? Who said that?" she demanded.

"Me," came a voice from about three people back.

"Come here," Charlie demanded.

The crowd parted and a short-statured man with strawberry blond hair and a wispy beard made his way to her. A lanyard hung from his neck with *TMZ* printed across the bottom of the laminated identification card.

"Dewayne, that's your name?" she asked looking down at his name typed in bold black.

He nodded, looking up to Charlie, who stood towering over him with her standard three-inch heels.

"Dewayne, you know nothing about me. You know nothing about Dominic. And you *obviously* know nothing about class. Now take your insulting comments and leave," Charlie said with venom in her voice. "And that goes for the rest of you too."

Charlie grabbed the door handle, slamming it closed behind her and relocking the bolt. Her heart pounded at the confrontation. In an instant, she was tossed back to high school and college—the whispers, the gossip, the judgment about the unlikely pair. She shouldn't care what people said about them, but it was a trigger that made her blood boil. Their status was no one's business, and now that their relationship had gone to the next level, she felt even more protective of their bond. Everyone wanted a piece of Dominic, and they were ruthless.

This was the exact reason she had never tossed his name around at work or in social circles. She wanted him to herself.

Her heart sank, wondering if she'd made a mistake. Maybe she did have boundaries after all. Maybe she should have learned her lesson from Gabe. And maybe she wasn't as tough as she thought she was.

CHAPTER THIRTY-THREE

Bianca

AWKWARD WAS AN understatement. Bianca had done her best to pretend like nothing had happened. But it had. Jane had caught her fucking the air conditioning guy in her dental chair. She had mentally retreated to a place of reflection—or maybe it was mortification—while she tried to sort out what the hell she was doing. It hadn't helped that she'd gotten an email first thing Monday morning that a court date had been set for her and Tom's divorce hearing for the following week. She was still boiling over his out-of-service phone and email, which her attorney had no information about either, since he was only communicating through Tom's legal counsel. At least the Luke situation had somewhat distracted her from that. Somehow, she was still working and managing to put one foot in front of the other.

Bianca was standing at the workstation in the hallway, typing in her patient notes, when Jane rounded the corner with a look of apprehension. Bianca knew her well enough to know that something was wrong.

"Dr. Moretti, Luke from Lowcountry Air is here to see you," she said in a low tone.

"Tell him I'm with a patient, please, Jane."

"I did, but he's refusing to leave without speaking to you."

Bianca was startled to see Luke walking up behind Jane.

She had no choice but to put her big girl panties on and address the situation. Nodding to Luke, she waved him into her office. "What the hell are you doing here?" she asked as she closed the door behind him.

"I'm sorry. I didn't mean to interrupt you at work, but you've barely responded to my texts. I've tried calling and you won't call me back. I want to talk to you and see what the hell is going on."

"Nothing is going on. I need time to think, Luke. And besides, let's call 'this' what it is," she said, pointing back and forth between the two of them.

"What do you mean? I guess the bigger question is, what is 'this' to you?" Luke replied, mimicking her motion.

"Honestly, do you really think we'd work out? We have absolutely nothing in common and live completely different lives," Bianca defended.

Luke's face dropped, and suddenly she realized maybe she'd been a little too harsh.

"Wow. I knew it. You think you're better than me. The rich oral surgeon would never be caught dead with the young mechanic, would she? I knew there was a reason you never invited me to your place. You're embarrassed by me, aren't you, Bianca? Or should I say, Dr. Moretti?" Luke's voice was rising, and she worried the staff would come rushing in. She needed to get him out before there was a scene.

"I'm sorry, Luke. It isn't going to work," Bianca said quietly, leading him to the door.

"Fine. Have it your way. See you around, I guess," Luke muttered.

Bianca closed her office door behind him. Tears streamed down her face as she sat down at her desk and placed her forehead down on the cold surface in front of her. She was an ass. A total selfish bitch. And never in a million years had she intended to hurt Luke.

She still had to somehow get through her day. The only saving grace was it was Thursday. If she could just make it to the gazebo, she knew Charlie and Sadie would make it all better.

CHAPTER THIRTY-FOUR

Sadie

"WHAT THE HELL has Dominic said about all this?" Bianca asked Charlie as Sadie unpacked the backpack cooler filled with appetizers and wine. Of all the Thursday nights they had gathered in this place, this one was on verge of being the most epic. Sadie doubted anyone would have guessed the current topics two years ago: Charlie dating her NFL superstar best friend, Bianca having a fling with a decade younger mechanic after Tom bolted, and her sleeping with Evan after Levi's death. Sadie hadn't filled them in on that part of the story yet, but she was hoping after a couple glasses of wine, she would have the courage to tell them. She had mulled over her delivery all day, though it probably wouldn't come out eloquently. But it had to happen. She needed their advice—or more importantly, their blessing.

"He's totally supportive, but he doesn't get it. He hasn't been a normal human in so long that he really can't grasp how much this is affecting my daily life," Charlie responded as Sadie handed her a full glass of wine. "White tonight?" Charlie inquired, taking a sip and nodding in approval.

"Figured we should mix it up a bit. It's summer after all, and summertime screams for a good white wine," Sadie replied. "Besides, Bianca and I had more than our share of champs the other night while we watched you in all your glory. I'm still recovering from that over-in-dulgence."

"You looked gorgeous, Charlie," Bianca added as she patted her friend's leg in support. "You and Dominic looked like the perfect pair. In all honesty, I was oozing jealousy." Bianca chuckled and batted her eyes.

"Well, I'm flattered. But there's nothing to be jealous about. It's just me, trying to focus on Dominic like I always have. The story's the same as it has been since high school, only back then, it was measly local report-ers, small-town fans, and jealous peers. Now it's a bigger crowd and the stakes are much higher," Charlie said with a touch of resentment.

"Charlie, you'll figure it all out. Like Dominic said, give it time. They'll move on to someone else next week, I'm sure." Sadie smiled through her words. "Bianca, I noticed you've been home all this week. What's up with you and Luke?" she asked innocently. "Trouble in Tybee paradise?"

"I think you might need another drink for this one, Sadie," Bianca responded, shaking her head. "I was hop-ing to save this story until we were at least a bottle of wine in, but since you asked, I'll divulge."

"Oh, hell. This sounds intriguing," Charlie said, leaning toward Bianca in anticipation.

"An understatement. So, in a nutshell, on Sunday, Jane caught me riding Luke in one of my operatory chairs," Bianca stated matter-of-factly.

Sadie spewed the gulp of wine she'd just taken straight out of her mouth.

"What?!" Charlie gasped.

"Yep. You heard me, ladies. I got busted. In the most embarrassing way possible. I somehow managed to make it through my teenage years without ever being caught making out by my parents, but somehow, I couldn't make it past my office manager. Nope. Caught bare-assed and red handed—or red faced is probably a better description," Bianca confessed.

"What did you do?" Sadie asked, wiping drops off wine off her chin and thighs.

"I got dressed, obviously," Bianca replied sarcastically.

"No. That's not what I mean."

"I tried to act cool. I played it off like it was nothing to Jane. And of course, I apologized for the unprofessionalism. But like she said, it's my office. I can damn well fuck whomever I want in it. But then a real problem surfaced," Bianca confessed.

"What's that?" Charlie asked.

"Luke. I was so embarrassed at being caught with him. Jane knows him. He's serviced our office numerous times." Bianca hung her head at her words. "I clammed up. I didn't talk to him all week. Barely answered his texts. Didn't answer his calls. I knew it would never work. We live two totally different lives. But apparently, he wasn't willing to give up so easily. He showed up at my office this morning and barged his way in to see me. I basically told him that I wanted to end it. It breaks my heart. I think he really liked me."

"Of course, he liked you, Bianca. What's not to like? You're pretty, smart, funny, and a great catch." Sadie stared at her friend. She could tell how bad Bianca felt, and she didn't want to throw salt in the wound but couldn't help but defend her friend's great qualities.

Bianca's face sunk in despair. "I never meant to hurt him. That wasn't my intention. I was selfish. He just felt so *good*. I really have had the best time with him. He's so easy, so…normal. But in the back of my mind, I just couldn't let myself give in to the idea of dating him seriously. I don't know what I was thinking getting involved with him…" Bianca trailed off. "Of all people, I know what it's like to be blindsided and hurt."

"Listen. Please don't beat yourself up. You're broken,

and broken people are desperate to quickly stop the bleeding from the gaping hole in their heart. You'll do all the 'things.' You'll have one-night stands. You'll screw your AC guy. You'll unintentionally hurt other people. And you'll cross every line you know better than to cross. But you'll also learn the difference between a Band-Aid and a cure. Band-Aids have their purpose, but they fail eventually. A cure takes more time. A cure supports you mentally, spiritually, *and* physically. It's patient, because it knows its goal: to heal. You'll know true love when you find it, my dear. It's the only cure for a broken heart." Sadie leaned into her friend and kissed her cheek. She knew it was her turn to confess her own story. "Speaking of crossing lines, I need to tell you guys something…" She watched her two friends look up at her somber expression. "I slept with Evan."

Neither Charlie nor Bianca moved. They stared straight at her without a flinch or blink. Finally, after an awkward lapse in time, she continued. "I know. It's weird."

"I knew it," Bianca crowed. "I knew it when his belt poked me in the ass."

"What the hell are you talking about?" Charlie asked with the most confused look on her face.

"On Saturday, I was at Sadie's watching you get made love to verbally on national television, and when I sat down on the couch, something stabbed me. Low and behold, it was Evan's belt buckle. Sadie made some lame-ass excuse that he had changed there for the gym. I knew something was fishy, and when I saw the look on your face while you were texting him, I knew something was up, Sadie. There was definitely more to the story," Bianca said.

"How did this happen? I mean, have you always had feelings for him?" Charlie asked.

"No. Absolutely not. I never thought of anyone but Levi. But over the past few weeks, things have sort of …I don't know, happened." Sadie hung her head. She honestly couldn't have explained the timeline or progression if someone held a gun to her head.

"Sadie, we know you love Levi. There's no doubting that. It's just…" Charlie trailed off.

"It's fucked up," Sadie finished her sentence.

"Yeah. Kind of," Charlie said.

"I would beg to differ," Bianca piped up to defend her friend. "I've had a little bit longer to toss this idea around in my head since my suspicious mind started to reel on Saturday night. Let me lay the facts out clearly." Bianca stood and started to pace back and forth over the wooden slats of the gazebo as she spoke, channeling her best impression of a defense attorney. "First, I can totally see why you'd be attracted to Evan. He's basically an older, taller version of Levi. Secondly, you're friends, and as we know from Charlie's recent stint with Gabe and Dominic, friends of the opposite sex seem to get their emotions all muddled. Thirdly, the boys *adore* him. What better man to bring into their life than someone they already cherish? And finally, Kate. She sucks. I can only imagine how envious Evan has been all these years, seeing you dote on his brother. I'm sure he watched in awe as you stood by Levi's side through the good and the bad, sickness and health," Bianca argued. "Just as a good wife should do."

"You know, B's right. Now that I think about it, you guys really *are* a perfect match. He's wonderful. You're wonderful. You deserve each other. I say go for it," Charlie said. "And, you won't have to change your last name if you get married," Charlie added with an enlightened tone.

"Well, that went over better than I expected. I wasn't quite sure how you two would react," Sadie said with relief in her voice. One confession down. One to go.

"Well, I must say, we've somehow gotten ourselves into

some pickles, now haven't we?" Bianca said through a chuckle. "As if the night couldn't get any more dramatic, let me add this update. It must have been a full moon or something on Sunday, because right before I was so embarrassingly caught with Luke, I got a weird rush of bravery. I woke up and decided it was time to finally confront Tom."

Sadie's stomach turned. It was the lead she needed to bring up the secret she'd been keeping for years.

"But when I tried to call him, his number was disconnected. So, I tried emailing him. No luck. It was sent back undeliverable. Do you think he's dead or in jail or something?"

"No, Bianca. I think Tom is a drunk," Sadie blurted out. The minute she did, she knew it had come out too harsh. That wasn't the empathetic delivery she'd practiced.

"A drunk? No, he isn't. I was married to the man for years. I think I'd know if my husband was a drunk, Sadie," Bianca replied defensively.

"Yeah, Sadie. What the hell are you talking about? Sure, Tom drank socially, but look at us right now. We're two wine bottles in and I wouldn't call us 'drunks,'" Charlie added.

"Bianca, please don't be angry with me if I tell you this. Promise?" Sadie asked.

Bianca nodded cautiously.

"Before Levi was sick, he would sometimes come home for lunch. One time, his truck battery died, and he made a surprise visit to your house for help from Tom…and he was drunk. Like hammered. In the middle of the day on a Tuesday. Levi made me promise not to tell you. He figured it was a random thing and we didn't need to meddle in your business. But with everything that's happened, I really think it's possible he had a hidden drinking problem," Sadie confessed. "I'm sorry, B."

Bianca just sat still, so still that it was unsettling. That wasn't the reaction Sadie had been expecting from fiery Bianca.

"B, are you okay?" Charlie asked.

"No, I'm not okay. It's not possible. You're wrong, Sadie. Your story might be true, but your assumption is wrong. There is no way on this earth Tom was an alcoholic and I was too checked out to know," Bianca said, her voice getting louder and quivering.

"Okay, B. Okay. You're right. I'm probably way off. It was just a hunch," Sadie said with remorse. She wished now that she'd kept her big mouth shut. Maybe some things were better left tucked away in the closet.

She pulled Bianca close to her into a tight embrace and eyed Charlie with concern over Bianca's shoulder. Charlie shook her head in disbelief. Even with the best of hearts and intentions, they had managed to get themselves into more drama than they had ever imagined.

CHAPTER THIRTY-FIVE

Charlie

HER MIND WAS still reeling from the bomb that had gone off in the gazebo. She wished she had been given some sort of warning about Sadie and Evan. And she was still felt flabbergasted by Sadie's theory that Tom was an underground alcoholic, or better yet, an attic alcoholic. She wasn't sure how much more drama she could handle…

And then she looked at her phone. There it was, plastered all over the sport news headlines: *Dominic Houston's girlfriend seen threatening the paparazzi.* An image of her and the little pip squeak that had degraded her relationship with Dominic stared her square in the face. She wanted to scream. How dare they accuse her of being the one in the wrong? She punched her mattress and threw herself onto her bed, steam coming from her ears. She suddenly felt sorry for every celebrity in the world. It was no wonder most of their relationships failed, having to deal with this shit.

Charlie sent a screenshot of the tabloid title to Dominic.

D: *Ha. Go get 'em, babe. That's my girl.*

C: *Dominic. You can't be serious. This is awful. I look like a crazy person.*

D: *News flash. You are crazy.*

C: *Not now. I'm serious.*

D: *Chill out. You are way overreacting. Who cares what they say?*

C: *I'm not you. I'm not that tough.*

D: *Charlie, you are way tougher than anyone I've ever known. You're really going to let this fake news get to you?*

C: *It's not fake. I did go off on him. He called us "friends with benefits."*

D: *Well, we are friends. And we do have amazing, toe-curling benefits.*

C: *Really? That's what we are? Friends with benefits...*

D: *Oh, come on... I'm kidding.*

Charlie's phone stared to ring. It was Dominic. She declined the call. She was too angry to talk to him.

D: *Answer your phone...*

C: *I don't want to talk to you right now.*

D: *Too bad.*

Her phone rang again.

And again.

Even more angry, she finally answered. "What?" she yelled, agitated.

"Simmer down. You're way off the mark here. You know damn good and well what we are. You know what we have. Why in the world do you care what some dumbass has to say about us?" Dominic demanded.

"I don't. But I do care about us. It's like we're right back in high school again. People whispering from their lockers when we walk by. Parents gossiping about us in the stands at the football games. So-called friends talking about us behind our backs at the sorority formals. It could have, and probably should have, torn us apart," Charlie's voice cracked.

"But it didn't then. Why would it now? Charlie, you're way overreacting. This is nothing. It'll be old news by tomorrow. I promise. You really want them to win? Please tell me that's not what you want. You're gonna let this silly paparazzi story get to you?"

"I know what I want. I want us…in a normal life. Kids and a Suburban and a white picket fence. But that won't ever be possible, will it?" she yelled.

Dominic was silent. She knew the answer and he did too.

"I'm tired. I've got work tomorrow. I gotta go," she muttered with her volume back to normal, knowing she wouldn't sleep a wink.

"Don't be like this, Charlie," Dominic pleaded. "I don't like getting off the phone like this."

"Dominic, it's late. I'm tired. I love you no matter what, okay?" Charlie said truthfully. The situation didn't change how much she loved him.

"I love you no matter what, too, baby."

Charlie's heart sunk at Dominic's words. She knew they were true. And she also knew she wouldn't survive another day without hearing them whispered in her ear. But the line of fire she would have to walk through to get to that point just might get the best of her.

CHAPTER THIRTY-SIX

Sadie

HER HEAD POUNDED. She wasn't sure if it was from the overconsumption of wine from the previous night, or the looming stress she'd recently incurred from a love affair with her dead husband's brother. Either way, she couldn't hide under her covers for too long. She had two hungry boys to feed.

"Mom, are you okay? We can get some cereal or something if you want to sleep in. It's fine," Tad sweetly suggested as he leaned in to kiss his mother's cheek. Sadie's heart melted. Her boys were so kind. There wasn't a thing in this world she wouldn't do for them.

"I'm fine, baby. What do you want? Eggs and toast?" she whispered sleepily.

"Oh, man, that sounds so good, Mom," Tad replied quickly. Sadie knew his offer had been out of kindness. It didn't take much to reveal her eldest son's true wishes—a full-on breakfast.

"Give me a minute. I'll whip something up."

She heard Max in the next room talking to someone. It wasn't but a second before a familiar figure made its way to her doorway.

"Tad, let your mom rest. Come on, son. I'll make you some breakfast," she heard Evan say.

"Yes, sir," Tad obeyed.

Sadie sat up quickly. She couldn't remember a time that

she'd ever slept in. She must look like some sort of lazy piece of crap to Evan.

"Nope. You rest. You'll need it," Evan commanded with a wink, then he smiled and closed the door behind him, leaving her by herself.

Holy shit, Sadie thought, sinking back into the sheets. *I think he implied I needed to rest up for him!* Her mind started to whirl as fiercely as her heart started to beat.

She jumped up and got dressed. She brushed her teeth and put on a dab of makeup. It wasn't anything like what he was used to with Kate—she was the queen of beauty products—but maybe he'd notice the effort and give her some grace. It was weird trying to impress someone. Even though she probably didn't have to.

"Out of my kitchen, you vandals," Sadie said in a commanding tone as she marched into the kitchen.

Max, Tad, and Evan all laughed and scurried away from their posts.

"How dare you come into my lair without permission."

Sadie saw Ava and Lainey sitting at the table, giggling at the boys being reprimanded.

"Mom, don't worry. We want *you* to cook us breakfast. Uncle E sucks at cooking eggs," Tad said, pointing to the mess that sat bubbling on the stove.

"Excuse me, sir. We don't use that language in this house," Sadie said, but knowing that he was right. Evan's skills did obviously suck. Bad.

"Yeah, but he's come a long way," Ava said in her dad's defense. "You should have seen the mess he made in the kitchen making our dinner the other night. And we had to clean it up, Aunt Sadie."

"Beggars need not be choosy," Evan mocked as he sat down at the table.

Sadie finished up the breakfast and couldn't help but beam with all of them there together.

"I have to head to work. You boys have a great day and please do the dishes for your mother," Evan directed as he grabbed his briefcase and headed to the front door. "Girls, let's go. You don't want to be late for cheerleading camp."

"Yes, sir. We will, Uncle Evan," Max said, giving his uncle a big hug.

"You boys have fun at basketball camp today. Don't forget to focus on the free throws. That was your dad's claim to fame in high school. Never miss a free throw," Evan coached, shaking his hands through Tad's hair, messing it up intentionally. "Talk to you later, Sadie," he continued with a secretive tone to his voice that ended with a long stare that reached deep into her soul. Sadie's heart pounded. For the first time in her life as a mother, she wished the kids were already at camp. She wanted nothing more than to take Evan to her bed and strip him down piece by piece. Their chemistry was palpable.

"Let's go, boys," she said, urging them to get their things. Her eyes never left Evan's as he stepped backward to his truck. She hoped Ava and Lainey didn't notice their love stare. It was obvious he was as hooked as she was. She closed her door, but not before giving him a coy grin. She hoped it was enough to let him know her intentions. "Go on and get in the car, boys. I have lunches packed. Don't forget your water bottles."

"Mom," Tad said, as he grabbed his athletic bag, "Uncle Evan sure makes you smile."

Sadie's heart stopped. She didn't know what to say.

"You know it's okay to love someone besides Dad, right?" Tad continued.

Sadie felt a lump forming in her throat. Never in a million years had she expected such words from her young son. She'd done everything in her power to protect him from any emotional rollercoaster she might be on, but kids were smart. And intuitive. She smiled at him and winked. "I know, baby. I know," was all she could get out. She couldn't drop the boys off quick enough at their camp. Her foot pressed hard onto the pedal as she bolted to the cemetery, her chest heaving from the tears she'd been stifling since they left the house. She had only one thing on her mind. She had one person left to come clean to, and that was Levi. As she pulled up to the headstone and stepped onto the grass that was fresh and bright green, she fell to her knees. Tears streamed down her face as her hands traced the letters of her last name on the granite: *Carson*.

"Levi, why did you have to leave me? I can't help but feel like this is some sort of test of my devotion to you," she said with a whimper. "You're the love of my life." Her chest felt like a vise was gripping it fiercely. "Please, *please*, let me know what I should do," she wailed in desperation.

Laying down on the cool green grass, something gave her peace. Sadie could feel him there, wrapping his tight arms around her. She curled up next to the headstone, her cheek on the cold gray granite. The weight of the past two years felt heavy in her soul. She needed a sign. A signal of any sort that it was okay to love again.

Within minutes, her prayers were answered. Sadie jumped hearing a flutter above her. In the same breath, she saw the most beautiful cardinal land on Levi's headstone. Sadie smiled. It was one of the things she remembered vividly from her childhood summers in the country with her grandmother: cardinals were our guardian angels in disguise, her grandmother had always said.

Chills zinged down her spine. It was Levi. She knew it was him, granting her permission to move on. To love again.

CHAPTER THIRTY-SEVEN

Charlie

IT WAS A good thing Charlie had packed a lunch. She'd barely made it into the office building without being stopped for a comment from some brave news reporter. There wasn't a chance in hell she was going out and facing that treacherous terrain again until it was necessary. She unpacked her chicken wrap and fruit and settled into the leather guest chair that she'd moved from the front of her desk to the window. Staring down below, she could see a handful of random people waiting outside the front entrance, hoping to get a glimpse of the crazy friend-with-benefits that had scolded a poor, helpless paparazzi reporter. *Ugh. So annoying.* Charlie's heart sank, thinking of how everything had taken a turn for the worse. One minute she had been snuggled up next to Dominic in a warm bed at the Ritz-Carlton, and the next, she was being blasted for that exact happiness all over the internet.

Dominic had texted her a few times that morning, trying to get a temperature reading on her after a good night's sleep. Unfortunately, the thermostat was still reading ice cold. She had responded, but used the, "I'm too busy at work to talk about this right now," excuse. She needed to think. This was the exact reason she'd kept her friendship with Dominic a near secret over the years. Hell, even Sadie, Bianca, and Gabe barely knew any details of her relationship with him. Charlie had learned early on in college what it was like to be associated with Dominic and his popularity. The college years had started to show fame's ugly side in the form of guys who invited her to parties, hoping she would bring along the star quarterback, only to be ignored when she showed up without him. Or girls that only befriended her to try and get their chance at meeting the superstar and catching his eye. It was all so fake. And exhausting. Like the current situation. Charlie leaned her head back, propped her feet up on the windowsill, and closed her eyes. Maybe if she prayed hard enough, it would all fix itself.

"Looks like you're really hard at work," she heard a familiar voice say from the doorway.

Her heart stopped and her eyes popped wide open as she jumped up. "Dominic! What are you doing here?" she exclaimed as she dusted off the crumbs from the front of her navy-blue pants.

"I came to talk you off the ledge," he said with a smile as he made his way over to her, wrapping his arms around her and planting a kiss on her lips that she feared still had remnants of chicken wrap. Charlie's face burned as she watched heads pop up in curiosity over the tops of their cubicles through the glass wall of her office. She was sure this would be the icing on the cake for Gabe. He would certainly get her thrown off the Sabo project now. He had made it quite clear on Monday that the distractions that came along with Dominic weren't welcome in the workplace.

"I'm not on a ledge. I'm at a crossroads," she corrected.

"Whatever you want to call it. Though you *were* sitting next to the window when I walked in..." He snickered.

"How did you get here? It's barely lunch," Charlie questioned.

"I took the first flight to Savannah this morning.

Booked it last night after you got so upset. I want to fix this. Set your head straight," he explained.

Charlie looked out the window, down to the street. The usual black Escalade sat parked on the curb at the front entrance to her building, currently swarmed by men and women with lanyards and cameras.

"I don't think you showing up here is fixing anything," she muttered as she pointed to the street. "How did you get in here without them seeing you?"

"I didn't. I waved at them and smiled." He shrugged. "I have nothing to hide, Charlie. And no reason to be secretive. As long as they don't try and get pictures of us doing the dirty, I don't care what they do."

"Well, I'm not that public, Dominic. I'm not like you. You know that." Charlie couldn't help the tears welling up in her eyes. "Maybe we should take a break from seeing each other for a while. Let everything calm down. You know, clear our heads and make sure this is the right thing to do," Charlie said through the heaves she was trying to stifle unsuccessfully.

"What? Are you serious? Take a break? No fucking way," Dominic said with agitation. His brows were furrowed, and his fists clenched.

"Don't be angry. It has nothing to do with how much I love you or how I feel about you," she defended as she grabbed his hand. She could practically see the wheels turning in his head.

"Life is so fucked up. I've spent my entire adult life with women falling all over me because of my fame. Now, the one woman I want won't have me because of it." Dominic shook his head in disbelief.

Charlie just stared at him, her heart breaking as she watched his pain.

"Okay, Charlie. If this is what you want, you got it. I don't ever want to push you into something you don't feel like you can do." Dominic pulled his hand back from hers and his demeanor shifted like the wind. She had seen that façade a million times: his stoic game face. It's what made him so successful. It was his quarterback sneak, his third down and goal, and his two-minute drill mental state. *Don't be rattled. Be tough. No emotion. Protect the ball.* Only this time, he wasn't protecting the football—he was protecting his heart.

Dominic stopped in her doorway and his eyes softened for a moment. "I guess sometimes soulmates aren't meant to be together. Maybe the universe couldn't handle that big of a love," he said, staring her straight into her soul. "But I can say with one hundred percent certainty that I would rather have been with the right person for a minute in time than the wrong person for a lifetime."

Charlie's heart sank. He was right. As the elevator doors closed, she watched as the man she loved slipped right through her fingers.

"Damnit, Charlie. What the fuck are you doing?" she said to herself. Kicking her heels off, she darted to the stairwell, rushing past wide-eyed coworkers that had seen more entertainment in the last week than on the streets during Mardi Gras. Shoving through the metal door to the main level, Charlie's heart raced as she gasped for air, her bare feet pounding on the cool tile floor. She could see the driver opening the door to the black vehicle as Dominic waited, surrounded by reporters.

"Dominic!" she called out as she burst through the front doors. "Wait!" Running to him, huffing and puffing from her race to catch him, she saw him turn to her, a stoic expression still plastered on his face. Pushing through the crowd that had now noticed who was causing the commotion, the group parted like the Red Sea, finally getting what they had been waiting for: live action. Charlie couldn't help but smile, knowing she was going to make it epic, in bold and fearless Charlotte Compton style. Wrapping her arms around his neck and jumping onto his waist, her legs with a tight grip around his back, she planted the most inappropriate kiss right on his mouth, tongue and all. As he wrapped his arms under her, holding her tightly to him, she finally pulled her mouth from his, and eyed his now beaming face. "I decided to give the fans what they want: a good juicy show, perfect for a headline." She giggled, nestling her nose against his as if no one was around.

"That's my girl. You never cease to amaze me, Charlotte Compton," he said, shaking his head with a coy smile.

"I've given it some thought, and I finally figured out how you can keep those restless football hands of yours busy in retirement," she said seductively. "Now let's get home and make up." Charlie unwrapped her legs and putting her bare feet back on the sidewalk. Turning to the crowd and being slightly blinded by the camera flashes, Charlie waved and sarcastically blew a kiss to a familiar face in the crowd: Dewayne.

As they both tucked into the third row of the Escalade and snuggled into each other's arms, Charlie's heart melted. The universe would just have to figure out how to handle their big love.

CHAPTER THIRTY-EIGHT

Sadie

THERE WASN'T A chance in hell that Sadie would be able to sort through all her thoughts on one long run. Even if she doubled her distance and super-charged her mind, it wouldn't help the reeling thoughts weighing on her mind. How would they tell the kids? What would Kate say? Sadie had hoped that she'd have a chance to talk to Evan alone, but the weekend hadn't allowed for it. This was the first weekend of the summer that Max and Tad didn't have sleepover plans. It probably wouldn't have mattered even if they had. Sadie had been at Bianca's emotional beck and call as she prepped for her court appearance the following week. It seemed that the only time she had to squeak in for Evan was quick texts and a secretive wink when the boys weren't looking on his usual stop-by visits. Sadie was, in a way, thankful for the distractions. A few moments of relief from the chaos in her mind were more than welcomed.

Sadie let her sweat soaked running clothes slap onto the tile floor as she undressed for her nighttime shower. Dunking her head under the stream of hot water, she found herself unable to hide from her own thoughts. Surely Kate would think this had been going on for years. The thought of tainting her marriage to Levi with assumptions of infidelity made her stomach turn. And what would their extended families think? The Carson lineage would surely be mortified at a family story worthy of *Jerry Springer*. Sadie rinsed her body and looked down at her frail figure. She in no way compared to Kate's perfect physique. There were no size D fake breasts or lasered bikini lines. Her toenails hadn't seen a pedicure in nearly a year, and there wasn't more than five minutes' worth of makeup on her face at any given moment in time, even during the most glamorous events in her life, which really only included her wedding day.

Why does he even want me?

She knew why she wanted him—that was a no brainer—but for the life of her, she didn't see what he saw. Wrapping her wet hair in a crisp, white towel and her body in a plush, gray robe, Sadie headed to her bedroom and picked up her phone sitting on the bed. Evan had texted only seconds before.

E: The boys asleep?

S: Yep. Crashed out like a light.

E: Good. Let me in.

S: What do you mean? Are you here?

Sadie's heart skipped a beat. She was in no way made up enough for Evan to see her.

E: Yep. Look out your window.

Sadie tiptoed over to her front window and peeled back the Roman shade. Sure enough, his truck sat parked on the street in its usual spot, headlights off. She could see the outline of his face from the light shining off his phone screen.

S: Evan, I can't let you in right now. What about the boys? What about the neighbors?

E: You said the boys were asleep. You and I both know that once they go down, a tornado wouldn't wake them up. And as far as your neighbors, I turned off my lights when I got to your street. No one will know unless they have no life. And that's their problem.

He was right. She could use a bullhorn to wake Tad

and Max and they would still sleep right on through it. Evan didn't know she'd spilled the beans to Charlie and Bianca, so them seeing his truck wasn't something she was worried about. And as far as the other little old ladies on the street, they had already been asleep for a couple of hours.

S: Okay. But be super quiet when you shut your truck door. And I'm not turning on the porch light, so watch your step.

Sadie made her way to the front door, unlocking it as softly as she could and motioning Evan in. He grabbed her hand as he tiptoed past her, pulling her into the only room in their view with a light on—her bedroom. Sadie closed the door quietly behind him, taking a deep breath of air and exhaling in relief.

"What in the world are you doing here?" she asked, adding a smile at the end of her words. She hoped her demeanor wasn't implying she wasn't happy with his company.

"I wanted to see you. But I suddenly feel like I'm back in high school, sneaking to see my girlfriend." Evan laughed through his words as he slipped his hand under the edge of her robe.

"You did that?" Sadie asked as her breathing became heavy and her heartbeat audible in her own ears with the touch of his hand.

"Maybe." He snickered, planting a firm kiss on her still-damp neck.

"Levi always said you were a ladies' man," Sadie whispered, suddenly knowing why he may have gotten that reputation.

"Hardly," Evan muttered as he lifted Sadie into his arms and placed her on the bed. He easily loosened the robe's tie from around her waist and pulled it open, exposing her body to his view. The towel around her head fell to the ground, revealing her wet, wavy locks.

"Evan, we need to talk."

"About what?" he asked, still running his hand down the front of her torso.

"About Kate. And the kids. And everyone else in the world that knows us. And I can't talk about it with you doing that," she stated, grasping his hand and holding it in a still position over her heart.

"Okay. Let's talk then," Evan agreed, kicking his shoes off and crawling beside her on the bed. His hand only left her chest for a moment, and then he placed it right where Sadie had guided it previously. "But before you start, I just want to say I couldn't care less about what Kate says."

"I get that. I really do. But we need to take it one step at a time. No one even knows you're separated. You haven't even told the girls. What if she comes back from California and she's changed her mind? What if she wants to work things out with you?" Sadie quizzed.

"We don't have to worry about that. She signed the separation papers. I got them last week," Evan admitted.

"I'm sorry, Evan. Are you okay?" Sadie asked, concern in her voice.

"Relieved is more like it. She and I talked on the phone. We have a plan to tell the girls. They'll be fine. I can promise you they won't be surprised. They aren't dumb. They know way more than we give them credit for," Evan stated confidently.

Sadie knew he was right. She'd witnessed it herself the past Friday when Tad had so blatantly called out her happiness around Evan. "And as far as Levi goes, I think he'd be okay with us too."

Evan's face contorted into a puzzled grimace.

"I visited his grave on Friday," Sadie said shyly, realizing how crazy all of this was about to sound. "And there was a bird—a cardinal to be exact—that landed on his headstone. I immediately felt a sense of peace. Like it was all okay."

"So, you're saying a bird told you it was okay for us to be together?" Evan asked through a chuckle.

"Damnit, I know it sounds stupid. But it's the truth. And my grandmother always said that cardinals were our guardian angels. When we saw one, we'd always take guesses as to who it was. I know that one was Levi. He was there, telling me to love again." Her eyes welled up with tears.

Evan's face softened. She knew he felt the weight of her words, as silly as they sounded. Whether the cardinal was Levi's soul or not, it had given her peace, and that, she was grateful for.

"Sadie, I believe you. And more than anything, I believe that Levi would want you to be loved. He would want you to be happy. And he would want you to be safe. There is no way in the world he would want you to spend the rest of your life alone. There isn't any other man on this earth that loves his boys more than me. And there certainly isn't any other man that knows how priceless you are," Evan stated firmly.

"I'm so sorry, Evan. I hate that you've been so lonely all these years," Sadie said as she rubbed her fingers through his auburn hair. She had always hoped that behind closed doors, Kate and Evan had their own secret love story. But unsurprisingly, she hadn't been wrong in her gut feeling that Evan had never been appropriately loved. "I know all too well how painful loneliness can be."

"I know you do. And I know how amazing of a person you are, and that you wouldn't allow yourself to be lying here with me if you didn't love me." Evan reached his arm around her waist, pulling her close. She could feel the heat from his body penetrating her still-exposed skin through his shirt. His head leaned down to her bare shoulder, kissing it softly then nestling Sadie's head up under his chin.

He was right. She did love him. And she decided the

best way was to show him. If there was one thing she had learned from loving Levi, it was that time was precious and love was priceless.

Sadie raised up, leaving her robe in its place on the bed, her naked body moving on top of Evan. His eyes were wide with amazement. It wasn't too often anyone had seen her in her queen bee persona. It was her secret weapon. There wasn't a thing in the world Sadie loved more than taking care of her loved ones. And this task was the ultimate pledge of devotion. Pushing her hands into the pillows as she straddled him, Sadie looked him square in the eyes, piercing his soul with raw honesty.

"I do love you, Evan Carson." Sadie's body went to work, and with every ounce of feminine energy she had, she made love to him, just the way he deserved.

CHAPTER THIRTY-NINE

Bianca

BIANCA'S FEET FELT like concrete blocks as she climbed the stairs leading up to the Chatham County courthouse doors. The building itself seemed to carry its own heavy weight. The gray cinderblock building with its linear black windows didn't fit in at all amidst the gorgeous historic Savannah buildings that were its neighbors. Bianca couldn't help but wonder how many lives had taken a complete one-eighty turn after entering its doors. Hers was about to.

She hadn't laid eyes on Tom in months. It was like he'd just vanished into thin air. As a matter of fact, she was finding it harder and harder to picture his image in her mind. She wasn't sure if it was from the fact that, with Sadie and Charlie's help, she had successfully purged her entire house of all pictures of him, or if it was her mind's way of instilling self-protection. Either way, she was more nervous about her visceral reaction upon seeing him than the actual court process. The damage was done. There was no turning back from the end of the story. Divorce was inevitable. But the body's reaction to trauma wasn't controllable, and Bianca knew that better than anyone. She had watched day after day as some of the largest, burliest men turned into sweaty-palmed babies upon walking into her dental office. No matter how tough or how many tattoos graced their bodies, their uncontrollable, innate fear reared its ugly head time and time again.

Her heels clicked a predictable rhythm as she coached herself to take one step after another toward the court-room to meet her attorney. She thought she was doing well holding it all together, despite the butterflies that swarmed in her stomach, until she rounded the corner. And there he was: her heartbreak in the flesh. He sat alone on a bench across from the courtroom doors, his legs spread wide, his forearms resting on his thighs as if he had just completed a marathon. His head hung low between his shoulders and his blond curls draped over his ears from the pull of gravity.

Bianca held her breath. She was hoping she might get lucky and make it into the courtroom without being noticed, but as his head lifted and he turned to see who the steps belonged to, their eyes met. And then she saw it: the pain.

There was something brutally satisfying to her to see him like that. It almost made her feel like she had the upper hand for half a second.

Standing quickly and straightening his tie, Tom flashed a forced smile. "Hey," he said nervously.

Bianca nodded at his greeting. Her feet stopped in front of his, her skin hot from the pain oozing from her heart.

"So, um, can I talk to you for a second?" he asked, motioning for Bianca to sit down beside him on the bench.

"You want to talk *now*? It's been *months* and you hav-en't so much as sent a text message. What's so important now?" Bianca asked with agitation.

"I have some things I need to tell you," Tom admitted.

"I hope it includes why you abandoned me and then practically fell off the face of the earth," she said snarkily.

"It does," he responded matter-of-factly. "But I need you to understand one thing before I start. I want you to wait until I finish. You need to hear the entire story. Please don't ask questions until I'm completely done. Okay?"

"Sure, I guess," Bianca said, annoyed. She sat down on the wooden-slatted bench beside him and crossed her arms, waiting for some lame-ass excuse as to why he felt justified in his actions.

"For starters, I love you. I don't expect you to believe me, but it's true. The problem is that I haven't loved myself for a long time. Bianca, I'm an alcoholic," Tom admitted.

Bianca's mind whirled. Sadie had been right. She wanted to crawl into a hole. Her heart pounded and her eyes filled with tears.

"I have been for years. And no one, not even my family or friends, knew."

"How—" Bianca tried to butt in.

"I said let me talk," Tom snapped.

Bianca stopped immediately, realizing that the words Tom was speaking probably needed momentum to continue to pour from his mouth.

"When you got home each night and started cooking dinner, I'd pop a beer. I might follow that up with three or four more through the evening. The truth is…" He trailed off, obviously gathering the courage to confess. "The truth is, I drank all day while you were at work. I'd pour myself a vodka—or five, depending on the day. I worked from home, so there was no one to notice, or judge me. About an hour or so before you got home, I'd stop drinking and eat, trying to sober up so you didn't notice. And you didn't. And that's not your fault. No one did. Bianca, I'm getting help. I've been in rehab since I left you. I didn't want to take you down with me. I wasn't strong enough when I left you to do it like a man. I was weak, and I ran. But I couldn't bring a child into a home that was built on secrets. I couldn't do that to you or a baby. It was terrible. I am so, so sorry," Tom whispered as tears dripped from his jawline onto the marble floor.

Bianca's heart sank. How could she have lived with

someone for years and not known they were drunk? She felt so stupid. Now it all made sense. The panic at the fertility doctor, the vodka bottles, the disconnected phone and email. She hung her head in defeat.

"I wish I would have known. I would have gotten you help sooner. I must have been such an absent wife to have never noticed," she said, flabbergasted still.

"Bianca, let me tell you something. You can hide anything you want, from anyone you want, for as long as you want. You couldn't help me. I had to do it myself. You were a great wife. You deserve someone who is kind and honest and will love you the way that I didn't." Tom grabbed her hand, squeezing it tightly in his.

For a second, she couldn't breathe. The elephant in the room had landed directly on her chest. She felt beads of sweat forming on her brow and her lips tingled with nausea just like the day he left her. It had only happened to her once in her life, but she was scarred enough to remember it. She was having a panic attack. Her heart pounded, her chest caved in, her vision became speckled with stars, and she felt herself slipping to the cold floor before everything went dark.

"Bianca, Bianca!" she heard Tom yelling from directly above her. She could hear the buzz of voices from her attorney and other strangers calling for help. Bianca batted open her eyes slowly, blinded by the fluorescent lights that shined above her in the drop ceiling tiles. "Just lie still, B. Help is on the way," she heard him say. His words were still a bit muffled, like she was in a tunnel. She did as he said. She was too weak to move anyway. Bianca could feel her heart waving the white flag of defeat. In that instant, she channeled the skill she had recently perfected with Luke: surrender.

CHAPTER FORTY

Bianca

"DAMN, GIRL. YOU sure know how to draw a crowd. I thought I was winning that race, but you're nipping at my heels," Charlie said through a laugh.

Bianca sat up in her bed. Her bedroom walls spun a little and she still felt groggy from the Valium the doctor had given her at the hospital. She hated taking any kind of medication, but she was currently thankful for the dose of calm that she was experiencing.

Charlie and Sadie sat on Bianca's bed, both staring a hole through her head.

"I'm assuming you'd like a play-by-play of what happened this morning," Bianca said.

Her friends nodded, eyebrows raised.

"That would be nice," Charlie said in a smart-ass tone.

"Well, I finally got answers. And they were a little overwhelming," Bianca admitted.

"Obviously. Overwhelming enough to have you splattered out on the floor of the courthouse," Sadie confirmed.

"You were right, Sadie. I'm sorry I didn't believe you. Tom *is* an alcoholic and has been for years. Like, since college to be exact. No one knows—not his friends, not his parents, *not his wife*," Bianca explained. "He's been in rehab since he left me, which is why his phone and email were cut off. It all makes sense now. He drank all day and sobered up before I got home. I couldn't smell it because it of his deliberate choice in liquor: vodka. And when he popped open his first beer at night, I assumed it was his first drink of the day."

"This is so fucked up. I am so sorry, B," Charlie huffed.

"He did you a favor, Bianca," Sadie said as she patted her friend's leg. "You have answers now. And you have a second chance at happiness, sweetie."

"It feels good to have closure. So much makes sense, and the pieces of the puzzle are starting to come together," Bianca said with relief in her tone.

"Well, if I know you, Bianca Moretti, you're going to take these pieces of the puzzle and turn them into a fucking masterpiece. And I can't wait to see the final portrait," Charlie said, clapping her hands together.

"I've definitely learned a lot about me and what I'm capable of living through," Bianca said with a shrug. She looked at her two friends and beamed with pride. They were a force to be reckoned with. Their hearts were broken, beautiful messes that only grew stronger and more loving with each heartache.

Their conversation was cut short by a knock at the door. Bianca looked at her two friends with curiosity. She wasn't expecting anyone.

"Sadie, can you grab that? It's probably Mrs. Gibson coming to check on me. News travels fast in this neighborhood." Bianca waited as Sadie answered the door. She didn't hear anything but a high-pitched Sadie voice coming from the foyer. She was probably thanking Mrs. Gibson for bringing some food or something. Much to her surprise, Sadie came shuffling back into her room with the biggest grin on her face.

"Please tell me I won Publisher's Clearinghouse," Bianca said snidely.

"No. Better. You have an unbelievably hot visitor here to see you," Sadie said with a wink.

"Who is it?" Charlie asked as she jumped off the bed and ran to the window to catch a glimpse. "Oh, snap. It's Luke van. I wonder if he's here to check on you?"

"What? I can't believe he would even speak to me after how I ended things," Bianca stated, confused.

"He knows about today. Jane told him. He has a bouquet of flowers in his hands. Get your drugged ass up and go see him," Sadie barked.

Bianca's mind whirled. Why was she so thankful he was here? Maybe there was more to her feelings for him than she had realized. Bianca jumped up, fluffing her hair and wiping the smeared mascara from her face. Hopefully there was some trace of makeup left from this morning's application. She was sure it wasn't in its original state, especially after an oxygen mask and wallowing in her bed, but it would have to do. There was no time to fix it now.

As she rounded the corner to her foyer, she could hear Sadie and Charlie behind her, shuffling to peek like two little kids trying to catch a glimpse of the tooth fairy.

There he was, sporting a big bouquet of wildflowers and a nervous smile. "Hey, you," the male voice said behind a smile.

"Luke, you shouldn't have," Bianca whispered sinking her nose into the gorgeous arrangement of lilies and roses.

"You once told me these were your favorite," Luke said shyly. "I took mental note hoping to get to surprise you someday. This isn't exactly the type of moment I had in mind." He chuckled. "Sounds like you gave everyone a scare today at the courthouse."

"News travels fast. Jane spilled the beans, I hear," Bianca added with agitation.

"Yes," Luke said hesitantly. "I know you are done with us, but I miss you. I stopped by to try and convince that stubborn head of yours to give us another chance, but the office was closed. She was there alone answering the phones. She was a frazzled mess. I just happened to be the only one around to help calm her down," Luke defended.

"So much for making her my emergency contact." Bianca chuckled. "Sadie!" she shouted back down the hallway, "you're now my emergency contact. And you two can come on out and stop eavesdropping." Bianca rolled her eyes as she turned back to Luke with a forgiving smile. "I guess now is as good a time as ever for you to officially meet my best friends." Bianca stretched her arm out to the two women making their way bashfully toward her foyer. "You met Sadie briefly once, I think."

"Yes. She barged in the first time I came here to service your unit," Luke confirmed.

"Is that what they are calling it these days?" Charlie said with a giggle.

"And that's Charlie, the crude one," Bianca replied sarcastically.

"Hey!" Sadie waved. "Nice to see you again."

"Nice to finally put faces to names. I don't want to interrupt you guys. Bianca, you need to rest," Luke said politely as nodded to the two friends. "But listen…" He trailed off, indicating the need for privacy. Bianca turned to Sadie and Charlie, and they caught the hint. She waited until they were out of earshot, back in her bedroom, before turning back to Luke. "Listen, Bianca. I know we are an unlikely pair. I know from the outside we aren't exactly Ken and Barbie, or whatever else you had in mind for your love life. All I know is that I like you…a lot. And that whatever you had before didn't work out, so maybe try something entirely different. Like me…"

Bianca watched as his eyes softened. He wasn't wrong. And she liked him too… a lot. Stepping close to him, she cupped her hands over his whiskers, pulling his lips to hers. "I don't deserve you," she whispered.

"Yes, you do, Bianca. Let me love you…appropriately."

"Okay," she said through a smile. She didn't have any more fight left in her. She was ready to surrender to him…to a chance at love. Even if it didn't look a damn thing like what she thought it was supposed to.

Bianca bid him good-bye after promising to call him later, and turned to close the door. Leaning back against it, she pressed the gorgeous bouquet up to her face, burying her nose in the amazing scent.

Her two friends rounded the corner running toward her, jumping up and down, clapping and squealing like teenagers. They had apparently heard the conversation in its entirety.

"Okay. I think I'm ready for adventure, but this time, maybe at more of a snail's pace," Bianca said with a chuckle.

"I'm in!" Charlie cheered.

Bianca wasn't surprised at that one at all. She eyed Sadie, waiting for response.

"Adventure awaits," Sadie confirmed with a confident nod.

Bianca wrapped her arms around her two friends. With them by her side, she could do anything. Together, they would jump bravely into love, two feet in.

THE END

ACKNOWLEDGEMENTS

With every great story comes some level of truth; and this one is no exception. This novel was only possible because of the fierce souls that dare to believe in finding true love. A huge thank you to my spit-fire friend, Diana Cicchiello, for your big, brave heart. To Korie Dunhoft Acord and Kristen Beeler Conner, our text threads keep me sane...and happy. Thank you for your unwavering support.

Caroline Tolley, my developmental editor, thank you for digging deep into the plot and helping this story bloom to its full potential. Jessica McKelden, as always, your line edits blow my mind. The details you nudge me to add are beyond anything I could recognize on my own. Your skills are truly remarkable. Jennifer Jakes, thank you for doing everything it takes to get a novel out the door and published. From proofing to formatting and everything in between, you are the whole package. I adore working with you. To Lena Yang, thank you for a gorgeous cover. It's beyond anything I could have ever dreamed of.

As always, thank you to my parents, Ronnie and Karen Cole, for cheering me on. You are my rock. And to my beautiful three children, you are my favorite gifts from above. Life is short and precious. May you always have the courage to go all in.

ABOUT THE AUTHOR

Growing up in rural southern Kentucky, Scarlett developed a deep love and appreciation for front porch conversations. It is from these bonds and personal life experiences that she gets her writing inspiration.

Scarlett received her Bachelor of Arts degree in Biology with a Minor in Women's Studies from Transylvania University in Lexington, Kentucky, graduating cum laude. In 2005, she graduated magna cum laude from the University of Louisville with a Doctorate in Dental Medicine. She is a full-time practicing dentist in Savannah, Georgia where she has resided for 16 years.

She is most proud of her toughest job, being a mommy to three hilarious and intensely loving kids. In her minimal free time, Scarlett enjoys yoga, running, and napping. She believes profusely in indoor hammocks, firm handshakes, letting her children make their own mistakes, and that words have the power to heal.

You can contact Scarlett via
ScarlettAdaire.com
Facebook.com / ScarlettAdaireWrites
@scarlettadaire

Made in the USA
Columbia, SC
14 October 2022

69451849R00169